# BLOOD IS BLOOD

# BLOOD IS BLOOD

## WILL THOMAS

MINOTAUR BOOKS ≋ NEW YORK

BLOOD IS BLOOD. Copyright © 2018 by Will Thomas. All rights reserved. Printed in the United States of America. For information, address St. Martin's Press, 175 Fifth Avenue, New York, N.Y. 10010.

www.minotaurbooks.com

Library of Congress Cataloging-in-Publication Data is available upon request

ISBN 978-1-250-17038-5 (hardcover)
ISBN 978-1-250-17039-2 (ebook)

Our books may be purchased in bulk for promotional, educational, or business use. Please contact your local bookseller or the Macmillan Corporate and Premium Sales Department at 1-800-221-7945, extension 5442, or by email at MacmillanSpecialMarkets@macmillan.com.

First Edition: November 2018

10  9  8  7  6  5  4  3  2  1

# ACKNOWLEDGMENTS

It's such a pleasure to write this series, and I couldn't do so without the support of so many people who contribute their skills and talents to this effort.

As always, I'd like to thank my incredible agent and friend, Maria Carvainis, for her superb guidance through the years, not to mention her fondness for Llewelyn and the Guv. I'm also fortunate to have Keith Kahla as my editor. Keith's great eye and sense of humor lend so much to the books and make the process enjoyable along the way. Hector DeJean, Alice Pfeifer, and the rest of the team at Minotaur help me (and my books) look our best.

My incredible family has long been supportive and involved. Many thanks to Caitlin, David, and Heather for everything. You are the best. And finally, my wife, Julia, my partner in crime. We write side by side, each in our own little world, then we share what we've written. She is the perfect helpmeet, sounding board, and partner. I could not do what I do without her.

# BLOOD IS BLOOD

# CHAPTER ONE

I detest Mondays with all my soul. I always have. They are the thug who clouts you in the alleyway, the friend who stabs you in the back, the offspring who casts you into outer darkness in your dotage. I have reasoned that fully one-seventh of all the terrible events in my life have occurred on that egregious day. No one in the history of mankind has ever uttered, "Oh, it's Monday! At last!"

The night before, I had enjoyed myself, heedless of what might lie around the corner. Sunday is a gentle respite, particularly for those of us who have but one day free of toil each week. At such a time, a change of scenery is in order: someplace calm, quiet, even contemplative, to consider the eternal conundrum. I'm speaking, of course, about the female of the species. Some men may choose to spend their evenings in public houses, surrounded by other blokes, discussing subjects they know little about. I'd much prefer staring at a pretty face, and trying to discern the mystery behind it.

Let us take Rebecca Cowan, for example. We were to be wed in a fortnight. I wasn't worried, as most grooms are. Now that our relationship was finally settled, it was a relief. All those years of searching for the right one, the heartaches, the misunderstandings, the outright blunders, they were behind me now. As a husband I would face an equal number of trials ahead, but just then, all was peace and serenity.

I was at Rebecca's home in Camomile Street, hard by the Bevis Marks Synagogue. We were in the small garden behind her house, and the sun was starting to set. There were beds of roses in their final bloom before the coming fall weather and there were more sturdy holly bushes that would withstand winter. We were ensconced in a circle of basket chairs in a small gazebo, enjoying the cool evening air. Dinner would soon be served, but I would not partake, for propriety's sake. It would be many a day before I got over the feeling that the bubble would burst and that she would see me for all my faults and drive me off, as any sane woman would. For now I would look at her and listen to her silvery voice as long as I could.

"Baby's breath," she said. "We should have baby's breath."

"Certainly," I agreed. "Loads of it."

Of course, I had no idea what baby's breath was, but my purpose in being there was to agree to everything she said. Once, I'd made an actual suggestion and she had patted my hand as if I were a five-year-old asking if we could please hold the reception in a sweet shop.

Her aunt Lydia was present as a chaperone, but she and I were already as thick as thieves. Lydia was the only member of the Mocatta family who didn't feel Rebecca was making a grave mistake in marrying me. Mind you, I had much to recommend me. I was a Gentile marrying into a family of Levites; a former felon, having served eight months in prison for theft; a widower, always a good recommendation; and thoroughly unable to keep her in the manner to which she was accustomed. Then there was the matter of my being a private enquiry agent, requiring me to go about London with a loaded Webley in the waistband of my trousers. I was not entirely certain that she was reconciled with the fact that I was in such a dangerous line of work. In fact, the only point I had in my favor was that Rebecca had also lost a mate and in the tradition of her people could marry whomever she chose. For some reason which even I found inexplicable, she chose me.

"You're not paying attention," she said. "I think you're falling asleep."

"I'm not," I replied. "It's just very peaceful out here. And your aunt Lydia always puts me at my ease."

"Our aunt Lydia."

"Darling, you must have some opinions. This is to be your wedding, too!"

"Well," I said, sitting up in the cane chair, "I like these little flowers here."

There were several small bouquets at our feet, while the two women considered which they preferred.

"Hopeless!" Lydia said.

Rebecca brought a hand to her head, as if I were giving her a headache.

"What's wrong?"

"Darling, that's baby's breath."

"Oh, that's what that is! I like it. That's an opinion, isn't it?"

Actually, there was one matter in which we differed, and that was my choice of best man. First of all, it was not customary to have a best man at all, but Rebecca, as a concession to our having a Jewish wedding ceremony, had encouraged me to select one. She had anticipated my choosing Israel Zangwill, my closest friend, but instead I had decided upon my employer, Cyrus Barker.

"I like Israel," I told her. "But if it weren't for Mr. Barker, I'd have been dead a thousand times over. He took me in when I was at my lowest, gave me a situation, a home, and a reason to live. Why, you and I met during our first enquiry together. We would never have met if it weren't for him. I owe the man practically everything."

She was terrified of him, I think, though she had not yet actually met him. His reputation, as always, had gone before him. Even Israel quakes in his boots whenever he is forced to come into contact with the Guv. I admit my employer is imposing. I don't think Rebecca was looking forward to staring across at him during our wedding ceremony, towering a head above everyone else in the synagogue.

I had a suspicion that Barker was as frightened as she, though he would never admit to it, either. He was afraid of nothing and no one. However, within her slight, demure, five-foot-one frame was the ability to affect his entire world. When we first became engaged, he had sent his ward, Bok Fu Ying, to get her opinion of my bride-to-be. The two women had become close friends, but it had still not allayed Barker's concerns. Rebecca was an unknown quantity, one of the few things he could not control. With mere words, she could influence how I thought and what I felt.

"What kind of boutonniere would you prefer, Thomas?"

"Whatever kind you would like, my dear," I told her, smiling. "You'll be the one staring at it all day."

The Guv had arranged his life the way he wanted it. It was black and white, right versus wrong. He knew his friends and enemies. Rebecca, however, was neither. She was a shade of gray that negated his entire system. She was right and good, and she made him nervous, something few people were able to do.

"I like your onyx cuff links," she continued. "They look good with a crisp French cuff."

"I'll have Mac polish them for me."

"You don't mind?"

"Why should I mind?"

"I really must talk to Jacob soon. We have a lot to discuss."

"Not if I have any say in the matter."

There was a second reason why Barker should be concerned about my fiancée. I had been a comfortable impediment to his own marriage plans, but now the prop was being pulled away. Well, perhaps not his plans per se, but Philippa Ashleigh's plans, which amounted to the same thing. The widow, Barker's lady friend, wished to bring him to the altar, and she generally got what she wanted. There was a theoretical date for their nuptials set for some time in the future, and he knew it. It was staring him in the face.

Rebecca leaned forward and tucked an errant curl behind my ear. Aunt Lydia raised a brow, but was not particularly scandalized. It was a casual gesture on Rebecca's part, and that was what I wanted, the casualness of it, the promise that she would still be pushing that errant curl back when it was gray.

I looked at Rebecca and she looked back at me. This was a time when I should confirm her decision about our marriage.

"Are you looking forward to the honeymoon?" I asked.

Both women looked scandalized.

"Palestine!" I corrected. "Will you like Palestine, do you think?"

"Of course," my fiancée replied. "Old Jerusalem, the Dead Sea, the ruins of Nineveh."

"And Greece and Italy."

"They are all ruins as far as I'm concerned," Lydia remarked. "And not particularly romantic."

"Don't worry," Rebecca said. "We'll make them romantic."

"If you want old rocks," her aunt continued, "you need to look no further than that pile by the east wall."

Intrigued, I stood and crossed to where she had pointed. There was a rock projecting from the ground like a bad tooth. It was totally incongruous with the shrubs and greenery that encircled it, as far as I was concerned, but obviously it bothered Lydia.

"Why don't you have it pulled?" I asked.

"We tried, but apparently, this is but the tip of it," Rebecca explained.

I took a jackknife from my pocket and scraped at it. It was not merely rock. I found old mortar as well. Stepping back, I looked up at the edifice of the synagogue beside us and pictured a map of Old London in my head.

"This isn't a rock at all," I said. "This is part of the original wall that encircled the City, the very center of London. It is an architectural ruin, just as you said, Aunt Lydia."

"Marvelous," she said, waving at it with a handkerchief as if it were a midge. "Just get it out of the garden, where it is making a nuisance. Is he always this academic?"

"Not always," Rebecca answered. "Sometimes he's poetic and romantic. Other times, he's dangerous and almost frightening."

"Apparently, I am a man of many parts, few of them useful."

Lydia leaned forward and touched my arm. "Just make my darling niece happy and I will forgive all your faults."

"I will do my utmost, if only to have you as a permanent aunt."

She looked at her niece. "Deft."

There was another matter to concern me. Where were we going to live? Rebecca had a perfectly fine home here in the shelter of the synagogue, not far from her married sisters and parents. It was a solid, attractive house, with a few male touches here and there, but it had belonged to her late husband, Asher Cowan. I knew their marriage had been loveless, arranged by her family in fear that she might become a spinster, despite several offers of marriage. In spite of my disappointment in their marriage, I hadn't disliked the fellow, whom I had only seen once or twice, giving one of his political speeches. I'd have voted for him had I lived in Poplar. Sitting in a chair that he had considered his was another matter.

He'd hung his hat on that rack, stood before that mirror to tie his cravat, slept in that bed. If I lived there with her after our wedding it would be grasping, as if I had married her in order to acquire the property. I could imagine women sneering at me and men slapping me on the back as if I'd made an advantageous investment, as though Rebecca herself were an appendage to the house. No, I didn't like it at all. But what was the alternative? I could not cram her into my spartan room in Newington under Barker's roof and expect her to accept it without complaint. She deserved better.

There was also the matter of Cyrus Barker and my work. He might require my presence at any moment, and were I off in the wilds of the City it might take over half an hour to arrive. In fact, anytime he needed me after hours I'd have to meet him, and there were plenty of cases that would not stay within the bounds of seven-thirty A.M. and six o'clock P.M.

One could say, in fact, that my life was a complete mess, were it not for the fact that I was actually content for the first time in my life. More than content. I was happy.

"I must let you go," I said.

"You had better not," she replied. "It took you years to propose the first time."

I kissed her hand, shook Aunt Lydia's, and went on my way.

One man shouldn't be this fortunate, I thought, and then I stopped myself. I really must learn to stop saying whatever I think as I think it. It tempts Fate; but then I've always jumped for the gold ring when the brass one was meant for me. The eternal optimist, I expect everything is somehow going to work out for the best.

I forgot Monday was coming.

The next day began as they generally do. There was nothing visibly ominous about it. Barker was up betimes and out in the garden, consulting with his Chinese gardeners. I was in the kitchen facing the window, slowly consuming a carafe of coffee. Our chef, Etienne Dummolard, was grumbling to himself while flipping an omelet in a copper pan on the Aga. Our factotum, Mac, was buzzing about like a bee, flitting from task to task.

I waited until the Guv donned his morning coat, then bolted toward the front hall. By the time he reached the back door I was waiting, bowler hat on my head and stick in my hand, as if I'd been there for an hour.

His pipe filled and the fire stoked, Barker chuffed out through the front door, under a full head of steam. We soon found and boarded a hansom cab, the great gondolas of London Town.

"How are you this morning, Mr. Llewelyn?" Barker rumbled.

"Quite well, thank you, sir."

"Did you see her last night?"

"I did."

Neither of them would use the other's name. It was as if each thought the other a momentary aberration of mine that soon would pass. Both mildly disapproved of my choices. Not openly, perhaps, and not in any great way, but it was there all the same.

We arrived in Westminster, turned north at the Houses of Parliament, and eventually docked in front of our chambers in Craig's Court. It seemed a typical Monday, not necessarily good, but not obviously malevolent, either. Something to get through. One wished it were still Sunday.

"'Ello, Mr. L.," our clerk, Jeremy Jenkins, murmured.

He was holding a wrinkled copy of the *Police News*, but his eyes were nearly shut. It is necessary to moderate the intake of sunlight between one's lashes after imbibing freely the night before.

"Good morning, Jeremy," I said, a trifle too loudly.

"Mr. B."

"Hmmph," our employer rumbled as he entered the chambers.

Really, a grown man sulking. Or worse yet, brooding. One can sulk for an hour or so, but brooding can take days. If the grunt were directed toward me, I certainly wasn't going to give up married life on the grounds that it would inconvenience him. He sat down in his large stuffed green leather chair, and I in my more modest wooden one. We can't have these assistants comfortable or they'll get themselves into all sorts of mischief.

We sat and the day began. A potential client entered minutes later with a request for our services. The man was looking for his eldest son, who had disappeared and was prone to melancholy. Mr. Barker promised he would look into the matter, but I sensed he was not enthusiastic. It was not the sort of case that attracted Barker's attention. Most of the cases he preferred to take had higher stakes or affected society as a whole, such as Irish bombings or the hunt for the Whitechapel killer.

He left after three-quarters of an hour and then we were alone. Unless we had a client, we had little to do, which I found irritating. Barker preferred to be working, up and about, but if need be he could sit in his chair and think for hours. However, an assistant must not be seen as indolent, so I shuffled papers, looked over the accounts, which I had already done the week before, and pulled various books down from shelves in an effort to look industrious.

I had just sat down with Kelly's Directory in my hand, looking for the office of the young man we were to find, when there was a muffled explosion that rocked the building. It caused a chandelier above the visitor's chair to shudder. It was as loud as a thunderclap, and for a minute, I lost my ability to hear.

Barker was calling me, but I could only read his lips, no easy feat due to his heavy mustache.

"Scotland Yard!" he shouted.

Years before, our windows had been shattered by a bombing nearby at Scotland Yard, but so far, our windows were still intact this time.

I called back to him. "Downing Street?"

Barker was standing now, and he put a cupped hand to his ear.

Then his desk collapsed through the floor, taking the Guv and his Persian carpet with it. The green leather chair was next, and the visitors' chairs, dropping into the cellar. Board by board, from the center of the chamber outward, the room began to come apart with a rending of wood that I could hear even with my damaged eardrums. Our entire chamber was disintegrating around and under me. The building which had been bombed was ours.

Have I mentioned how much I despise Mondays?

# CHAPTER TWO

T he floor of our chambers finally collapsed beneath me. I
 barely had time for a single thought beyond that of simple
 self-preservation. Pulling myself up into my American
rolltop desk, I rolled the top down as far as it would go. Any criti-
cism I had ever made of the Americans I now regretted. They
make a fine piece of furniture. A second later it tipped forward
and I, too, fell atop the shattered wood and debris in the basement
below. The desk tumbled over a few times before settling. Squashed
inside, I tugged open the drawer and peered out, coughing. The
air was charged with plaster like a fine ash. The desk was prone,
so I wormed my way out among the rubble, trying to stand as I
bawled my employer's name. My feet shifted among the loose
boards and my ears still were not functioning properly.

A hand fell on my shoulder and I turned, hoping it was my employer, but it was Jenkins. He must have climbed down after me.
I looked up into our offices overhead, the bookcases lining the

walls intact for the most part, but books flung in every direction and everything else destroyed.

"Are you all right, Mr. L.?" he shouted, though I could barely hear him.

"I think so," I said. "But the Guv's buried under there!"

Frantically, we began digging through the rubble, lifting lengths of shattered planks and tossing them to the side. Jenkins, a slight, lanky man, looked ready to fall over. He is generally the worse for wear in the mornings and reanimates as the day progresses, but he was now wide awake, more wide awake than I had ever seen him. He was as terrified as I that Barker might be dead, though neither of us would say it. We pitched together and began the process of unearthing our employer. As near as I could judge, we had at least six feet of debris to dig through before we reached him. Six feet, the depth at which a corpse is buried. I felt ill at the thought. But he couldn't be dead. He just couldn't, not Cyrus Barker. Anybody but him. It didn't bear thinking about. I tugged my handkerchief from my pocket and tied it about my mouth. Then I set to work again.

"Oi!" a voice called from overhead.

"Down here!" I yelled. "There's a man trapped here!"

A crowd had gathered from the surrounding buildings of Whitehall and a few of the men let themselves down as best they could, and began to help. I recognized some of them as other detectives from Craig's Court, such as J. M. Hewitt, who often accepted cases which, for one reason or another, we were forced to forgo. I was grateful for the help.

"Someone go for a fire brigade and an ambulance!" I shouted. "Mr. Barker is buried under this rubble!"

It wasn't merely his life at stake but my own as well, I realized. For six years, I had been pulling this one cart, and now it seemed I had become no good for anything else. What I had hated when I first filled the position I now had come to love. No two days were alike. I wasn't chained to this desk or this building. We were out of the office often. Sometimes we would work around the clock and other times we would go home early. I enjoyed a freedom most scribes and clerks around the City would envy. Most of all, I enjoyed the opportunity to work with such a unique fellow as Cyrus Barker. He was a law unto himself. Often he exasperated me, and just as often I did the same to him. It had not occurred to me before that very moment how easily this house of cards could topple. Barker was in a dangerous profession. He could be gone at any moment. Him, and all my prospects with him.

"Sir!" I bellowed into the pile of rubble as I struggled to keep my balance. "Mr. Barker, can you hear me? Say something if you can! We'll get you out, sir. We've sent for help and we're removing this debris as quickly as possible!"

There was no response, no sound save for the planks being thrown about and the hush of settling plaster.

Between the nails and the splintered wood, my hands were soon battered and bloody and I was in a panic. Everything I owned was tied up in this one man. Layer by layer, we picked our way through the rubble. I threw lumber about so carelessly that men were forced to duck flying boards. A full dozen of us were now trying to unearth the Guv. I thought surely it could not be long now before we found him, but it was.

Finally, we uncovered the edge of Barker's desk, and when we lifted it off its side there was a muffled groan. I found an expanse of dusty waistcoat studded with buttons. I lifted a few more boards and uncovered his face, powdered white, including his mustache.

"Oh, crikey!" Jenkins muttered.

Barker's limbs had been pinned under the desk. There was a puddle of blood beneath him, and I saw the end of a bone protruding through his torn trousers. He would not be walking away from this attack. But he was alive, and that was the main thing.

There was a ragged cheer from among the men. Barker was respected here. He was not necessarily one of them, perhaps, being a wealthy man, but he leant a posh air to their businesses, owning the first and best one, just past the Cox and Co. Bank facing Whitehall Street. Their respect for him did not automatically extend to me. Most of them wanted my situation, and the salary that went with it.

There was a commotion overhead, and I looked up to see a brigade of firemen in their shiny hats. We must have looked like a roomful of ghosts, covered in plaster as we were. The captain climbed down and, stepping amongst the rubble, inspected Barker's wounds.

"All right, boys! Get down here!" he shouted. "Drop a rope and mind your step!"

He sent for more firemen. Aside from his injuries, Barker is a large man, over fifteen stone, which would not be easy to lift, and he was unconscious, which meant so much dead weight.

I explained to the captain who my employer was and what had happened to us. One of the firemen pointed to some black sooty marks on the walls under the joists. I recognized them for what they were: scorch marks left by a dynamite charge. Someone, for whatever reason, had crawled through the tunnels of the telephone exchange at the far end of Craig's Court with the deliberate intent of blowing us out of our seats. From what I could see, the charges had been just powerful enough to weaken the supports. The weight of our furniture and gravity had forced the floor to collapse upon itself.

One of the firemen pulled a small bottle from his back pocket and handed it to me. It was laudanum, the real stuff. No alcohol, or syrup, or even sugar, just full extract of poppy. I knew what to do with it. The Guv was my employer, and I would have to administer the dose myself. Carrying him up tied to a litter, with at least one shattered limb, was going to be excruciating. The firemen were not going to chance that he would wake in the middle of being lifted and begin to struggle against the intense pain.

"Mr. Barker?" I called, no more than a few inches from his face. I lifted his head onto my knee. "Can you hear me? I'm afraid I'm going to need to give you some laudanum. There's been an accident, but you're going to be all right."

I opened the bottle and poured a few drops into his mouth at a time. At one point he coughed, but I suspected it was involuntary. Somewhere inside that six-foot-two frame was a drawer in which his consciousness was stored, ready to open again at the proper moment. That is, if it ever opened again at all.

There was a change of light overhead and the room suddenly became darker. The electricity had been cut by the explosion, which was another thing that would have to be repaired before our offices could be opened again. I heard voices overhead, and then there were men in white uniforms swarming down the ropes to where we stood. I noticed the insignia on one of their uniforms: ST. JOHN'S PRIORY. Gone were the days when victims, living or dead, were thrown onto a police hand litter and wheeled off to a nearby hospital. Modern times required modern services. St. John's Priory was a private hospital that ran the first ambulance service in London. Cyrus Barker had been treated there before, and it was one of the places he endowed with his money, an ancient charity. The change of light must have been the ambulance wagon blocking the court.

Their presence relieved me a little. A fire brigade is good for a number of things, but I suspected lifting an injured man from a pit was not one of them. The two men assessed the situation, saw that Barker was unconscious, and then reset the bone, with all of us standing over him. Just the sight of them pushing the broken bone back in place was enough to make even the most hardened veteran look away. There was a loud groan from Barker, but no more response than that.

By then we had cleared the debris completely from around his body. He had not only been buried in heavy rubble, he had fallen eleven feet onto a cement cellar. It was a wonder he was even alive.

The hand litter was lowered by another rope, and we set it beside the Guv. Carefully, he was rolled up onto his side and a woolen blanket placed under him, then rolled to the other side while the blanket was straightened out. A few of us seized the blanket like pallbearers, and at the command of the captain of the fire brigade, we lifted Barker's body, groaning under the weight. There were red faces among us, none more than mine, being the smallest of them all. We set Cyrus Barker on the litter, and then strapped him onto it.

"Oi, there!" the captain called, looking overhead.

He gave a thumbs-up gesture and then we heard a metallic clicking sound. Someone had set up a small winch outside. We watched as the rope went taut, protesting under the weight as we had, and then began to lift my employer inch by inch from the debris. There was no cheer this time, but plenty of back slapping.

After the Guv had been lifted to the ground floor, I seized the rope and swarmed up the side. I followed the handcart out into the street. There, I watched them loading him into the back of the ambulance van. I would have gone with him, but there was no room for another man inside the vehicle. With a crack of the whip, the horses strained, the wheels rolled, and my employer was carried off and away into Whitehall alone.

I thrust two fingers in my mouth and blew as loudly as a man can with a throat full of plaster. A cab pulled to the curb, took one look at me, and rattled off. When the second arrived, the horses shied and the cabman shrugged his shoulders. I looked down at myself. My best suit was ripped and chalky white. I shook my head and watched a fine powder rise into the air.

Pulling a shiny guinea from my pocket, I lifted it high, letting the morning sun send the message to passing hansom cabs: despite his disheveled appearance, this man has money. One stopped and I clambered aboard.

"Take me to the Priory of St. John," I shouted, and with a click of his tongue, we were on our way.

The priory is in a section of London which had become gentrified since the days when Charles Dickens set his novel *Oliver Twist* there. It is a small medieval street spanned by an arched gate and is run by the Order of St. John of Jerusalem in Great Britain. Originally, the building was built by the Knights Hospitaller during the Crusades, and it hasn't changed much since. There is the ambulance brigade, a hospice, and a dispensary, but Barker was occasionally brought here to recover from one wound or another. I suspect it was due to the donations he made to various associated charities, as well as the fact that Barker belonged to a modern organization calling itself the Knights Templar. In history, the Knights Templar and the Knights Hospitaller had merged centuries ago, hoping to survive the whims and machinations of kings and popes.

That sounds academic, but I wasn't feeling academic at the time. As we clopped through the City, I became agitated again. What if my employer died? Or what if he didn't die, but was incapacitated? He could lose that crushed limb. Cyrus Barker would have rather lost his life than lose a limb. To be unable to do what he does, to end this reason for living, searching the city for injustice and uncovering what has been cleverly concealed, would destroy him. He would destroy himself. I was afraid he'd take one of his innumerable revolvers and put a bullet through his own brainpan. He will accept no sympathy and damned little advice.

I entered the monastic halls of the priory and told the head orderly who I was and why I was there. So far, the doctors were still examining him, as I had expected. The only information the orderly was able to give was that my employer was still alive. I found it cold comfort.

Two hours later I was sitting on a hard chair in the hall, thinking I should be out doing something. We had been attacked, but it had been unsuccessful if the purpose was to kill us. There was a very real chance the bomber would try again. Should the explosion have been meant to warn us of something, perhaps to stop an investigation, it was useless. The Barker Agency is intractable. We won't be warned away, frightened away, or driven away. If one of us is injured, heaven help them, we shall repay tenfold. We may be momentarily beaten, but the war was ours, or we would die in the process.

I was sitting and waiting for word, still coated in dust, when I heard a loud echo in the hall. It was the sound of a woman's boots clicking in fury. Every man on earth is acquainted with the sound; it is instinctual. I looked up just as Philippa Ashleigh stopped in front of me. She bent forward and pushed a glove-covered finger into my face.

"You did not call me!" she barked.

"The telephone lines are down," I answered. "There was no way to reach you."

The truth was, I had been so distraught over what had happened, it hadn't even occurred to me to call her.

"Then, pray, how was Mr. Jenkins able to inform Mac that Cyrus was at death's door?"

"I have no idea. As you can see, I'm not at the offices."

"Surely they have a telephone set here," she reprimanded.

"No, it is a priory. They don't have modern conveniences."

She shook that finger in my face again.

"If he dies," she said, "he'll be treated like a pharaoh. And don't think I won't have you walled into his tomb!"

Mrs. Ashleigh in her wrath is a terrible force, yet beautiful in her fury. There is a belief that redheaded women are more volcanic than their sisters, more raging, more vindictive, more clever and ruthless when thwarted. I never considered that old superstition true until then. Perhaps it has something to do with being the brunt of other women's envy.

"Hello, Mac," I said to our butler, who had walked up behind her.

As far as I was concerned, he had informed against me.

"Mr. Llewelyn."

"Thomas, what have they said?" Mrs. Ashleigh demanded, unwilling to be put off.

"They haven't told me anything," I answered. "One of his legs has been broken, perhaps both. I assume he is in surgery to reset the bones."

"You're filthy," Mac remarked, as if it were a crime.

"That happens when one has been blown into cellars. I'm glad the two of you have arrived. You watch him. I've got to get back to number seven and make some sense of the place. I must find out who did this."

I carried some fury of my own, I'll admit. Being blown apart before lunch was not how I expected the week to begin. There was a wedding in a fortnight. I didn't need a crisis on top of it, not now of all times. If this affected the date in any way, that was it. I would seize the Rock of Gibraltar in both hands and shake it until the earth crumbled to nothing but rubble floating through the heavens.

Eventually I reached Craig's Court again, and made my way to number 7. I found the door locked, and a sign, obviously created by our clerk, was pasted inside the pane of the door.

*The offices of private enquiry agent Cyrus Barker are currently under reconstruction. Please direct any enquiries to number 5, Craig's Court.*

There was an arrow pointing west.

"Number five?" I demanded of the locked door. "What in hell?"

# CHAPTER THREE

I opened the door immediately adjacent to number 7. There was a small vestibule and a set of steep stairs leading upward. I'd glanced in once or twice before, but the glass was thick and distorted, the product of a Georgian glazier. Climbing the stair, I reached the first floor. There was an entry table there and a dusty chair, with one door facing west. It was the office directly above ours. I walked in.

Jenkins was seated at a desk not very different from the one below, reading yet another copy of the *Police News*. He looked up as I entered.

"You're back, Mr. L.," he said.

"Back, my blessed mother!" I said. "What are you about? And why the dickens are we in number five?"

"Mr. B. owns it. Always has. The entire building, in fact. There was an office here years ago now, but he didn't like the sound of footsteps overhead and rousted the residents who were leasing it.

As you can see, it's like the chamber below, only without the bookshelves. How is Mr. B? Has he awakened yet?"

"No. Not even close, I imagine."

"How is his leg?" Jenkins asked, clearly as worried as I.

"That's the question. You know how heavy that desk is. I had a close look at the bone and whoever operated better have his wits about him, or the Guv will have a peg leg."

"He wouldn't like that," the clerk said.

"True, but he is fortunate to be alive." I paused. "Why is it number five? Shouldn't it be seven-B?"

He shrugged his bony shoulders. "You can dig up the architect and ask him if you like. All I know is three is above us and seven is below. I assume number one is the Cox and Co. Bank next door."

I raised a brow and pulled the notebook from my pocket where I always keep it. It was time to organize my thoughts and go on from there.

"Now, let's see. First of all, we need an inventory," I said, sitting on the edge of his desk. "We'll require a carpenter and a contractor. The panes in the bay windows are cracked, so we shall need a glazier, as well. We must purchase new furniture, ordering duplicates of the originals, if possible. You know how particular the Guv is. Some items, like his desk and chair, he may wish to have repaired. I suppose I can climb down and find the manufacturer somewhere on that giant chair of his."

"The electricity is out," Jenkins said. "That will have to be fixed first."

"We could both do with a bath and a change of clothes," I remarked. "You look like a bandicoot."

"No less than you, Mr. L."

I shook my hair, trying to get the plaster out, and brushed down my suit with my hands. Then I wiped my face with my handkerchief. The transformation was negligible, but at least I had made the effort.

"We'll have to climb down into the cellar and retrieve our files, too. The cabinets will be smashed, no doubt."

"Is that important now, sir?" he asked. "I mean, they're just files. There must be a dozen things we should be doing besides that."

"Not if I'm going to find who did this. Someone who had a grudge against the Guv must have done this, and I'm going to track the fellow and make him pay."

Jenkins looked at me blankly. "Without Mr. B.?"

"Do you see him visiting the offices anytime soon?" I asked, my nerves a-jangle. "I understand what you're saying, but in theory, I have a skull filled with more than porridge. I've been educated by the best, and I don't mean my time at Oxford. Besides, I can't simply follow Barker about forever without doing enquiries of my own. We'll take this logically and see what we uncover, starting with those files."

"Are you sure? Why not wait and let him solve it?"

"Because I suspect Mrs. Ashleigh won't let him come back for some time. She nearly bit me at the priory because I had forgotten to call her. Unfortunately, Mac hadn't. On top of that, I walked out in a huff. I'm as jumpy as a cat."

"That was my fault," Jenkins said. "I should have called her first. Anyway, why all the rush?"

"In case you've forgotten, I'm getting married in a fortnight. Our honeymoon begins immediately afterwards. I'm not going to hand a half-finished case to an injured employer. If I can't solve one case, if I cannot do what Mr. Barker does, what good am I? I might as well resign."

"Good luck," he said, putting as much doubt into the words as he could.

"I'm not going back to the priory to face Mrs. Ashleigh right now. Why don't you go and bring me a report of the Guv's condition?"

"Righto," he said.

I shook my finger at him, much as Mrs. Ashleigh had just done to me. "And no stopping at a public house on the way."

"It never crossed my mind!" he called from the stairwell.

I went downstairs to number 7 again. If anything, it looked worse than before. There was a limp rope suspended into the cellar. Slowly, I climbed over the side, knowing that if I fell and injured myself no one would be there to save me. A thick layer of dust had settled over everything and motes hung in the air. I moved boards about until I found what I was looking for: our broken filing cabinet.

One doesn't wake one day with a whim to blow up a private enquiry agent. There had to be a reason. Barker had trod on someone's toes and now that person had taken his revenge, someone who'd had a long time to stew over it, and if he was worth his mettle, he would keep coming until the Guv died or submitted. I began collecting files. I had been proud of that cabinet: every case docketed, reams of neatly typed notes in folders. Now it had been dashed to pieces and our files scattered everywhere. I'd need something, a bucket perhaps, to lift them to the first floor, where I could try to make sense of the loose, scattered papers.

I heard a low whistle, and a composed voice overhead asked, "Some doings, eh?"

I looked up and saw a well-built man in a cutaway coat. I knew he was from Scotland Yard, but it took me a moment to identify him.

"Chief Constable McNaughton," I said.

"I've been out all morning," he remarked. "I only heard about the accident when I got back to 'A' Division about a quarter hour ago."

"It wasn't an accident."

"Poor choice of words," he replied. "Disturbance, then. How is your employer? Is he going to pull through?"

"I have no idea. I left the priory before the diagnosis was tendered. Not good, certainly. One of his limbs was shattered. I saw the bone myself."

He looked down into the gaping hole. "What do you know so far?"

"The blast was set deliberately. There look to have been four charges, according to the captain of the fire brigade. He thinks the dynamiter used just enough charge to blow out the major supports, and then the floor fell in upon itself. It's obvious the bomber knew what he was doing."

"Finesse," McNaughton said. "Most dynamiters over-charge, blowing themselves to bits. Any prior notes or warnings?"

"None," I admitted.

The chief constable put his hands in the pockets of his trousers and considered. "You're on your own then, without your employer. What are you going to do?"

"I'm going to go through our files to see who might want revenge against Mr. Barker," I answered.

"That could be a very long list. He certainly didn't open this agency to become beloved."

"True, but most of the suspects are incarcerated and have no one willing to put themselves out for them. I'm hoping I can create a list of those who seem likely or capable. Perhaps one of them has been released from prison recently and wants to kill the man who put him there."

"That's where CID would start," the chief constable admitted. He was in charge of the Criminal Investigation Department, which was considered the best in Europe.

"This could take awhile," I said, looking at the jumble of papers before me. "First I'll have to decide what papers went in which files."

"If you'll get me a list of possible suspects, we'll find where they are at the moment," he offered. "If any of them are in prison, we'll see if anyone suspicious has come calling."

"I would appreciate that very much."

"You understand this was a crime against a citizen," he said, looking down into the hole again.

"Two citizens. What's your point?"

"Only that we'll be looking into the matter ourselves. Would you provide information for us as well, since we are doing a favor for you?"

I considered before I spoke. We are a private agency, but we had worked with the CID before. It was always a good idea to stay in their good graces.

"Done."

"Right, then," he said. "Cheerio."

He left me with the giant pile of wood and plaster and the mountain of papers. I surveyed the room, thinking there must be some better way to get the files out of the basement. I didn't want to swarm up the rope every time. A ladder, I realized. That's what I needed. A ladder and some crates that were not too large.

I pulled myself out of the hole and visited an ironmongery in Charing Cross which was willing, for a good fee, to deliver the ladder and crates immediately. When I returned, Jenkins was standing, arms akimbo, staring into the hole again. It had a certain fascination to it.

"Do you have any word about Mr. Barker yet?" I asked.

"I do," he said. "One leg is shattered. The other is badly bruised but intact. He's cracked a few ribs and took a good thumping to his cranium. Concussion, the doctor called it. He hasn't awakened, yet. He'll be in hospital for the foreseeable future."

"He's lucky he survived the fall," I said.

Jenkins nodded his head, still staring into the hole. "He may be confined to a bath chair for a while. When he wakes, he won't be happy."

"Yes, well, if he keeps angering people, he should expect something like this," I said. "And I should as well. I've rarely thought about what happens after someone has been arrested because of one of our investigations, or about the trial and the punishment afterward."

The ladder and crates soon arrived, and we spent the next hour carrying boxes of loose papers up to the ground floor. That would be the easy part, compared to matching each with its brethren. It was like a child's game, a jigsaw puzzle.

As Mac will attest, I am not the most orderly of persons. I would hate to contemplate how my room would be without him to straighten things. It is my private place and, to some degree, I prefer it disorderly. My work, on the other hand, requires my being able to lay hands on one file or one piece of information at a moment's notice, because the Guv demands it. Heaven help me if I'm found rummaging around searching for a date or address and turning red under his steely scrutiny.

That was in the ash heap now. I must do what I could with what was in front of me and hope it would be enough. Could I actually compile a list of likely bombers with a deep hatred of Barker? Even that seemed difficult.

Looking through the files, I found many that warranted interest: the Spring-Heeled Jack case, for example, or the Ludgate poisonings. However, neither left a criminal free to threaten enquiry agents such as ourselves. The Irish Republican Brotherhood case in which Scotland Yard was bombed certainly qualified, but all of the bombers were currently in prison. Were the Irish attempting another campaign with our offices as the opening salvo? They were no less likely than a French anarchist named Perrine, who had threatened to blow Barker's head from his shoulders. I would definitely add his name to the list.

Of the Guv's more well-known adversaries, Sebastian Nightwine, was dead, Seamus O'Muircheartaigh was rumored to be, and Mr. K'ing, the casino-owning husband of his ward, Bok Fu Ying, was in a sanitarium to overcome an addiction to opium.

The problem was that people had relatives to aid them, or money enough to buy confederates willing to do practically anything, so in a way no one could be ruled out. If a criminal died due to our machinations, how were we to know that a relative had enough anger festering inside him to warrant an investigation? For that matter, a prisoner who swore death to Barker and myself one minute might have totally forgotten it the next. Having reckoned the costs, another might have come to the conclusion that going against the agency was not the wisest of ideas, but he wouldn't send us a note informing us of a change of heart. The only thing I could hope for was a workable list of names, knowing it might not be all-encompassing.

I looked about me at the packing cases holding files and the ones full of loose papers. Sooner or later, I would have to go through everything. I was not looking forward to facing that anytime soon.

"Six boxes," I said, looking at the crates on the empty floor when I was done.

"We only began with three."

"Yes, but they were heavily packed. I should know. I packed them myself."

Over the next several hours, thanks to a number of telephone calls by Jenkins, a parade of workers descended on number 7, lifting boards and unearthing furniture.

Meanwhile, I sat in a chair behind the temporary desk that was not yet Barker's and tried to assemble his papers again. Fully half had fallen out of the broken cabinet in order, and those went into two of the crates.

I had the desk covered in tall stacks of papers by then—all it could hold as far as space was concerned. I was in a world of words, sentences which trailed off into nothing, to be united with a paragraph that had no beginning. After three hours, I was beginning to make some degree of progress and had created a working list of men who had threatened us. They included Jacques Perrine, the French anarchist currently residing in La Santé Prison in Paris. The case had occurred before my time, but the Guv had actually gone to Paris for several weeks, posing as another anarchist. Barker told me Perrine was a hardened killer.

Next was Henry Strathmore, a corrupt financier whom we had only recently brought down. He had created a scheme to bilk dozens of MPs and aristocrats of their fortunes. He had been less dangerous than Perrine, but I myself had heard him tell Barker to set his affairs in order.

Third was Joseph Keller, a man who had slaughtered his entire family: his wife, his children, and two sisters. Barker had helped track him, and when he was caught, he called a blood oath that my employer would feel the point of his knife. Like Strathmore, he was in Newgate Prison. Unlike him, he was soon to hang for his crimes.

Then there was Dr. Henry Thayer Pritchard. He had sunk three wives into various bogs about the country in order to collect the insurance money. It was one of Barker's older cases, but he'd told me about pursuing him. He had hoped to see him hang, but a clever barrister had successfully pled for a long stay at Burberry Asylum on the grounds of insanity. He had not threatened Barker per se, but he seemed to belong on the list, as far as I was concerned.

Finally, there was Jack Hobson, leader of a notorious gang of brothers in Shoreditch who had beaten two constables nearly to the point of death. Barker was not happy with the light sentence Hobson had received. I had been present when he passed us in chains and said his brothers would "do for him."

That was the lot, five men who had threatened Cyrus Barker. One of them had made good on his promise, almost. I needed to stop him or he'd try again.

"Jeremy!" I called. "Could you take this list to 'A' Division and make sure Chief Constable McNaughton gets it?"

"Yes, sir, I will, but you have a visitor."

Looking up, I saw a young woman enter the room, clutching her reticule and looking in bewilderment at the empty walls and the dusty man shuffling papers about.

"May I help you?" I asked.

# CHAPTER FOUR

I was up and out of my seat in a trice, not because the young woman was pretty, although she was, but because the office and its occupant were far from being ready for visitors. There were two exceedingly hard wooden chairs, a desk, and a basket chair, and that was all there was in the way of furniture. There were no rugs, no fabric on the bay window, nothing that announced that the room was ready for a client, if client she was.

"May I help you, miss?" I asked. "I mean, ma'am?"

I noticed her ring. It's important to notice things like that in our business. She wore a dress and matching hat in a color that was neither light gray nor light green, but a mixture of both. She wore a—well, I'm no fashion reporter. She was dressed well. We need not go into details.

"Has something happened?" she asked, looking about.

"An accident," I replied. "A gas main exploded and we were forced to move here temporarily. Please excuse my dusty appearance."

"Are you Mr. Barker?"

"No, I am his assistant, Mr. Llewelyn. How may I help you?"

"I was recommended by someone to see Mr. Barker. If he can't find Roger, he can't be found, they said."

"Who is Roger?" I asked.

"He is my husband. He's gone inexplicably missing."

She brought a handkerchief to her eye. Belatedly, I lifted a hand toward one of the dusty chairs.

"I'm sorry to hear that, Mrs.—"

"Archer. Camille Archer."

"Won't you have a seat?"

Mrs. Archer had a pale, comely face, and gray eyes almost exactly the shade of her ensemble. The feature that made all the difference was her nose. It was turned up and delicate; in profile, it had an intriguing bump at the end. It made her look impudent, even saucy. Despite her expensive clothes she'd never be mistaken for an aristocrat. On the other hand, I could picture gentlemen of the middle class fighting over her as a prize. To a merchant, no bangle would ever decorate an arm as well as this young woman with the upturned nose.

"You say he has gone missing?" I asked. "For how long?"

"Five days!" she replied, grasping the arm of the chair with emotion. She seemed to be holding in a great deal of pain and worry.

"What is your husband's full name?"

"Roger Alan Archer."

"And what is his occupation?"

"He is a contractor," she said, with a note of pride in her voice. "He builds private residences."

"I see. Under what circumstances did he go missing?"

"He went to his office early last Tuesday, in order to collect some plans. He told the clerk that he was going to one of the properties in Mayfair. No one noticed until the latter part of the day that he never arrived."

"So, he could be anywhere in London, or even in Europe. He could be halfway to America by now."

She held the lace handkerchief to that bewitching nose of hers. I was still taking impressions. Her hair was a light chestnut color, very full, and the curls were pinned up. She wore pearl earrings, and the pearls were large, attesting to her husband's wealth. She was perhaps three-and-twenty. From appearances, Roger Archer must be quite successful, and was likely older than his wife.

"Yes, sir," she said, as if ready to cry.

"Madam, I'm afraid we cannot undertake such an investigation. Mr. Barker has been injured, and we have not enough staff for the kind of enquiry you seek."

"Oh, please, sir!" she pleaded, pulling herself to the edge of her seat, perched no more than an inch or two from the edge. She reached out to touch me, but at that last minute pulled back, aware it would be inappropriate.

"I'm very sorry," I told her. "Even if Mr. Barker were here, I'm afraid he would not accept your case. Between the two of us it would take at least a week to track all the possible leads. We'd have to stalk London, visit all the ports and steamships, and talk to every cabman in the city. Then there are the Undergrounds."

"How can I persuade you to change your mind?"

"You cannot, I fear."

She actually seized my wrist then, in her hand.

"Oh, please, I implore you!"

"I'm sorry, Mrs. Archer," I said, disentangling myself. "For such an enterprise, Scotland Yard would be the only one to consult. They have the resources. We do not."

"But the scandal!" she cried. "It could endanger his business prospects."

"Can you think of anyone who might mean your husband harm?"

She nodded, and sniffed. "As I said, he is a contractor. Contracts are won by undercutting others. Roger calls it a 'cutthroat business.' Many competitors are trying to solicit the same clients. My husband is ambitious. He frequently overworks himself to stay competitive, sixteen or eighteen hours a day, because his agency is relatively new and he's eager for it to grow."

"Could it be possible that he is attending to other business elsewhere? Does he have other offices or clients outside of London? It's possible that he found he had to take care of something that has taken more time than he had expected."

"There, you see!" she said, clutching her bag and leaning forward imploringly.

I looked away, unable to take the searing glance she was giving me. It felt overly personal. "I'm afraid I don't."

"You're so resourceful. I hadn't thought of that. Of course, you're right. It would wreak havoc upon the business if he had a lead he didn't pursue. Do you think he is all right, then?"

"I don't see why not. If, as you say, he is a contractor, in a world of plans and parquet floors, I don't see how he could be in any real danger. Most likely he was called away for something involving his work."

"But what if it's the alternative?"

"That he might be in danger?"

"No!" she cried. "That he left because of me. He left me because I was a disappointment, a poor wife. I know I'm not a very good cook, and I haven't had much schooling, but I've tried to impress the associates he has brought home. Is it me? Am I so repulsive that he must disappear in order to—"

"That's not possible, madam," I answered. "Believe me."

"You don't think I'm . . ."

"Mrs. Archer, you have nothing to worry about on that score."

She wiped her nose with the handkerchief, which was totally inadequate to stanch the salty tears rolling down her cheeks. I gave her mine. She sat for a moment, calming herself, twisting the wedding ring on her finger nervously.

"How long have you been married?" I asked, if only for something to say.

"A year. A year and a half, actually."

"Ah. You have two options, as I see it. Notify Scotland Yard, or wait for your husband to return."

She looked up at me with those greenish-gray eyes of hers. When she spoke, her voice was rough.

"You really won't help me, then?"

"It's not a question of will I, but of *can* I. I'm but one man. You'd require at least a dozen agents to follow so many possibilities. And I don't have Mr. Barker's permission to start such a case."

"Oh, bother Mr. Barker!" she cried, then stopped herself. "Forgive me. I'm overwrought. Is he badly injured?"

"I don't know yet. He certainly was injured."

"But not near death, I trust."

"No."

"So there's at least a small chance he might take my case?"

I shook my head. Her hopes were misplaced.

"Ma'am, at this moment your husband could be anywhere in the country. Every tick of the clock could take him farther away. And if he is in London, there are tens of thousands of garrets to be searched."

"I understand," she murmured, staring at her hands. "Forgive me. I'm sure you're right."

"I would recommend most of the detectives in this court, if that is your preference."

"Thank you. I was recommended to Mr. Barker as the most professional and the most discreet. If word were spread it would mean the end of our business and our fortunes. But you have no part in that."

"I fear not," I said, rising.

"Thank you, Mr. Llewelyn. I-I won't take up any more of your time."

She stood, took a deep, straining breath, and left the room. I could hear her dainty shoes on the stair, and the sound of the latch.

Shakespeare said it best. "By the pricking of my thumbs, something wicked this way comes." As soon as she was gone, my mind began calculating. Mrs. Camille Archer had asked almost nothing about the state of our rooms. She had come into a bare office and sat, while most women would have left in search of a more prosperous-looking agency. She had leaned forward a little too often, in spite of the knowledge that I was doing my best to put her off. In effect, she had flirted with me. I know a woman at the end of her rope might do just about anything, but I doubted this was one of them.

"What a corker!" Jenkins called from the other room, but I was distracted.

It was a ruse. She had been hired to ascertain if Barker were alive or dead and I had unwittingly told her. After years of training, I had been tricked by an adorable nose and a bit of lace.

I turned and, without a word to Jenkins, ran out of the chambers and down the stairs into Craig's Court. I dashed into Whitehall, looking right and left. A cab was just pulling away on the north side of Whitehall Street. It might be hers and it might not, but following it was better than doing nothing. Hailing a cab, I jumped aboard and told the cabman to follow the one ahead. He snapped the whip and we began to move into the bustling traffic.

It was a stupid mistake, I told myself. It never occurred to me that someone might try a second time to harm Barker, or even me, now that I thought of it. She could have easily reached into that reticule of hers for a lace handkerchief and pulled out a pocket pistol instead. She could have put an end to my incompetence, a well-deserved end, no doubt.

The hansom bowled into Charing Cross, heading toward the station there. I assumed she would be leaving London, but at the last minute, the cab turned into a smaller street, coming to a halt in front of a private hotel. Bradford's Family Hotel, to be precise. I watched her descend and go into the building. She had indeed chosen that cab, so I wasn't a complete idiot. Telling her Barker's condition was incredibly imprudent for a trained private enquiry agent. At least I had not said where he could be found.

I paid the cabman and alighted. Family hotels are a misery for enquiry agents. They offer propriety to families coming into London, and safeguards their identity. Their clerks won't tell one anything, and one is not permitted to wander the halls or converse with guests. One is stopped at the desk and driven back out into the street again.

In spite of that, I approached the desk, and spoke to the clerk. "A young woman came in just now, wearing a gray dress. I need to speak to her."

"Who might I say is calling?"

"A friend of her husband. A business associate, in fact. She is upset over the disappearance of her husband."

"So I understand, sir. She arrived last night. I'm afraid she was near tears this morning at breakfast."

"What room does the woman occupy?" I asked. "I have been hunting her husband for her and would like to give her some information."

"I cannot say, sir, and you cannot go upstairs. This is as far as you may go."

"Would ten pounds change your mind?"

"Bless you, sir, ten times that amount would not keep me from enforcing our guests' privacy. I am the son of the owner. Our living is based upon it."

"But since I cannot go upstairs, what is the harm in knowing the number?"

"It is policy, sir."

Our interview was reaching the point where it would be easier to punch him than to continue the conversation. I also had a pistol in my pocket, a snub-nosed Webley to track a snub-nosed girl. But no, it wouldn't do to have it thrown about that Thomas Llewelyn, Cyrus Barker's assistant, had assaulted a humble desk clerk, in a family hotel, no less. Bribing a clerk, on the other hand, might still be tolerated.

"A shame," I said. "Me with so many pound notes in my pocket, and you with your family honor. That won't keep you warm at night."

I laid down a five-pound note. And then another. I stopped at twenty. He snatched them up and they disappeared into his pocket.

"Actually, she left this morning, sir, bags and all."

"But I just saw her enter this establishment!"

"Yes, sir, she entered through the front door, then exited out the back."

I cursed, pushed past him, and ran out the back door. There I found a brick wall and a narrow alley. At the end of it, one side went back to the street, while the other looked narrow and disreputable. She'd soil and snag her pretty ensemble on those walls.

Angry with myself, I ran into the thoroughfare, but she was gone. Frustrated, I turned and went into the hotel again, to the same desk and the same clerk.

"Let me see the ledger, please."

"I'm afraid that's strictly forbidden, sir."

I opened my jacket and put my hands on my hips where my pistol was secured in my trouser pocket and glared at him.

Wordlessly, he opened the ledger. I scanned the list. There was no Mrs. Archer written in the book, but there was a Miss Camille Llewelyn. The last name was printed in large block letters. She had done it on purpose, I realized. I was nothing more than a pawn in her hand.

The chances of my finding her now were remote at best. There was nothing more I could do now but return to the offices. As I hailed a cab, it began to rain. I climbed aboard, watching the familiar view while the downpour fell like a curtain in front of me, buffeting me with its fine spray. Rain dripped from my hair. I shook it off, realizing my bowler was probably in the cellar at Craig's Court.

As I rode, I admitted to myself that I had been rude to Mrs. Ashleigh at the priory. I'd taken out my ill temper on her. I decided to have Jenkins order some stationery so that I might send her a note of abject apology. I had no excuse and no defense. My only choice was to throw myself on the mercy of the court.

When the cab arrived in Craig's Court, I sprinted to the front door and up the stairs.

"Jeremy, order some stationery—" I began, but one look at our clerk stopped me in mid-sentence.

Our clerk seemed to be having some sort of fit, a case of St. Vitus's Dance, perhaps. He was twitching his head in the direction of the office. Pulling my Webley, I stepped into the chamber, wondering if Mrs. Archer had returned. Perhaps the bomber was working his way to the roof, one floor at a time. I expected anything, anything in the world, except what I found: a full-size, living, breathing American cowboy, straight out of one of Ned Buntline's novels. His oilskin coat was dripping on the wooden floor.

"Well, that's not friendly," he remarked, his eyes trained on the gun in my hand.

"Sorry," I said, although I kept it in my hand, pointing it at the floor.

"You're the runt of the litter, aren't you?"

He was a full head taller than I, in a long brown slicker and a wide-brimmed hat. His hair curled on his collar, and his long mustache was shot with gray. His eyes were shrewd and even mean. I saw a gun belt on his hip.

"Why, that comes as a shock," I remarked, shrugging my shoulders. "Nobody's ever commented on my height before."

He crossed his arms and gave me a crooked smile.

"Who the hell are you?" he asked.

"I'm Thomas Llewelyn, Cyrus Barker's assistant," I said, raising my pistol again. "But this is my pitch, not yours. Who in hell are you?"

The cowboy raised his hands, not in the least afraid that I was armed.

"The name's Barker," he said. "Caleb Barker. What have you done with my brother?"

# CHAPTER FIVE

M ay I see some proper identification?" I demanded of the
man. "Someone has already tried to blow me into the
cellar and dupe me today. I consider your sudden arrival
suspicious."

He reached into his pocket, and my hand naturally raised the
pistol again. His hand withdrew nothing more dangerous than a
sheaf of papers, which he held out to me. I opened them and was
arrested by the legend printed across the top of the letter.

"Pinkerton Detective Agency!" I said.

In response, he lifted the lapel of his coat. On the inside, a pewter shield was pinned to it, with the agency name printed upon it.

"Here are your papers," I said, handing them back. "I'll accept
you are whom you claim to be, for the moment."

The truth was, I could tell it was Barker's brother. Caleb was
tall, although not as muscular as my employer. They had the same
strong jaw, though their mustaches were different. I could have
picked him out of a crowd.

"My brother," he growled again. "Where is he?"

"Our offices were bombed this morning. He is in hospital."

"How bad is it? Was he seriously injured?"

I hesitated. I had just given this information to Mrs. Archer and was still castigating myself over it. But in truth, he was the Guv's brother and deserved to know.

"He has a shattered limb and a concussion."

"I'd like to see him."

"He's been drugged. I doubt he'll be awake tonight."

Caleb Barker put his hands on his hips and frowned fiercely at the floor. After a moment he spoke. "Fine. Then tell me what you're doing to catch the man who did this."

"I've culled a list of people who might have cause to do the Guv harm. Scotland Yard is confirming their whereabouts."

"The Guv?"

"It's what we call him," I said. "Some of us, anyway. I'm not sure who started it. Anyway, I've spoken to Scotland Yard, and they'll confirm the location and condition of each of the suspects."

"Was it a large blast?" Caleb asked, pushing back his hat.

"No. As far as I can ascertain, it was four small devices, each set in a corner, with just enough charge to bring the room down. The Irish, for example, would have blown out half the block."

"I've had dealings with the Irish before in Pennsylvania. They don't do things by halves. Well, you've got a start. Has Cyrus been awake?"

I was momentarily nonplussed by hearing my employer referred to by his given name. That would take some getting used to.

"Not to my knowledge."

"What are you doing now?" Caleb asked.

"I'm waiting for Scotland Yard to contact me."

"What'll I do while you wait for them? I didn't come here to sit on my thumbs. He's my brother. Blood is blood. You go against me, you go against us all."

"I have no idea why you're here. You're being very circumspect."

"Mr. Llewelyn, it's none of your damned business what I do."

"It is when I'm in charge," I said.

"You, in charge? Ha! You're just an assistant. I'm an operative, with twelve years' standing."

I crossed my arms and glared at him. "Perhaps in America, where there are no standards, and just anything or anyone will do."

"That's big talk from a tadpole still wet behind the ears," he growled.

I'd been sitting behind the temporary desk, but I rose at his last words and rested my knuckles on the surface.

"A tadpole trained by the best enquiry agent in London. Now get out and don't come back until I talk to Mr. Barker in the morning."

"You keep talking, boy," he growled, "and I'll have to wipe that smirk off your baby face. Why in the world did my brother hire someone like you?"

"You'll have to ask him about that, but you're welcome to try me if you're man enough, without your guns and spurs. Otherwise, you can get out of here and take the next boat back to America. Slaughter some more Indians for their lands."

"That tears it!" he growled.

Caleb came forward then, hands out, ready to pummel me. It was all I needed. I charged over the desk and caught him full in the chest with both boots.

I've spent too much of my life facing men who are larger than I. I've studied various fighting schools in vain for some kind of help in my predicament. Finally, I cobbled together bits and pieces of many arts into my own unnamed creation, collected just for myself. For the most part, there is only one useful tool, and that is precision. Taller men may throw a wild hook, punching securely in the knowledge that if it misses its intended target it will still cause damage. I have no such luxury. My speed, my muscles, my height and weight must all work together to reach one specific spot with all the force I can muster. If it succeeds I can incapacitate my opponent. If not, I must escape his clutches as quickly as possible and search for another opening. It's not ideal, but it is all that I have, which means serious men my own size must train twice as hard in order to survive.

As I said, I came over the desk and caught him full in the sternum with both heels, pushing the air out of his chest like a bellows. He staggered back and swung that left hook my way, which I was able to duck in time, punching him just under the nose. It sent a shock through his skull and would make his teeth feel loose for days. His response was a straight punch to the gut of a man half his size. It caught me in the chest and knocked me back over the desk again.

I didn't stop. I couldn't. The feet reach terra firma and one leaps and attacks again. Someone must learn that you are serious, resolved, even adamant. There will be no retreating. The only way by me is through me. There is no time for subtlety in a fight. If you attack me, I must assume you are trying to kill me. Therefore I must kill you.

I jumped and reached for an ear, which had been pushed outward by the wide-brimmed hat he wore. An ear is mere flesh and cartilage. It can come off. He batted me across the collarbone, flipping me into a tangle of loose limbs, skittering across the dusty wooden floor to the wall.

He came after me then, taking me by the collar, preparing to give me the solid right punch that would end it. However, just as there are few moves a man my size can inflict, there are few a taller man can use against an opponent my size. I slid low, just under his reach, and delivered a vertical kick to his cobbles.

There are parts of a man's anatomy that cannot be strengthened, that have little muscle. The eyes, for example, or the throat. There are bundles of nerve there, the chinks in the dragon's scales.

Caleb Barker staggered back, cursing like a sailor. I scrambled to my feet and attacked again, hoping to catch him under the chin with my knee, since he was bent over. I missed.

He caught me on the chin and then twice in the stomach. I felt the edge of a fist against my temple that had been meant for my nose. Then came the hook again, which caught me full on the left cheek. It felt like he'd torn my head off.

I heard rather than saw him step toward me. Growling, I leapt, practically climbing the man. My limbs were wrapped around his chest and I attacked, ripping, scratching, punching, pulling hair, biting, giving him all that I had, all that I had learned—no Queensbury Rules, just dirty fighting from the close alleys of Canton, Edo, Marseilles, Damascus. I knew the coup de grâce would come soon and it would lay me flat, and I wanted to inflict what damage I could while I still had time.

As expected, it came. The next I knew, I woke stretched flat on the floor, pain roaring in every limb. I blinked at the ceiling and hoped for death. It was a couple of minutes before either of us spoke.

"Where in the Sam Hill did you learn how to fight like that?" he demanded, rubbing his jaw.

I tried to work out who Sam Hill was, then concentrated on the gist of the question.

"Your brother taught me," I said, trying to sit up. "He trained under a teacher in Canton named Wong Kei-Ying. It's very effective."

Caleb leaned against the wall, still nursing his jaw, which I had elbowed.

"Must be, if I fought a kid to a draw."

"You have a good left hook," I said.

"Thank you. It feels good to bust someone's head now and then. It's therapeutic."

"Where did you learn a word like 'therapeutic'?"

"I do have some education, Mr. Llewelyn. In America, there

are towns that swear by their mineral water to cure anything from lumbago to a cold in the pants. Now, tell me who's on this list you're making. Has anyone sworn vengeance on my brother in the last few years?"

"A few," I admitted. "There was a financier who promised to destroy him, though I think he meant financially. There's a fellow named Keller who swore he'd kill Barker, but he's going to be hanged in a few days."

"A fellow might take exception to something like that," he said.

"The problem is that most anyone who goes up against the Guv either dies or finds himself in prison, and you can't blow up a man's offices while in prison."

"No, but your friends can."

I considered the matter. "I'd have to really like someone to dynamite a building for him."

Caleb nodded. "It's been my experience that most prisoners don't make very good friends."

"True."

"That's all you've got?"

"Sir, this only happened at half past eight this morning. My employer is injured, my offices are gone, I had a strange woman in here just before you arrived and I followed her to a hotel due to her suspicious behavior. Then you arrived. I haven't had time to solve the case. In fact, I haven't even got the plaster out of my hair."

"Fair enough," he said. "I'm cutting myself loose. I'll see you in the morning. Where can a man find a good meal and some beer around here?"

"The Clarence. It's one street to the south."

"Near Scotland Yard? I think not. I'll head north and see what I find for myself, thank you."

In a moment, he was gone. I heard the door click shut.

"Five-thirty, Mr. L.!" Jenkins called from the outer room.

"Thank you for telling me. Good night, Jeremy."

"Good night, sir."

I was alone at last in the peace and quiet. Somewhere in the distance I heard the quaint sounds of old London Town, but it didn't soothe me as it otherwise might. I put my forehead down on my desk. The plain wood was not as cool as Barker's glass-topped desk, but it was cool enough for my fevered brow.

Should I follow after Caleb Barker and see what he was doing, perhaps catch him in a criminal act? No, I believed what he'd said about the meal and the beer. It was wise not to trust him, but I did not want to be lured off-task by what could prove to be a fool's errand.

I didn't sleep exactly, but almost immediately Big Ben chimed six. I stood, looked about the dusty room, and then went downstairs to lock the door. Out of doors, everything seemed louder. I made my way to the Underground and eventually came up the stairs into Newington Causeway. After five minutes' walk, I was home.

"What has happened today?" Mac asked at the door, overwound like a spring.

"Where to begin?" I asked.

Sighing, I took him through all that had occurred since that morning, including a certain annoying fellow who had informed against me to Mrs. Ashleigh. He was less than contrite.

"A brother," he murmured when I was done. "I knew he had one, but somehow I never imagined he would come here. America is so far away."

"I wish he had stayed there. He's an unpleasant character. If you are fortunate, perhaps you will avoid his company entirely."

"What about this Mrs. Archer? What is her game, do you think?"

"I got the impression that she enjoys toying with men like a cat batting about a mouse."

"A coquette, you mean?"

"No. Something darker, I think. I don't want to know how much darker."

"Are you hungry? I can make a sandwich, or even a casserole, if you like."

I considered the subject. "What kind of pie do we have in the larder?"

"Lingonberry, I think."

"I'll have a slice of that," I said.

"Just that? No meat? No vegetables? That's not very substantial."

"Then give me half the pie. Is that substantial enough? And some milk. Do we have any in the house?"

"We do."

"There you are, then."

"It's still not a proper meal."

"Mac."

"Have it your way, then."

"I intend to."

I sat in our opulently appointed dining room, possibly the most formal room in the house, at the end of a long table, eating pie. Pie cannot fix everything, of course, but it has never ruined anything, either. I ate the entire half with a tall tumbler of cool milk and stared at the wall opposite me. Then I had a bath. After that, I called Mac.

"Look, I'm sorry. It's been a beastly day, but I shouldn't take it out on you."

"You haven't. To tell the truth, I'm amazed you are even lucid. You've had a day."

"Thank you, Jacob. I have, indeed. What o'clock is it?"

"Half past seven."

"I believe I'll go upstairs and read a book," I said.

It was almost a challenge. Neither of us had the Guv to tell us what to do. I felt numb. What was I going to do about Caleb Barker? Should I let him visit his brother? And why in the world did I eat half a pie for dinner?

"Oh," Mac said. "Yes, read. Get your mind on something else."

I hadn't realized how steep our staircase was and how many steps it had. Inside my comfortable room, I lifted a novel from my bedside table, a collection of stories by Mr. Kipling. Then I collapsed on the bed and promptly fell into a deep sleep.

# CHAPTER SIX

Blessed Tuesday began with a ruckus downstairs. I pulled on my dressing gown and descended the staircase in my stockinged feet. Stepping into the kitchen, I found Caleb and our chef, Etienne Dummolard, nose to nose in the middle of an argument.

"I like a cigarette as much as the next man, it's true, but it's not a goddamned condiment! You drop one more ash in my egg and I'll plug you so bad you can read newsprint through your chest."

"You cannot 'plug' me with a meat cleaver in your head, Cowboy *Américain*. You reach for a gun and I will split your skull."

I looked into the skillet and shook my head, wondering how long Caleb Barker had been in the house and how he had gotten there. I hadn't given him our address. "Those aren't ashes, Caleb. They're truffles."

"Well, what do you call that?" he asked, pointing to the side of the pan.

"Er . . . Well, yes, that's definitely an ash."

"I just asked for a couple of eggs without all the fancy folderol. Is that too much to ask? Some spuds and a bit of bacon? Surely that's not beyond your skills, is it, Cookie?"

"Who is this 'Cookie'?" Etienne demanded, looking at me. He is a bearlike fellow, unshaven, slovenly, with a nose like a radish. His temper is legendary.

"He called you a cook," I said.

"A cook?" he cried. "A cook? I am a chef, trained in Paris at the greatest school in the world."

"That's the problem, then," Caleb said. "Those places breed the taste right out of you. Everything has a sauce. Have you ever had a real beefsteak before, man? I mean a fresh one, pink and rare? You don't need sauce, you don't even need salt. I suppose that's too much to ask."

Etienne began cursing simultaneously in two languages, while reaching behind him. I knew what he'd do and he didn't disappoint. He untied his apron and threw it at Caleb. Then he did the same with the pan. Caleb ducked just in time, though he was spattered with egg. The pan burst through the picture window, and plummeted into the koi pond behind the house, no doubt scaring the fish.

"I quit!" Etienne bellowed.

He marched toward the hall door. As he did, he glared my way, and I thought he might strike me, but he didn't. I'm blessed if he didn't wink instead. Then he was gone.

"Sensitive fellow, isn't he?" Barker's brother asked, picking egg off his shirt and eating it. "Hmm. Not bad. I've had worse."

"This is a fine kettle of fish. What are we going to eat now?"

"I've worked a chuck wagon before. I'll make some eggs, if you toast the bread. Is that the pantry?"

"It is."

"Where'd you get the Frenchman?" he asked, dropping butter into a copper pan.

"He came with your brother. He was a galley cook aboard the Guv's lorcha, the *Osprey*."

Caleb looked over his shoulder, an egg in each hand. "Wait. Cyrus had a boat?"

"Yes. He was captain of a merchant vessel. Hokkaido to Singapore," I said, toasting bread over the stove top.

"Last time I saw him he was afraid of the water."

"Really?" I asked, trying to sound casual. "What was he like as a child?"

"Like most brothers, I reckon: short, skinny, and irritating. We had no idea then that he'd get so big."

I was silent, waiting for him to speak again. His brother was not half as loquacious.

"Our parents made us dress like the Chinese. Being missionaries, they thought it would make us fit in. I was already too tall, but Cyrus could lie low and not be noticed. One day he came home with a pair of Chinese spectacles. The next day he gave our mother a conniption by shaving the front of his head. You'd think he was just another orphan running through the alleys of Foochow. His Chinese was perfect, though he learned it in the street. Our father had to cane him once or twice for his language. He and I didn't really get along, I'll admit. Some of that might be my fault. I didn't have much time for a scrawny little brat tagging along. Strange one, too.

"Our parents sent me to a boarding school in Shanghai. I begged, I guess. I didn't care for China, and I got into a lot of fights. In Shanghai, I was with other European boys my age. And girls. I was very interested in girls. Still am."

"No doubt," I said.

"Anyway, it all went to hell, didn't it?" he continued. "Our parents died during a cholera epidemic. I suppose, being missionaries, they thought themselves proof against disease. Cyrus disappeared and I assumed he was dead. Then the Taiping Rebellion reached Shanghai, and our school closed. They weren't too particular if you were a seventeen-year-old student or an adult, especially if you spoke Chinese. I had a few close scrapes. The war was a disaster. Nobody knew who was in charge, the English, the Americans, or the Ching government. There were skirmishes all over but no organization. It was difficult to tell one side from the other, since few of us wore uniforms. Anyway, I got shot in the chest during a battle. I'd been interpreting for the Americans, a squad called the Devil Soldiers. Their general got killed and they retreated, taking me with them.

"Apparently, after they got the bullet out, I had a fever, and I woke up in the middle of the ocean halfway to America. As far as I knew, I had no family ties, no money, and no prospects. After I healed, I worked on the docks in San Francisco for a spell. I followed the railroads as an interpreter for the Chinese workers, then became a cowpuncher. I got in a spell of trouble, but I was offered a job as a deputy marshal in Dodge City. I did that for a few years, then I got fired."

"Fired?" I asked.

"Sacked. It was politics. Our dispute reached the newspapers. Bill Pinkerton read about it and offered me a job. I've been working for him ever since."

"Where do you work?"

"I'm based out of Chicago, but I go all over. New York, District of Columbia, Montana, California. Plate."

"What?"

"Plate!"

I handed him my dish and he slid some scrambled eggs onto it. I lay the toasted bread on top. We sat and began to eat.

"Did Barker, I mean your brother, try to reach you?"

"He sent a postal card, last year, but I was on a mission at the time. It was a shock to hear that he was still alive. I sent him a card about six months later, saying we'd get together sometime, but of course we both knew we never would. Then I got an assignment to protect another agent in England, and here I am."

"Did you remember your brother's address or did you just come upon the sign?"

"Boy, do you ever give your tongue a rest? Don't think I don't know I'm being squeezed like a pump handle."

"Pardon me. I'm naturally curious."

"You're naturally irritating, more like."

I poured some coffee and took a gulp. Immediately I began choking.

"What is this?" I croaked.

"What do you think it is? It's Texas coffee. I made it myself."

"What's in it?"

"Coffee, a little water, molasses, egg shells, some chewing tobacco, gunpowder for taste, and salt. Oh, and cayenne pepper."

"Surely you're joking," I said.

"Of course I am. There's no cayenne pepper over here."

I dared another sip. Something was left on the tip of my tongue. Eggshell. "I've been poisoned."

"Drink it. Say, are you aware there are men in the garden?"

"They are Chinese gardeners."

"Really? I think I'll go get acquainted. My Mandarin is rusty."

"We're leaving in three minutes," I warned.

"You can't rush talking to a Chinaman. It's poor manners."

He left and went outside. I watched him from the broken window. Jacob Maccabee came in a moment later.

"Where have you been?" I asked.

"Hiding. He called me a varmint. What exactly is a varmint?"

"I haven't the slightest idea."

"Did he break the window or did Etienne?"

"Both between them. Oh, and don't drink the coffee."

He raised my cup to his nose and quickly pulled it away. "What's in it?"

"You don't want to know."

"That window is the most expensive thing in this entire house. Do you know how hard it is to make a single pane that large?"

"I have no idea. I've never considered breaking it."

"He's so unlike his brother!"

"In some ways. And yet in others, he is exactly like his brother."

"Oh really? How do you mean?"

"To begin with, I wouldn't want to go up against either of them."

"Does he carry a gun?" Mac asked.

"He was just guarding another Pinkerton agent. I doubt he did it with a jackknife. Why?"

"He looked like he wanted to shoot me."

"Don't worry, Mac," I said, patting him on the shoulder. "I've wanted to shoot you for years and yet here you stand."

"I'm keeping my shotgun by my door just in case."

Caleb Barker came in then. Mac turned and left the room.

"You might consider not terrorizing the staff, unless you prefer to do laundry as well as cooking," I said. "You don't work well with people, do you?"

"As I said, I prefer my own company."

He wasn't the only one, I thought.

"America's big enough that you can ride all day and not see a single soul," he said.

"I can't even imagine what that's like."

Caleb Barker pulled a watch from his canvas trousers and consulted it. "Three minutes, didn't you say?"

"You did."

"Let's go, then. Tempus fugit, as it says on the clock in your hallway."

In Newington Causeway, we found a cab and climbed aboard. When we reached Clerkenwell, I told the cabman to wait while we went inside. I couldn't gauge Caleb's mood. I suspected he was concerned about speaking to his brother after all these years and that he might feel guilty for not tracking him down before now, but that might not be the case.

We entered the room. Barker was still lying immobile, and Mrs. Ashleigh was sitting in a chair close by, embroidering a spray of bluebells in a small hoop.

"Thomas!" Mrs. Ashleigh said.

"Good morning," I said. "How is the patient doing?"

"He sleeps a good deal, but wakes for a few minutes every hour."

She was speaking to me, but looking at my companion.

"Mrs. Ashleigh, this is Mr. Caleb Barker of America. Caleb, Mrs. Philippa Ashleigh of Seaford, Sussex."

Philippa's eyes shot open but they returned to normal very quickly. She is famous for her aplomb.

"Why, Mr.·Barker, how lovely to meet you. Your brother and I have talked of you many times."

Caleb came forward, took her hand, and bent over it.

"Madam, I am most pleased to make your acquaintance." He looked at the Guv, who lay very still behind those black-lensed spectacles he wore. "Is he awake?"

"I am," the Guv rumbled. "Good morning, Caleb."

"Good to see you again, Cyrus. It's been awhile."

"You sound like an American," the Guv said. "What's become of your Scots tongue?"

"Didn't suit me," he replied. "I'm sub rosa most of the time, as a Pinkerton agent. A Scots accent would stick up like a nail."

My employer shifted in the bed. He looked like he was in a good deal of pain, not that he would admit it.

"What brings you to England?" he asked.

"The SS *Kintyre*. I was accompanying a witness that America was too hot for. He was peaching on a local secret society, and they weren't very happy with him. I have a few other errands for Mr. Pinkerton while I'm in London."

"Have you been to the office?" the Guv asked.

"I have."

Barker turned his head slightly in my direction. The movement made him grimace. *He's getting by on sheer will*, I told myself.

"How bad is it?" he asked. I realized he'd been unconscious since the bombing and had no idea of the extent of the damage.

"I'm sorry. The floor is gone, sir," I answered.

"We'll have to rebuild. Until then you'll have to find temporary quarters."

"He has," Caleb answered. "He set up camp above your office."

"I'm hoping to salvage some of the furniture, sir," I said.

They weren't listening. I watched as the two men regarded each other.

"You look like Father," Caleb continued.

"And you favor Mother's side of the family. Long and rangy."

"Brass tacks, lads," Caleb said. "Who did this and what are we going to do about it?"

"What do you mean 'we'?" Barker asked. "I'm sure you have work of your own to do."

"I do, but this is clan business." Caleb Barker grinned. "Are you still thumping your Bible, Cyrus?"

"If by that you mean am I comforted by scripture, the answer is yes."

"I go to a Christmas Eve service now and again if I'm in a city. Mostly I'm working, though."

"Mother would not approve," the Guv rumbled.

"In case you haven't noticed, Cyrus, Mother's dead. Father, too. Do you need my help? I've got things to do if you've got no use for me."

They both had a temper, I thought. Looking over, I saw Mrs. Ashleigh staring over her embroidery, enthralled. This was a part of Cyrus Barker that she had never seen.

"Stay for a few weeks," Barker said. "Until I'm better. Move into the house if you wish. I've got plenty of room."

Caleb Barker gave him an ornery smile.

"Much obliged, little brother, but no, thank you."

# CHAPTER SEVEN

W hat do we do now, sir?" I asked, though I was reluctant to ask the question in front of his brother.

I had plans of my own, of course, but I wanted to
let him make the decision if he could. I was certain once he was
fully awake, he would be even more eager than I to find whoever
was responsible for the bombing.

"What have you done so far?" the Guv asked.

I told him of examining the remains of the blast with the fire
captain, accumulating the files, the details of Mrs. Archer's visit,
the arrival of his brother, and the list of suspects sent to Scotland
Yard.

"What made you suspicious of Mrs. Archer?"

"There was something about her manner. She didn't seem as
grieved as one might be if one's husband was missing. In fact, she
had a coquettish manner and there was a look in her eye, as if she
was capable of anything."

"You were wise to follow her. It's unfortunate that she escaped before you got some solid answers."

"Can you think of anyone who might hate you so much as to do this?" I asked.

"I must consider the matter. Caleb?"

"Still here, Cyrus."

"Can you track?"

"With the best of them. What do you need me to do?"

"Try the tunnel under the offices. It's possible the bombers came through there."

"There are two problems with that, sir," I interjected. "The tunnel has been blocked off with boards, and the clerk at the desk won't let anyone pass."

"Oh, Hell's bells," Caleb said. "As if some flimsy wood and an even flimsier clerk are going to stop me."

"Take the lad with you to the tunnel."

Barker's brother flipped a thumb over his shoulder in my direction. "Lad?"

"Sir," I said to my employer, "I'm twenty-six and about to be married. Don't you think we can do without that word?"

"You're not married yet, laddie," he said in his Lowland accent.

Caleb stood. "Come, laddie."

I gave my employer a withering look.

"I'll meet you outside," I told Caleb.

When he left, I turned to my employer. "That man is impossible. He's trying to run the investigation himself. What do you want me to do?"

"Suffer his presence as best you can. Come in to see me as often as possible to discuss what's happening." He paused and gave me a hard stare. "Oh, and Thomas, do not trust that man under any circumstances."

"Yes, sir," I replied.

I took my leave from the room and found Caleb out on the street waiting for me, one hand in his pocket and the other holding a cigarette.

"Got a question for you," my companion said, putting on his hat again. "Between you and me."

"What is it?" I asked, hailing a cab.

"Is he any good?"

"Mr. Barker?" I asked, surprised. "He's very good indeed. His methods aren't usual, but they're effective. He's often in competition with Scotland Yard if he isn't working with them. He considers it a point of honor to try to reach the solution first."

"So it's not a matter of putting an ad in *The Times*."

"Wait," I said after we had climbed aboard the hansom. "You said you'd seen the sign on the door by accident."

"Did I?" he asked, not the least put out by being caught in a lie.

That was all I needed, another brother as secretive as the first. Who was this fellow, anyway? Of course, he was Barker's brother, and a Pinkerton agent according to his papers, but we knew nothing of him or what he had done over the past twenty years. He could have been one of those desperados I had read about.

"How did he make his money?" Caleb asked. "That house of his is pretty fancy."

"I have no idea. He won't talk about it."

Two could play at being secretive. I knew Barker had made his fortune diving for sunken ships, but I was under no obligation to tell it to anyone else. Caleb looked as if he didn't believe me.

"Do you have experience tracking?" I asked.

"I was a tracker for the U.S. Army during the Modoc War."

A few minutes later, we arrived at the office. Caleb directed me to light a lamp. Then, carefully, I climbed down the rope to the basement with the lit lamp in one hand. It was far more difficult than I had anticipated. I was relieved when I finally reached the rubble-strewn floor.

"Look out!" he called, sliding down the rope to the floor. I stepped back to give him room, raising the lantern high.

"They've nailed a sheet of birch over the tunnel," I said. "We'll need to get some tools."

He lifted a trouser leg and retrieved a knife from inside his boot. "This should be all I need."

"What is that?"

The knife was long, practically a short sword, with a wide heel tapering to a sharp point. The handle seemed to be made of some kind of horn.

"It's called an 'Arkansas toothpick.' Good for any number of things."

He slid the point by the edge of the board and began to pry it loose. Once the first corner gave way, the rest followed rather easily. We moved the heavy board and stepped into the tunnel.

The ceiling was low, and most of the area was taken up by pipes and cables, providing the heart of London with communication. Beside it was a narrow corridor. Caleb appropriated the lamp and squatted down, looking at the dusty concrete floor.

"The tunnel's empty," I said.

"Quiet."

He scrutinized the ground inch by inch, picking up anything that wasn't part of the tunnel itself: nails, bits of wood, etc. He took infinite care, which meant, as far as I could see, that he was wasting my precious time. There were files to examine and I had neither the skills, the patience, nor the desire to crawl about in a tunnel all day.

Caleb Barker grunted and pulled something from a crack in the wall. It was a small bottle, of the sort which carried patent medicine, the kind that was almost pure alcohol. Obviously, some of the employees of the telephone exchange were not as morally upright as others. Barker's brother lifted the bottle to his eye and peered inside with the aid of the lamp.

"Dry," he said, setting it carefully back where he had found it.

Then he moved on and examined another bit of ground. At that rate we would still be there at midnight.

"Can't we go faster?" I asked.

He looked scornfully over his shoulder. I'd accused my employer from time to time of being ill-tempered, but I was beginning to wonder if he was the more genial of his family.

We pressed on another few feet, inch by irritating inch. I'd have simply left him there and gone back to work like a sensible person, but the Guv had sent us on this fool's errand. He had settled the question of who was heading this enquiry very quickly: he was. If there was any comfort to be had it was that I was accustomed to standing in Barker's shadow, both figuratively and physically, but his brother was not. He was used to being out on the prairie, running an investigation all by himself.

We were at least a dozen yards down the tunnel, and by a sharp turn south, when he actually found something. It was the fag end of a cigarette, smashed by the heel of a shoe. He picked it up and examined it, holding it very close to his eye. I suspected he needed spectacles, but knew better then to suggest it.

"G-A-U-," he began.

"Gauloises," I said. "French cigarettes. Our chef, Etienne, smokes them."

"Are they common in England?" he asked.

"I shouldn't think so. There must be a tobacconist that sells them in London, for French expatriates, but I've never seen them. Perhaps Etienne knows."

Caleb raised the cigarette end to his nose and sniffed it, then he rolled it between his fingers until the small morsel of tobacco inside fell into his hand. He sniffed that as well.

"No more than a day or two old," he pronounced.

We crawled around the bend in the tunnel, and came upon a second find, a spent lucifer. He gave it much the same treatment as he had the cigarette.

"There you go," he said.

"Where, exactly?"

"You can't move about in an unlit tunnel in the dark unless you're a mole. This man stopped and lit a lantern or a lamp here, unless he merely used the match to see where he was going."

"That makes sense. And look over there! Another cigarette."

"We're not there yet. Don't jump ahead."

He crawled, nearly on his stomach, until he reached the cigarette. I looked over his shoulder.

"The end here," he said. "It's been bitten. It was held in the teeth. The other was perfectly round, with no teeth marks. It was smoked by someone holding the end between his lips. I'll bet—"

"There were two smokers."

"Yup."

"Two men to set the charges," I continued.

"It's easier that way."

Caleb crawled on until he came to the stairs at the far side of the tunnel. He examined each stair, and then pressed on the diagonal door leading outside to the embankment.

"It's locked," I said. "It would be now."

"It's still worthwhile to check."

"This tracking business brings taking pains to a higher level."

We returned through the tunnel to the rope and began to climb. Caleb was older than Barker by several years, but had little trouble scaling the rope. In a couple of minutes we were standing in front of Craig's Court.

"How long is a Galywas?"

"Gauloises. Not very long at all," I replied. "Half the length of a British cigarette, but strong. Why?"

He ignored my comment but made a request.

"Could you take me around the other side of that door?" he asked. "I still need to follow the trail."

I sighed. "Fine. Come this way."

There's a narrow exit through Craig's Court to the Embankment behind. I led him through until we came to the Thames, and around the long east side to the diagonal door. He continued to search the area thoroughly. The man was part bloodhound.

"Here you go," Caleb said, pointing down to the ground beside an elm. I came closer.

"Two more cigarette ends," I said. One was flattened and the other had burned down to the filter.

"One man stepped on his. The other flicked it away."

"Two men," I agreed. "And the match was to light a lamp or something."

"Two Frenchmen," he corrected. "Unless there are two Englishmen in London who enjoy torturing themselves with French tobacco."

"What's wrong with French tobacco?" I asked.

"Not much, except you might as well have used the match to burn your tongue. I'm American. I know good Virginia tobacco, and not this inferior weed here."

"Etienne likes them."

"Just because he knows food don't make him an expert in tobacco."

I tried to keep from smiling, but I'm not sure I succeeded. "Is that it? Can you track out here?"

"They took this stone path along the river. A few hundred people have walked along here since then. Any sign is long gone."

"The Frenchmen."

"Yup. Look for Frenchmen on your list. You're welcome."

"Thank you."

I fell into step beside him, his long stride almost as difficult to keep up with as his brother's.

"Have you ever met a Frenchman?" I asked. "Besides Etienne, I mean."

"No, but I have met their little cousins, the Creoles. Been down to Storyville after a case. The men are fops, but the women are uncommonly pretty."

"You've been all over America, then," I said.

"Most of it. My line of work has taken me all over, including north to Canada and south to Mexico."

We summoned a cab and clambered aboard.

"You must have a lot of stories after your travels."

He bristled then. "This isn't a campfire and my history is nobody's business but mine."

"I didn't mean to pry. I was merely curious."

"Curiosity can get you shot in the Territories."

"Then I'll remind myself never to visit the Territories."

The man actually chuckled. "You do that. Don't want to see that head of hair of yours decorating the end of a lance."

"They really scalp people? I thought that was a myth."

"I wish it were. See, they take a knife and cut around the hairline like so, from above."

He drew a line about the edges of my hair with his finger.

"After that, they tug back the flap in front just an inch. Then they yank on it and pull it right off. Some seize the flap between their teeth and rip it off that way. Believe it or not, some men survive it."

"What happens to them?"

"They wear a lot of hats and are not presentable to polite society."

# CHAPTER EIGHT

I had a list of suspects, and I thought it likely that researching them would result in enough evidence to incriminate one of them in the bombing. That was the process of enquiry work, though in his eccentric orbit about each case, Cyrus Barker never did the expected. He didn't plod. That was Scotland Yard's forte, and they did it well. My employer used flashes of inspiration to bring cases to a close quickly, generally within two weeks. During an investigation he would eat wherever and whatever he came across, sleep little, and work around the clock. I had learned to do the same, if only to accommodate my employer. He enjoyed it, I think, the work. It was a challenge.

I was about to follow leads across the country, verifying the location of each suspect, and questioning them, if possible. Caleb had disappeared, on another of his innumerable errands. That still left one fly in the ointment: Mrs. Archer. She could lead us on a merry chase and, quite frankly, I didn't have time for it. Who did she work for? A young woman like that did not have a personal reason to hurt Cyrus Barker. Was she the relative of one of the men, or was she paid? She was an enigma, and I hate enigmas.

Climbing down the stair from number 5, I turned into Craig's Court, around the east side of the telephone exchange, to the diagonal door housed in an old mansion known as Harrington House. Just before reaching it, I opened a door on the wall opposite ours and stepped in. The office was empty, but a call brought a man from the back room. He wore no jacket and his sleeves were rolled to the elbows. He'd been washing his hands.

"J.M.?" I asked. "Are you busy?"

"Thomas, come in!" he said, waving me inside the room. "I was just working on a brief. How's the old man?"

J. M. Hewitt was a detective who had given up a profitable career as a barrister to track information and question suspicious people. Normally he worked exclusively for law offices, but from time to time he'd take on a case we were too busy for. As detectives go, he never had a wolf at the door, but then he specialized in a specific and wealthy clientele.

"First of all," I said, "he's no more than ten years older than you. But he's not in good shape at the moment. His shin bone is broken."

"Bad luck. Give him my best the next time you see him."

"Thank you very much for helping yesterday."

"It was the least I could do. Push has been very good to me."

"Push" was the term many of the Underworld, which unfortunately includes detectives, called my employer. Somehow he'd acquired the moniker "Governor," which was translated into criminal patois rhyming slang as "Push-comes-to-shove," and then later shortened to "Push."

"So what can I do for you, Thomas?"

"I'm looking for a girl."

"Aren't we all?"

"I mean a girl detective. Sarah Fletcher. Do you know how to find her?"

"Of course," he answered. "She's finishing a case for me at the moment. She's good. Very good."

"So I hear. Could you send her word that I would like to use her services if she is available?"

Hewitt wiggled his eyebrows, which was wholly unnecessary. He's of average build, with dark, wavy hair, and a bland face, and his expression was always halfway between comic and serious. He was a likeable chap and his mild manner gave him the unique ability to not be suspected as a detective.

"And you practically a married man."

"You are a humorist, sir," I said. "You should write for the *Idler*."

"I'll let her know that you require her services. She's due within the hour."

I thanked him and returned to the office. I must admit it was good to sit without the constant and infernal scrutiny of Mr. Caleb Barker. Leaning back in the single office chair, I put my foot up on the corner of the desk, and thought furiously about everything. Sometimes one must gather ideas hither and yon, and see how they fit together. An hour later I was still at it, without making much headway, when I heard a light step on the staircase. For a second, I wondered if Camille Archer had returned. I jumped from my seat and awaited my visitor.

"I say, is anyone there?" a woman's voice called.

"Up here, Miss Fletcher!" I replied.

She climbed the stair and entered the room. She was no more than five foot three, with dark hair and a narrow waist. Small eyes and the kind of expression that society would say was due to too much thinking marred an otherwise handsome face.

"Mr. Llewelyn! How good to see you."

"And you, Miss Fletcher. How have you been?"

"Quite well, thank you," she replied. "As a matter of fact, I have been considering opening an agency of my own, handling strictly female clients."

"That sounds splendid," I replied. I gestured to the chair opposite the desk. "Let us know if you require any help. Mr. Barker will act as a reference if required."

She came forward and settled into the visitor's chair, still with that air of caution, as if I were a benign lion that still might spring at her if the mood suited me.

"What can I do for you, Mr. Llewelyn?"

She was very businesslike. I admired her composure. I sat down behind the desk and moved papers out of the way.

"Miss Fletcher, a young woman came into our offices yesterday morning, seeking someone to find her husband. Within a few minutes, I began to suspect her story was fabricated, although I wasn't sure why. Afterward, I followed her to the Bradford Family Hotel, but she disappeared through the back door with her luggage. To add insult to injury, the name she signed on the registry was Camille Llewelyn."

"Is there a Mrs. Llewelyn we don't know about, sir?" she asked, as if it were the height of humor.

"Ask me in two weeks," I said.

"Ah, yes. I hear congratulations are in order. Another sister reduced to meeting the needs of a man."

"I forgot that you are a suffragette. Very well. For you, and possibly for my fiancée as well, I promise to be a more enlightened husband."

"That would be at least one in London," she replied. "Tell me, can you describe the young woman for me?"

I knew better than to assign some degree of beauty to the visitor. Best to just stay with the facts.

"She was of average height, about five foot three. Her hair was voluminous, and an odd shade of almost chestnut red. Her eyes were green. Her lips were full and her nose was upturned. Almost impudent."

"Pretty?"

"She was attractive enough, I suppose, but there was something unsettling about her. I could not quite put my finger on it. She was coquettish, which was completely against type. One does not flirt while looking for one's missing husband."

"She flirted with you?" Miss Fletcher asked.

"Oh, rather."

"And you did nothing to encourage her?"

"Believe it or not, miss, I am a professional, for six years now. I would never flirt with a client."

"Some have and said they didn't."

"You said you were aware I am betrothed."

She gave me a prim look, perhaps even judgmental. "You know very well that does not stop some men."

I stifled a smile, and even a sense of indignation.

"I agree, it doesn't. I cannot convince you otherwise without evidence, but I can give you a kind of defense, even if it were merely a feeling."

"Very well, Mr. Llewelyn. If you have an impression I may not agree with it, but I shall hear it."

"Thank you, Miss Fletcher. Now I forget, but what is that substance some fast women are wearing on their eyes these days? It's not kohl."

"It is called mascara. It's French."

"Exactly. Thank you. She wore mascara, very dark, but no rouge. Her face was very pale and her lashes dark."

"Very well. And what happened after you spoke?"

"I followed her at a discreet distance to the family hotel. I spoke to the manager for a few moments, trying to convince him to let me speak to her, but meanwhile Mrs. Archer slipped out the back. By the time I reached the street she was gone."

"That's unfortunate," she said.

"Worse than that, when I looked at the register, what do you think she wrote after her name?"

"I cannot imagine."

"'Camille Llewelyn, of Cwmbran, Gwent.' That is my birthplace, Miss Fletcher. It means she has looked into my background. I feel her out there somewhere, perhaps watching me. She's under my guard with a knife, trying to decide which ribs to stab between."

"You are very forceful with your language, Mr. Llewelyn," she replied, raising a brow. She smoothed her skirt and regarded me.

"No, Miss Fletcher, I am precise. If I say she is dangerous, I am willing to lay down money that you shall find her the same."

She appeared to doubt me, but she stood as if willing to offer me the benefit of the doubt, if only for professional purposes.

"Very well," she said, closing her small notebook and returning it to her reticule. "I shall go to the hotel and see if I can follow her trail from there. I will report back as soon as I know something."

"Wait. There's a second matter I would like you to undertake."

"Yes?"

"My employer is currently in hospital, which leaves his friend Mrs. Ashleigh unprotected. Do you think you could both search for Mrs. Archer and watch Philippa Ashleigh at the same time? I think she would be more comfortable with a female operative and I am far too busy with our current case."

"Very well."

She stood and turned to leave.

"Miss Fletcher, I must implore you not to underestimate this woman."

"Thank you for the warning, Mr. Llewelyn. I am armed."

"I am glad to hear it."

"Is this in relation to the explosion yesterday?" she asked, turning back toward me.

"That I cannot say," I answered. "One followed the other but that does not necessarily prove a connection."

"I see."

"However, neither can I prove that they aren't connected, so one must prepare for either eventuality."

"I will keep that in mind."

"I understand you are otherwise employed. If you wish, you

should finish Mr. Hewitt's case. Mine is not a priority, and I don't consider it likely that Mrs. Archer will return."

"Based upon what, Mr. Llewelyn? Intuition?"

She was baiting me. She hoped I would equate intuition with the fairer sex.

"You are correct, I have none. Thank you."

She was mollified for the moment. "How is Mr. Barker faring?"

"Not well. He was badly injured. I have hope, however, that he will make a full recovery."

"Based upon?" she asked.

"The words of his physician, not the conviction that everything will work out for the best in this, the best of all possible worlds."

"I didn't know detectives read Leibniz," she said.

"I am a private enquiry agent, and I attended Oxford."

"That explains it, then."

"That explains what, Miss Fletcher?"

"Your hiring."

I was tempted to change my mind about engaging her services, but instead considered the list I had given to Scotland Yard. I dismissed her from my mind. A minute went by. Eventually she would understand.

"Mr. Llewelyn, pray forgive me."

"For what?" I asked, looking up.

"For allowing my feelings to interfere with this investigation."

I looked at her now. "It is the last thing that I expected from a woman—a detective, rather—who prides herself on her objectivity. Apparently, your reputation for professionalism is unmerited."

"I—wait. You're playing with me!"

I smiled, though my eyes had returned to my list.

"I am, miss, but it is no less than you deserve. What precisely have I done to draw your ire?"

"I applied for your position but was summarily dismissed. It isn't that he won't work with a female operative. It must have been your education. I didn't know you were an Oxonian."

"Miss Fletcher, my education consisted of less than a year in Magdalen, followed by Oxford Prison for eight months."

She was mystified.

"What was the reason he hired you, then?" she demanded.

"I have heard several explanations from him, and I don't believe any of them. I truly believe he thinks he works by the Holy Spirit. Certainly I needed the work, but I cannot give you a single reason why he chose me over you. You are obviously more qualified than I. The only thing I can say in my defense is that I have survived six years with the most contrary employer in London. Perhaps your refusal was a blessing in disguise."

Slowly she unbent. Perhaps "thawed" was a better word.

"Miss Fletcher, I would very much like to retain your services. You came highly recommended, but if we cannot work together, I will show you to the door and solve this without your aid."

"I understand," she said.

"So which is it to be?"

"You're not teasing this time, are you?" she asked.

"No, Miss Fletcher, I am not."

Two spots slowly blossomed on her cheeks. "I apologize, Mr. Llewelyn. I was rude."

"Thank you. Now, do you want to take on this enquiry? I would still prefer a female operative and I hear you are the best in London."

"I would, sir."

"Excellent. Do you require any more information?"

"No, Mr. Llewelyn."

"Very well, then. Good day, miss."

She nodded and took herself off. I heard her footfalls on the steps and the door closing behind her.

"My word," I muttered.

# CHAPTER NINE

I went out for a ploughman's lunch and no sooner had I returned than I was accosted in the street. My nerves were still raw, and I did not care for being approached by a perfect stranger, but the one who summoned me had the appearance of a junior clerk somewhere in Whitehall Street.

"Mr. Llewelyn?"

"Yes, I am he."

"Might you be able to spare a few minutes?" he asked. "Mr. Humphrey would like to speak with you."

I was impatient, and perhaps a trifle tired. I wanted to sit in my chair, hard as it was, and not move for half an hour altogether. Such things were not to be, however.

"Pray, who is Mr. Humphrey?" I asked.

In answer, he pointed up to the large white edifice beside our offices.

"The bank manager, sir. Cox and Co."

"Ah. Has he had you skulking about, waiting for me?"

"He has, sir. I promise it won't take over half an hour. Mr. Humphrey is a busy man."

"So am I," I told him. "You said it would only be a few minutes."

"I can't really say how long precisely, sir, but he does have an appointment half an hour from now, so it can't be any longer than that."

I looked at him. The clerk was younger than I, his face blotched with acne. He had been ordered to find this enquiry agent and he'd been pacing around Craig's Court ever since. I felt sorry for him.

"Oh, very well, take me to him, by all means."

The clerk exhaled and his shoulders fell in relief.

"Thank you, Mr. Llewelyn. Please follow me."

For a moment, I thought of a time six years before when I was without situation, and waiting near this very spot for an interview with Mr. Cyrus Barker, private enquiry agent. For all this fellow knew I had been born to this profession and was highly successful, successful enough to have an account at Cox and Co.

I followed him around the corner into the bank. It was impressive. So many tons of marble, quarried in far-off Italy or Portugal, and brought here by boat, by train, by cart, to be assembled at this absurdly out-of-the-way spot so that people here would be impressed enough to have this firm safeguard and make use of their money. Was a marble bank safer than a brick-and-mortar one, and if so, how?

Under normal circumstances, visiting a bank manager, any bank manager, would cause a moment of concern, but after being unceremoniously dropped into a cellar the day before, and battling away since then, I began to consider there are things more intimidating than bankers. The clerk led me along as if tied with an invisible rope, past customers, clerks, bank cages, tables, private offices, and the like, and then the two of us climbed a grand staircase into the gallery above. As it happened, the managers' offices were such that should he have had a window in the east wall, it would have looked down over our narrow courtyard and offices.

The gangly youth who led me finally stopped in front of a secretary who guarded the manager's offices. He sent the boy away with a hard look, and banished me to a chair harder than the marble floor. I tried not to make faces at him, but promised myself that if he ever came for our services I would make him come and sit in this very chair until I found myself willing to see him.

At last a door opened behind the secretary, and an unctuous fellow came forward and said, "Mr. Llewelyn! I'm so sorry to keep you waiting! Would you please come into my office, sir?"

"Of course," I said, following him into the room.

"Sit here. Robert Humphrey, sir. Very pleased to make your acquaintance! Cigar?"

"No, thank you."

I was all at sea. Normally, bank managers were like the cat who got into the heavy cream, but this fellow seemed actually nervous. Why else, for example, would he be so polite to such an insignificant fellow as I? True, I had an account there, with my own few pounds collecting interest, and Barker had his, a substantial amount, but not by comparison to Her Majesty's Army and Navy, whose accounts make up the bulk of Cox and Co. assets. Why all this bowing and scraping?

"What can I do for you, Mr. Humphrey? I have many duties today. No doubt you are aware that our premises were damaged yesterday."

"I was here, sir. I heard the rumble, but I know not from whence it came or in what direction."

Humphrey was stout, choleric, and side-whiskered. His watch chain sprawled across his prosperous waistcoat, and his pince-nez spectacles attached by a ribbon to the boutonniere eyelet of his gray lapel. He did not look comfortable, and I almost felt sorry for him, as I did for his clerk. I spared no pity for the secretary.

"Why am I here, sir, if I may be so bold to ask?"

"Yes, well. Mr. Llewelyn, I was aware that Mr. Barker has an account in this bank, but that as his clerk—"

"Assistant," I corrected.

"Excuse me, as his assistant you handle all his financial matters. Money is placed here at irregular intervals, and the account accrues interest."

"Yes, that is essentially according to Mr. Barker's wishes. Continue, please!"

"Mr. Barker does not come here, although I have met him once, as I recall. His appearance is not unknown because of the proximity between our offices. Therefore, his general appearance is well known to many here."

"And . . . ?" I asked, wishing he would get on with it.

"Yesterday morning, mere minutes after the explosion, a man came into our bank answering your employer's description and claiming to be him. He made a substantial withdrawal and left the building."

I sat for a while taking it all in, or trying to. "Withdrawal? From Barker's account?"

"Yes, I'm afraid so."

"How substantial?" I finally asked.

Humphrey leaned forward and consulted a sheet of paper. "Four thousand, nine hundred and eighty-seven pounds, five shillings, and six pence."

I cleared my throat, still reeling at the thought. "That amount is both random and highly specific," I said.

Humphrey leaned forward and laced his fingers on the desk, trying to look businesslike under difficult conditions.

"It isn't when one understands that we have safeguards in place for a withdrawal over five thousand pounds. Your thief is aware of banking regulations."

"Ah," I countered, "but I have no thief. I'm sure a bank of the reputation of Cox and Co. would have replaced the missing amount from the emergency funds or what-have-you, and called Scotland Yard."

"We have."

I nodded. "I expected as much. Is the teller who completed the transaction in the building?"

"He is, Mr. Llewelyn."

"I should like to speak with him and to see the spot where the transaction was made."

"But, sir, you are not Scotland Yard. You are private agents. You have no authority in a bank."

"Then give me that authority. I merely want to interview one man. The fellow who strolled in so casually yesterday must have had some connection to the attempted murder, or rather, murders, since I was present. Mr. Barker would be here now if he could, doing what I am doing. Any delay could mean that this thief is escaping London."

Humphrey drew in his breath, then nodded.

"Fleet!" he called.

The odious secretary rushed into the office.

"Yes, sir?"

"Get Smithers in here."

"Right away, sir!"

Fleet rushed back out again.

"We'll have this matter arranged to your satisfaction, Mr. Llewelyn," the manager assured me. "I would not want to see a falling-out between our agencies. We try to keep harmony between the various businesses in Craig's Court. Just yesterday we were working with the telephone exchange to get the lines restored. We had heard a rumor that the explosion came from some electrical problem there. We did not hear for several hours that Mr. Barker, one of our own clients, was injured. By then, the thief had come and gone, with nearly five thousand pounds sterling."

We heard a knock on the door.

Humphrey leaned forward. "Yes?"

Smithers was pushed in from outside, like a Christian being fed to the lions. He was a pudgy fellow, with receding hair and spectacles.

"You wanted to see me, sir?"

"Come in, Smithers. This fellow is Mr. Llewelyn, assistant to

Cyrus Barker. The real Cyrus Barker. He is here to investigate the imposter you spoke to yesterday."

There was an underlying tone implying that this humble clerk was solely responsible for the entire incident. *Poor chap*, I thought to myself.

"Mr. Smithers," I began. "Could you describe the man who came to you yesterday morning?"

"Yes, sir. He was tall and well built, with a heavy mustache and dark spectacles. I have seen your employer once. He was pointed out to me in passing. This fellow looked very much like him. It did not occur to me that our visitor might not be he."

"What kind of hair did he have?"

"He wore a bowler hat the entire time."

"Did he carry a stick?"

"He did, but I did not notice what kind, regrettably."

He looked up and flinched at Humphrey's expression. Apparently, clerks at Cox and Co. are expected to notice everything, not unlike private enquiry agent assistants.

"Was he lean or heavily built?"

"He tended toward lean, I should say. Wait! Yes, I did notice the stick. It was very thin and black, one of those wand types that are fashionable these days. With his physique I thought the stick looked too thin."

"Excellent. Was it a cane or ball end?"

"Ball, sir."

"Very good, Mr. Smithers. Now his clothes. What can you tell me?"

"He wore a morning coat, double breasted, striped trousers, and pumps."

"Collar? Tie?"

"I don't remember the collar, sir. I'm sorry. The tie was red. It was an ascot. Very smart. There was something wrong with the hat, however. The crown was very high. It did not go well with the suit. In my opinion, sir."

The last was directed toward his employer.

"Tie pin?"

"Nothing notable, I'm afraid."

"You spoke to him for how long, would you say?"

"Ten minutes at most. Had it been a lesser amount, we would have filled it immediately, his being a client in long standing."

"I was out of the building," Mr. Humphrey assured me, removing himself from any blame in the matter. "The approval was given to my assistant, Carruthers."

I did not want to be in Carruthers's shoes, either, although I might be if I did not handle this case correctly.

"So you engaged in a conversation, then?"

"He was not a talkative man. For the most part he merely waited."

"Did he have an accent?"

"Yes, sir. Scottish."

"Could you tell if it was Highland or Lowland?"

"That's the thing I've been turning over in my mind, Mr. Llewelyn. I was in a play once, sir. A bit of amateur theatrics, you might say."

He looked sheepishly at his employer that he would dare have once indulged in such frivolity. The latter seemed to agree.

"Anyway, my role was a Scotsman, and it was difficult to attempt, if one does not have the knack. Looking back to yesterday, his accent seemed put on. It sounded like the one I affected, which was neither Highland nor Lowland, but what a London audience might think a Scotsman sounds like."

"You are doing well, Mr. Smithers. Can you add any other detail to your account?"

"Well, sir, when he came toward my desk, his walk was unusual. He sort of rolled from side to side."

"Was he bowlegged?"

"He might have been. As I said, he wore a long coat."

"Anything else?"

"He was very at his ease. Being there did not appear to fluster him. The hand he gave me did not shake in the least."

I stood. "Thank you, Mr. Smithers. You've been very helpful."

The teller nodded at his employer and began to scurry away. I called after him.

"Excuse me, sir. Did he have a scar?"

"No scar, sir!" he called as he hurried out the door.

"Good man," I said to Mr. Humphrey.

"Yes, less dull than I expected."

"That conversation was all that I required."

"Will you let us know Mr. Barker's condition and his progress?"

"I shall."

We both understood that the fellow had no real interest in Cyrus Barker's condition and that I had no plan to inform them of it. It was merely a way for him to end the interview and get me out of the room in time for his next appointment. I nodded, took up my hat and stick, and left his office.

At the front entrance I stopped and turned about, surveying the room and the path he must have taken. Smithers was at the front desk, past the line of tellers. I tried to picture the man crossing to the desk. The problem was I had little trouble picturing it. The imposter in my vision was Caleb Barker.

# CHAPTER TEN

My employer's brother returned an hour later, transformed. His hair had been cut short, his mustache trimmed, and his clothes made respectable. He wore a brown suit and a matching bowler. I couldn't help but think that somehow he seemed diminished.

"That's quite a change," I said.

"As a Pinkerton agent, I don't want to stand out in a crowd," he said in an accent that could almost pass for English.

"Is this your true speaking voice, or has the American become more familiar?"

Caleb Barker nodded, curling his fingers around his lapel.

"A fair question. I adopt whatever language I need wherever I am. It has become second nature. However, I'll admit being in the United States for so long has flattened my natural way of speaking."

"I wish you would choose one accent and stay with it."

"I'm not here to please you, son, only to help Cyrus. Have you finally made a plan about how to catch whoever tried to kill my brother?"

"I have. We're going to Scotland Yard to get information. While we are there, I will introduce you to some colleagues."

Caleb frowned and crossed his arms. "That's not the best of plans, Mr. Llewelyn."

"You don't wish to visit the greatest detective police force in all the world? You, a Pinkerton agent?"

"Not while they are hunting for me," he said.

Now I understood why he'd been so ill-tempered and secretive. "Was this in connection with the case that brought you here to England?"

"It was," he muttered under his breath.

"What happened?"

"A simple difference of opinion. I thought two men should die and they disagreed. As you can see, I won the argument."

"Was it murder or self-defense?"

"They were wasting bullets as fast as I was," he said.

"Where did this take place?"

"Sussex," he replied.

"I see."

"Don't expect me to walk in and surrender myself."

"But you can't walk about London with impunity," I answered.

"Hence the new suit, Mr. Llewelyn," he said, beginning to pace the room. He strode back and forth like he was already in a cell.

"Look," I said. "Your brother and I have friends at 'A' Division. We've even worked there on a case or two. The name 'Barker' has a certain reputation in London."

"You can't expect me to stroll in and say 'Good morning! I'm the fellow you are looking for.'"

"They're not stupid. Sooner or later they'll catch you. Wouldn't it be better to go and surrender yourself? Isn't that the way a Pinkerton agent should act?"

Caleb's temper got the best of him again. "Don't lecture me on what a Pinkerton should do. You can gamble with your freedom, but I'd prefer to choose what I do with my own, thank you."

I shrugged. Some people won't listen to reason. Not that I haven't been accused of that myself once or twice.

"Do as you like," I said. "I've got business to do. I'll see you later."

"Wait, give me a minute to think on this," Caleb said. "You can't just spring this on a man, and expect him to trot along behind."

Caleb Barker was becoming something of an impediment. He wished to be consulted about everything. This was not his case, and to some extent he was hindering rather than helping. I wondered if that were his intent. If this man was being deliberately obstinate, he was doing a fine job of it.

"Suit yourself," I said, standing. "That's me, then."

"Oh, very well. It might be worth it to see the face of Scotland Yard's finest when I walk in the door."

I led him round the corner to Great Scotland Yard Street and through the gate to the new "A" Division. As usual, the first face I saw upon entering was that of Kirkwood, the bewhiskered desk sergeant.

"Hello, Mr. Llewellyn," he greeted upon our arrival, looking my companion up and down. "Whom have you brought us today?"

"This is Mr. Caleb Barker, my employer's brother. He is connected with the business that occurred in Sussex earlier this week."

"Ah, the Wealden murders," he replied. "Three men dead in a display of firearms, all Americans. It is as if they come from the womb with a gun in each hand."

Caleb looked ready to defend his adopted country, but bit his lip. He gave me a look which told me he regretted being brought here. While a constable was dispatched for an inspector, he dropped into a chair and offered me a Sobranie from a new cigarette case, which I refused, and lit one of his own with a match.

A few minutes later, Chief Constable McNaughton came to the

front desk with his hands in his pockets. It's true, I do have a reputation for bringing the unexpected into their building, but I am
only doing the Guv's work.

"Hello, Mr. Llewelyn," the chief constable said. "Is this the
gentleman you were referring to?"

"It is. This is Caleb Barker, my employer's elder brother."

"I hear this is the man we've been combing Sussex for. And
you just marched in off the street?"

"I'm here, aren't I?" Caleb said irritably.

"Is it true that you are an agent of the Pinkertons?"

"What's your best guess?"

"Friendly chap, isn't he?" the chief constable said to me.

"Oh, he's just bags of fun."

"Gentlemen, let's go back to my office."

We followed him through the wide, sand-colored halls of the
new "A" Division, which were so much better than the cramped
quarters of their previous offices.

"Here we are," McNaughton said as we entered the room. It
had the usual dull furnishings but a number of racing prints on
the walls where one expected photographs of criminals. He waved
us into chairs and closed the door, to keep others out, and his suspect in.

"Now, Mr. Barker, I understand you were accompanying
Mr. James McCloskey to England. For what purpose, may I ask?"

"Mr. Pinkerton felt that America had become too dangerous
for him. He was being pursued by members of a group calling
itself the Knights of the Golden Circle."

"Were the two gentlemen found dead in the house you rented
members of this party?"

"They were, sir. Mr. Josey Anderson and Mr. Bodie Calhoun."

"What was your purpose in coming to England?"

"To protect Mr. McCloskey, obviously."

"You're not very good at your occupation, then, are you, sir?"

"Apparently not," Caleb said, stubbing out his cigarette in a
glass ashtray on the desk.

"Where were you during the shooting?"

"Getting supplies."

"How came all of you to possess firearms?" McNaughton asked. "You have no permits to carry any here."

"I'm not armed, and I have no idea how McCloskey or those dirty rebels got theirs."

"Do you believe the two men were shot by Mr. McCloskey?"

"I couldn't tell you. As I said, I was out getting supplies. Coffee. Bacon. Flour for biscuits."

"There was no chance, then, that Mr. McCloskey was shot by these two gentlemen and in turn you killed them both?"

Caleb smote the arm of his chair with the palm of his hand.

"That's what it was, Chief Constable. It looks like you got your man. Now why don't you run down to the American embassy and inform them that you are holding an American citizen against his will, after he came in voluntarily to help Scotland Yard with an investigation."

"Out of the goodness of his heart."

"Well, naturally. Cyrus and I were raised by a fine missionary mother."

"Chief Constable," I said, "Mr. Barker here has been instrumental in helping me search for the two men who bombed our offices. Apparently, he was some sort of tracker in America. He wants to find the men who nearly killed his brother out of a sense of family honor."

"That's right," Caleb replied.

"Mr. Barker, if Mr. Llewelyn is willing to vouch for you in your brother's name, I will allow it. However, you may not leave London."

"Chief Constable, may that be extended to England?" I asked. "We are involved in a case which may yet take us out of town."

McNaughton leaned forward and glared at me with the full authority of the Metropolitan Police Force on his shoulders. "We had an agreement," he said, "but that didn't include a murder suspect."

"I brought you the most wanted man in England," I replied. "Surely that is worth something."

"I've a mind to toss both of you into a cell and let the commissioner decide what to do."

"You can, but we will merely summon the American ambassador and Mr. Bram Cusp to release us. It would be a wasted effort."

Cusp was our solicitor, who liked nothing more than dragging men from the clutches of the Met. McNaughton inhaled slowly through his nose and out through his mouth.

"You realize the American legation will be looking for you. We've informed them of the incident."

"They'll have to catch me first," Caleb said, as if it were a herculean task.

"Mr. Barker, the only reason you're not cooling a bench in a cell right now is because of our . . ." McNaughton had begun to say "respect," but looked for another word. ". . . previous working relationship with your brother. Don't make me regret my decision."

"No, sir."

The chief constable looked at me but pointed at Caleb. I understood what it must be like to be a lowly constable dressed down by him.

"Now, I have some information for you regarding your list of suspects," he said.

I nodded. "The first was a French anarchist named Jacques Perrine."

"He's been in La Santé Prison for several years, thanks to your employer. Then there's the financier, Henry Strathmore, who is in Newgate, along with Joseph Keller."

"The fellow who is about to hang."

"That's correct. The next one is Henry Thayer Pritchard, who murdered his three wives. He's still in Burberry Asylum, which, as far as I'm concerned, is the perfect place for him. And finally, we had Jack Hobson, the East End gang leader. I'm afraid I have some news on that score."

"What is it?" I asked.

"Unfortunately, he's been released from prison and we don't know his precise whereabouts at the moment. C.I.D. was not warned before he was released."

"I appreciate your effort to locate everyone, sir," I said.

I stood to go. It seemed that Hobson was our primary suspect, but I thought it best we visit all of them, anyway.

McNaughton cocked his head toward Caleb. "Keep this one close to you, Mr. Llewelyn. Whatever trouble he gets into, I hold you responsible."

"Yes, sir."

We were halfway down the corridor when I heard McNaughton's voice calling after us.

"Wait!"

I turned about. "Sir?"

"You said two men bombed your offices," he said. "How did you know that?"

"Mr. Barker here led me through the telephone tunnels under our offices and pointed out two sets of footprints."

I didn't mention the French cigarettes. He needn't know every detail of the case.

"I see. The tunnel, you say?"

"Yes, in the basement where you found me."

"Ah."

Much as I wanted to, I did not smirk. What the Yard had not thought of was the first thing the Guv had.

I waved at the sergeant on the way out, and we were soon in Great Scotland Yard again. I led Caleb to the Rising Sun across from the old Criminal Investigation Department and ordered two pints of bitter.

"Do you ever get Englishmen out there in the plains?" I asked.

"From time to time a lord will come for the hunting, though the buffalo are gone now. I've shown a few Englishmen around, being able to comprehend the language."

"Did you tell anyone you were Scottish?"

"Mr. Llewelyn, you should know by now not to tip your hand. Silence, as they say, is golden."

He was right, and though I didn't trust him fully, I did learn a few things. I'm far too gullible. It is a habit I need to grow out of. I also trust too much. There must be some way, I told myself, to talk easily to someone while at the same time assessing their words and character. I should be, well, let's face it, more like my employer, which was a sobering thought.

We split a steak and mushroom pie between us. Afterward, he hooked a bootheel over the other knee and lit another cigarette.

"I prefer Texas beef and Virginia tobacco," he said. "But I can't fault the ale."

"Of course not. It's Watney's."

"Do you think your list will bear fruit?"

"I suppose it's possible for a man to bear enough ill will to blow up your brother without saying a word, but it is more likely that ill will shall manifest itself somehow."

"You've had some education yourself, I see."

"I spent a short while at Oxford," I said.

"I've always wanted more education than I had. I'd have liked to have finished my schooling, but it was cut short by the Taiping Rebellion in Shanghai. After the American Civil War, I was hired by Mr. Pinkerton, and I've been traveling ever since."

"Travel broadens the mind."

"Not as much as books. I generally keep one in my saddlebags. I'm a great enthusiast for Marcus Aurelius."

"With good reason," I said.

"When's Cyrus coming home?"

"Soon, I hope. He doesn't convalesce well. It isn't in his nature to lay about."

"No," Caleb said. "It isn't. Our mother used to keep us in during the monsoon season. You would have thought she was taking a hot poker to his feet the way he carried on."

"It's so strange hearing you talk about his childhood days. I rather thought he'd sprung to life at forty."

"He'd have preferred we treat him as an adult at ten."

"And you?"

"Me? I've never much regarded anyone's opinion of me one way or the other."

"I rather suspected that," I said.

He gave me a rare smile, the corners of his eyes crinkling, but he gave no answer. The two brothers were alike in one way, at least.

"So, what do we do now, Mr. Private Enquiry Agent?" he asked.

"As I said before, I am a humble assistant. Perhaps it is time to talk to your brother. I'm certain he has some ideas."

# CHAPTER ELEVEN

I had verified the whereabouts of everyone on the list except Hobson, but it still wasn't my case. I had to talk to Barker, to see if he wanted me to chase down the leads out of town. The day before had been a whirlwind.

Caleb had taken himself away. He still had business to transact for his employer, William Pinkerton, as I had with mine. As it happened, I didn't mind. He was distracting and irritable, and I had a case to solve.

Stepping from my cab, I came to the ancient St. John's Gate and went into the priory. I doffed my hat, and ran a hand through my hair. Then I walked down the corridor, my steps echoing in the halls. As I reached the doorway, I saw that Barker was asleep, as was Mrs. Ashleigh, in the hard chair beside his bed. Between that torturous chair and the accoutrements of female beauty, she must have been in a good deal of discomfort.

I cleared my throat and she awoke instantly, like a lioness on the savannah, ready to protect her young. She relaxed when she recognized me, and hid a yawn behind her lace glove. I came farther into the room.

"How is he?" I asked in a low voice.

"He's fine, thank you," the Guv growled from the bed. There he was, flat on his back, buried in a mound of flat pillows, his left leg encircled in a contraption of wooden splints and hardware, and it didn't matter. Cyrus Barker was in charge. He wasn't a wounded animal in a corner. He was Henry the bloody VIII on his throne, about to take off heads. One of them, I suspected, was my own.

"Philippa," he rumbled. "Go have a cup of tea."

He was even short with her. He was never short with her. I often suspected he thought of her as a full-size Staffordshire figurine, a shepherdess or lady, who would shatter if not handled with care, but this time, he didn't ask her. He ordered her.

She didn't argue, but when she turned to leave, she glanced in my direction. I read the look as easily as Caleb Barker had read the signs in the tunnel the day before. It said, like the legends on antique maps: be careful. There be sea serpents here.

"What have you been doing?" he asked shortly. The pain was causing him to be in an ill mood.

"Sir, I went to Scotland Yard to find out where each of the suspects is presently."

"To whom did you speak?"

"Chief Constable McNaughton."

"Why not Poole?"

Chief Detective Inspector Terence Poole of the Criminal Investigation Department was an old friend of ours. He and the Guv had known each other for years and he was Barker's trusted source for information and advice. Once or twice he'd gotten himself in trouble for revealing secrets to Barker, or not revealing secrets of Barker's. He even tolerated me.

"I've developed a good rapport with McNaughton," I answered. "He doesn't actually loathe me, or if he does, he hides it well."

"Poole is a senior officer and may be privy to more information."

"Let's face it, sir," I argued. "Terry Poole has crossed the threshold. He's not a beat inspector anymore. He spends most of his time out of 'A' Division, attending various meetings. He's a good man and a fine detective, but McNaughton, well, he's got a lean and hungry look."

Barker grunted. I had actually prepared my case and proven it. The Guv had become a shadow of his former self. Still, you don't walk up to a wounded lion, smite him on the back, and say "Wotcher!"

"How are the repairs coming along?"

"They're like a team of beavers," I said. "I've never seen so much fresh timber. I made a few suggestions. Beech paneling in a lighter shade of mahogany. The room was too shadowy. The painters say they could darken the paneling if you don't like the result."

"Mmph."

We were down to monosyllabic responses already. It was not a good sign.

"And my brother?" he continued.

"As it turns out, he has been on the run. There was a gun battle in Sussex, and Caleb was the only man to survive. I had to sell my soul to convince McNaughton not to toss him in jail."

My employer shifted his weight, and grimaced in pain.

"Keep your eye on him, Thomas. Who knows where the man's been these twenty years? Prison as likely as not. That Pinkerton badge could have been purchased from a pawnbroker in Arizona."

"How would I—"

"Quiet. Let me think."

I let him. It was preferable to being bawled at.

"Give him his lead," he ordered. "Let him come or go as he likes. If you find yourself with any time, follow him. Don't reveal our plans to him. On the other hand, get him to reveal his. You are naturally loquacious. That should not be difficult."

"Yes, sir," I said.

"Is there anything else to report?"

"There's an important thing I didn't get to tell you yet. A woman came to the offices shortly after the bombing, posing as a prospective client."

"And?"

"And there was something strange about her. I can't quite put it into words. She reported her husband missing, but then behaved in a way that was unbecoming for a concerned wife. I didn't trust her, and my instincts turned out to be correct. When she left, I followed her to her hotel, but she had already checked out. I gave chase but by the time I reached the street she was gone. She gave the name Camille Archer, but the worrisome thing is that she had the cheek to sign her name as Camille Llewelyn in the hotel register, so she knows who I am."

"That is troubling, indeed. It was certainly no coincidence."

"I took the liberty of hiring Miss Sarah Fletcher, the female operative, to search for Mrs. Archer."

"Miss Fletcher," he said, considering. "Excellent move. I hear she is competent."

I wanted to warn him, but I held my counsel.

"What about the tunnels?"

"It was an excellent suggestion, sir. Caleb and I walked the tunnels for an hour searching for clues."

"Get on wi' it."

When Cyrus Barker lapses into Scots, he's at his most elemental.

"We found two sets of footprints in the tunnel, one with a turned nail in the sole. We followed the trail to a spot near the Embankment, not far from Cleopatra's Needle. There were some fag ends of cigarettes there."

"Let me see them," he said.

"We didn't keep them, sir."

"Blast. What sort were they?"

"Gauloises, sir, like Etienne's. They had been only recently smoked."

"I think it's time for you to visit the suspects. See what they are up to."

"Should I take Caleb?" I asked.

"That's a fair question, lad. Should we? He might learn a secret or two, but we'd know where he was."

"He's wearing on my nerves, sir. He's playing a game, but I'm not sure what kind. Do you suppose he's trying to scoop the case from under us? Another successful case completed by the Pinkerton Detective Agency?"

"He's welcome to it, Thomas. There's little reason why a professional detective would take such a case."

"I'm not surprised."

"There's an old seafaring term that describes Caleb well: a loose cannon. He goes wherever he likes and leaves destruction in his wake. Be careful, Thomas. He'll try to save his own skin first. Don't expect him to save yours. Hand me the list."

I gave it to him, aware that in doing so I was abdicating the case. It was his case, his agency, and he had a right to go after whomever he wished. He perused the paper, mumbling to himself as he did so.

"Excellent work, Thomas," he said, handing it back. "Good list. I can neither add nor subtract from it. Perrine, for example. You must discover if he is still incarcerated."

"Sir, he's in Paris," I answered.

"Then go to Paris."

"When?"

"Now. Or tomorrow morning will do, I suppose."

"I promised McNaughton I would not take your brother out of the country."

Barker lay back on his pillows for at least half a minute. The bottle of laudanum was still at his elbow. I wondered if he had fallen asleep.

"Sir."

"Don't let him see you, then."

"All right. What if Caleb refuses to come?"

My employer snorted. "Refuse Paris, that cesspool of sin? The trouble will be in getting him to return."

"Is that everything, then?"

"You're coming along, Thomas. Go to Paris. Be certain to check in with the Deuxième Bureau."

"Yes, sir."

"And send in Philippa on your way out. I have been trying to get her to leave. One would think I was in triage at the Battle of Bull Run."

"That was in America, wasn't it, sir?" I asked.

He gave me a withering look.

"I'll go find Mrs. Ashleigh."

After I had located her and given her the message, I left the priory and returned to Craig's Court, where I found myself in sole possession of the office, for once. It was possible that Jenkins had drunk himself into a stupor over the turn of events and was out with a headache. I didn't blame him. I wish I had thought of it myself. An idea occurred to me then. I picked up the telephone and spoke into the receiver, giving a number. Eventually I was patched through on the line.

"Mocatta residence," a maid answered. Rebecca's was a strictly female-staff residence.

"This is Mr. Llewelyn. Could you please relay a message to your mistress, asking her to call me at her next opportunity?"

"Yes, Mr. Llewelyn."

"Thank you. Good day."

Rebecca rang a few minutes later.

"What is your schedule like?" I asked.

"Nothing that cannot be rearranged."

"Would you care to have an early tea? At a respectable ABC, of course."

"I'm a widow," she said. "You needn't be so circumspect."

"Propriety, madame. I would not be seen pursuing you vehemently for your fortune."

"It's hardly a fortune."

"Your husband left you a fair amount of money, not to mention a house in town."

"Which you refuse to move into once we are married. In less than two weeks, may I add, in case it didn't make your timetable."

"Oh, is that when it is? Tea, then?"

"I'll put Drusilla Goldman off again," she said. "I don't really enjoy her company. Four o'clock?"

"Four it is."

An hour later we were in the tearoom, where I sat across from my intended. I could stare at that face for the rest of my life. Wavy dark hair. A white dress with a narrow waist. A thin face that framed two lovely brown eyes. Her smile, it was a second sun. I tried to work out whether I preferred her face straight on, in profile, or three-quarter, but decided it was impossible. Perhaps I'd hire an artist to paint her. Or engage a photographer for a portrait. But no, a photograph really wouldn't do justice to her pale olive skin.

She was enumerating a list of changes to the wedding ceremony, or something like that. I wasn't paying attention. I was thinking of the wedding night, in general terms at least. Perhaps I was a little nervous. I am no Casanova, though no one can fault my ardor.

"And I'm relieved to know your family is coming," she said.

"Rebecca, you know that is impossible. My family and I are estranged. After being released from prison, I was too ashamed to return to my family in Gwent, knowing there was nothing for me there and no employer willing to hire a disgraced scholar."

"Nonsense! Your sister came to town and said everyone was all a-twitter. Some of your friends and acquaintances are making the journey just to fill your family's pews."

"My sister came to London?" I asked, shocked. "When?"

Rebecca smiled and put down her cup. "Yesterday afternoon. She was wonderful. She told me stories about your childhood, Thomas. You were quite a rascal in the town, according to her."

"Well, perhaps," I admitted. "Which sister was it? Mara? Bronwyn?"

"Neither. It was Camille. Such a little charmer."

Nothing has ever shook me to the core so quickly in all my life. Forget convention. I wanted to turn over the tables and barricade the doors, and hunt down my pistol, which I had stupidly left in the desk drawer because it didn't match the Aerated Bread Company's decor. Looking about the room, my professional eye searched for weapons I could use: the curtain rods, teapots of scalding water. I would throw the Spode if necessary. Was there a back door? Did the windows have shutters? Should we move to the wall? Could this table withstand a bullet were I to throw it onto its side? I stood and scanned the entrance, my heart thumping in my chest.

"Thomas!" she cried, reaching out for my hand. "What are you doing?"

I sat down again, turning my chair so that I could watch the door. "Describe her."

"Who?"

"My 'sister.'"

"She was very pretty, with enormous green eyes. Her coloring, I must say, did not resemble yours." Her brow furrowed. "What precisely are you telling me?"

"Rebecca, I have no sister named Camille. A woman came to the offices trying to secure our services this week. She gave the name Camille Archer."

I watched as she tried to take in what I'd told her.

"Camille Archer? But—"

"I realized as soon as she left that she wasn't trying to hire us at all," I interrupted. "She was trying to find out if Mr. Barker had been killed in the blast. I followed her to a hotel, and although I couldn't catch her, I discovered she had registered there as Miss Camille Llewelyn. She even spelled my name correctly. She was flaunting her deception in my face."

"That's unconscionable," she said, shaking her head slowly. "I don't know what to say. There was no reason to doubt her word."

"Did she set a date for a second meeting?"

"She was hoping to help with the decorations. She said she would ring."

"No doubt."

There was no one near the door, but I became fixated upon it. Would an assassin enter and shoot us? Would conspirators distract me enough to seize my intended and spirit her away? There were too many theories to contend with.

My blood was up. "I'm not sure you should go back to the house. If you do, you mustn't let anyone through that door."

"You're frightening me, Thomas."

"Unfortunately, that might be the very thing to keep you safe."

# CHAPTER TWELVE

I was a poor companion at tea. I'd been nervous and distracted and I wondered now whether I should have postponed telling Rebecca that I had no sister named Camille. More than anything, I was incensed that Mrs. Archer, or whoever she was, had come close enough to actually touch my intended bride. If she thought she could threaten me with impunity I would disavow her of that notion quickly.

Back in our offices, I looked over the state of repairs in the rooms below and found myself satisfied. The temporary offices above, still mostly empty, now had crates on the floor containing all the salvageable items from our damaged chambers. Barker's old coat of arms, for example, was leaning against the wall, none the worse for wear. We would get through this temporary interruption. The agency would survive and go on as before.

Caleb had not yet returned. I leaned back in the chair behind the desk and put my feet up, facing the window, as Barker sometimes did. I even tried scratching myself under the chin thoughtfully like the Guv did. Nothing happened. It was as if a bit of fluff was caught in the old cogs. Then, finally, they began to turn.

Staring out the window, I worked out what I would say, where I would go, what I would do in France. It was not a perfect plan, but I had the Guv's blessing, and it had to be done. I waited impatiently, considering what might come next, when Caleb Barker strolled in in his confident way.

"Was your work successful this morning?" I asked, not having any idea what it entailed.

"We'll find out."

"Do you have any plans for tomorrow?"

"None I can't shift," he said. "Why?"

"I thought we might have some breakfast."

"And then?"

"And then go to Paris."

He thought about it a moment, then nodded. "Never been."

I placed a call to Mac, informing him of our plans and the need for a valise for a day or so. We had no intention of dawdling or sightseeing. Finding and interviewing Perrine was my only objective.

The next morning, Caleb arrived and we broke our fast while Mac finished packing. I kept a careful watch on Caleb and Etienne, lest they break into another fight. My customary view was blocked by planks that covered the window. I went to my room and retrieved the times table for Dover and the ferry to Calais. We had scant time, but we would get there, barring another attack. We arrived at St. Pancras station just as the express whistle was blowing, and hopped aboard. As was always the case, even with Caleb, I found myself in the smoking car. I'd be breathing fumes all the way to Paris. Caleb's cigarette was wedged in the corner of his mouth, under the eaves of his mustache.

"What is Paris like, in terms of safety?" he asked.

"It has wide boulevards cutting through cramped neighborhoods and narrow streets. Then there are the apaches—local gangs in some areas."

"What else?"

"The Sûreté, the Paris police, is generally considered one of the best on the continent. As for the rest, you'll have to see for yourself."

"I intend to," he replied. "I assume there's an entertainment district. Opera or the more earthly kind?"

"Both, I suppose."

Caleb nodded his pomaded hair. "Good to know."

We reached Dover in plenty of time to take the ferry across a placid Channel, and met the express to Paris in Calais. I looked about to see if we had been followed or if there was anyone sinister on the train, but nothing was out of the ordinary. It all seemed safe so far.

I've always liked Paris. It's so un-English. People sit at outdoor cafés and try to decide whether they shall return to work or take the rest of the day off. Italian or Spanish circus performers blow flames into the air or dance with chained bears in the open squares. Africans stroll about in long caftans. It's a breath of fresh air after being beached in London.

We located a café, where we ordered a meal. As I turned to help my companion, he looked up at the waiter.

*"Garçon, vous pouvez m'apporter blanquette de veau, les haricots verts, et un bouteille de Bordeaux, s'il vous plaît."*

"My word!" I exclaimed. "You speak French! But your accent is strange."

"Creole. As I said, I spent a lot of time in New Orleans, keeping an eye on the Italian district. There were some feuds down there between rival gangs from Sicily."

"What did you do?"

"I invited them to adopt a more civil tone in the United States of America. New Orleans doesn't put up with that kind of nonsense. The trees there bear strange fruit, as the Creole say."

I stared at him, puzzled. In answer, he raised an arm and mimicked a man being hung. A chill went over me, wondering what it would be like to be a detective in such a wild, wide-open country, where one made one's own rules and death could come at any time.

After lunch we summoned a cab and told the driver to take us to the Deuxième Bureau. As we bowled down the street, we saw the new marvel, the Eiffel Tower, a giant steel structure, reddish brown, that dominated the city.

"Looks like it's about to pull up stakes and walk around the town," Caleb remarked.

I couldn't decide if it was an eyesore or a work of genius, not that anyone cared for a Welshman's opinion.

A quarter hour later, we arrived at our destination, a granite building, anonymous save for a flag, and just enough architectural bonhomie to blend with the rest of Paris.

"What exactly is the Deuxième Bureau?" Caleb asked.

"It's the office that handles statistics and counterespionage."

"Why aren't we going to the Sûreté?"

"They'll know more about Jacques Perrine here, and his time in prison. In the past, he has gathered anarchist materials from Saint Petersburg. The files say he may have a link to the men who assassinated Alexander II."

With some trepidation we entered the building. The whole of the French government seemed to be represented in that single edifice. Inside, the building looked like the grand château it had once been. We were directed to a room that had been a ballroom a half century before. It was now divided into desks for statistics, and a man was awaiting us.

"*Messieurs,* welcome to Paris," he said, rising. "My name is Gerard Dacre."

We introduced ourselves and he led us to a desk encircled by chairs. On the wall there was a map of Paris, covered in pins. There was a single file on his desk, which he opened.

"Have a seat, gentlemen," he said, extending a hand. "Hmm. Jacques Perrine, anarchist, provocateur and dynamiter, sentenced to six years for his connection to an attempt upon the life of the emperor, Napoleon III. Captured with the aid of English detective Mr. Cyrus Barker."

"Scottish," I said.

"It appears M. Barker infiltrated a loosely organized group of anarchists, posing as an Irish freedom fighter. He was consulted after the group easily recognized all of the agents of the Sûreté and the Second Bureau. His work was deemed satisfactory."

I find Frenchmen quite entertaining, and Mr. Dacre was no exception. He was a sharp-faced fellow, all angles, with a big head and a small mustache. It seemed that every man in Paris had one. Somewhere in Paris there must be barber shops with diagrams of the various types.

"He was released by order of the French government."

"What?" I cried. "Jacques Perrine was released?"

"*Oui,* six weeks ago. He's served his sentence and was a quiet prisoner. There was no reason to continue his incarceration."

"Did you keep a record of anyone who visited him while he was in prison?"

"Of course we did," Dacre said. "Here it is! Just as M. Bertillon's methods of identifying criminals has revolutionized detective work, our statistics will revolutionize tracking them. Thieves tend to use particular methods. All their procedures are carefully taken down. For example, the areas which are most frequently robbed are recorded and marked on a map, like this one here. Thieving along a certain street is cross-referenced with released criminals known to live in the area. Scientific, you see. It will revolutionize everything."

"You French are known for your revolutions," Caleb drawled.

Dacre took it as an insult, bristling slightly.

"So, who came to visit him at La Santé?" I asked.

"Only his daughter and son-in-law."

"And their names?"

"Monsieur and Madame Alphonse Mercier."

"Where is Perrine now?" I asked, to turn their attention back to the matter at hand.

"He was in Paris until last week," Dacre said. "One of our agents tracked him to Calais, suspecting he was going on to Russia. He—"

Dacre turned the page and read with his finger on the paper.

"He escaped. They lost him on the train. They suspect he jumped from it before it reached Calais. He is forbidden to legally leave the country. We assume he has gone on to Saint Petersburg to meet other anarchist associates."

"I'm sure that's not going to stop him," I said. "Do you have his last known address?"

The French statistician took a slip of paper and copied the address on it and then handed it to me.

"I hope this is helpful," he said.

Caleb Barker rose to his feet in that informal American way he had.

"I hope so, too," he said.

We left the building feeling a little crestfallen.

"If we came all this way for that, it wasn't worth the fare," Caleb growled.

"Let's visit this neighborhood, then," I said, tapping on the paper.

We jumped onto an omnibus that would take us near Perrine's last known address. In a few minutes, we had arrived in the Rue Gris, a draggled, down-at-heel street in the 14th Arrondissement. It was not yet evening, but streetwalkers stood looking bored on the street corners, awaiting their first clients. Cats attempted to rub against one's ankles and horses pulled carts through the narrow streets. We reached Perrine's door, and knocked upon it. A small, wizened woman, likely a concierge, answered the door.

*"Oui?"*

"Is Monsieur Perrine here?" I asked.

*"Non. Il a disparu,"* she said dismissively.

Disappeared. Of course, we knew that.

*"Avez-vous un paquet pour nous?"*

"*Non.*"

He'd left nothing behind. I asked if we could go upstairs to see his room, but she refused.

"*Ce n'est pas possible.*"

I asked if he had any friends nearby, but she was finished answering my questions. She shrugged and slammed the door in our faces.

"Very interesting method, Mr. Llewelyn," Caleb said.

"I thought you were going to ask her something."

"You were charming her all by your lonesome. Let's go."

"Where to?" I asked.

"Up and down the alley. Maybe we can uncover something."

"It's better than nothing," I said.

We walked along the street from one end to the other several times. Unfortunately, we were obvious, two men in expensive suits patrolling a dingy street full of dilapidated buildings. We might as well have walked about waving our arms and shouting. It wasn't getting us anywhere.

Then a young man came down the street and stopped, observing us. He had a dark complexion and a wispy chin beard. He wore a cloth cap, a scarf stuffed into his waistcoat, and cracked French military boots on his feet. He was as down-at-heel as the street he lived in. Also, he was particularly interested in us.

"There is another behind you," Caleb said in a low voice.

"I hear him."

They climbed from stacks of old packing cases, dark alleys, and door eaves. Their leader, if such he was, was still a youth. None of them looked older than eighteen.

"*Donne-moi ton porte-monnaie.*"

He wanted our money.

"No, you little cur," Caleb replied.

All the boys stepped forward. There were more of them than I anticipated, perhaps a dozen. And they had knives, every one of them.

"Apaches," I said in a low voice to Caleb.

"I've dealt with apaches before. These are no apaches."

With a gesture from their leader, all of the youths stopped. Each of their hands were held up near their heads, a blade in the right, and they moved with the stiff gait of *savateurs*, French pugilists. The dark one came forward as if we, the gang, and the entire quarter were his.

Caleb muttered an oath under his breath. The boy cursed and pulled a blade from his pocket, a large jackknife with a yellow handle. He came forward, weapon poised, until he was mere inches from Caleb's chest.

"You don't understand what you're doing!" I wanted to shout, but I held my tongue.

Suddenly, Caleb was upon him, kicking his feet from under him and clutching him from the knot in his scarf. He pushed the boy to the ground and straddled him. Pulling out his own knife, he pinned the lobe of the youth's ear to the cobblestones. The lad screamed in surprise.

Two youths jumped onto my back, trying to cut my throat. One actually nicked my chin. I tossed both to the ground. When they tried to come at me again, I pulled a pistol from my waistband and aimed it at them. The two immediately ran away. So much for resolve. Or their leader's orders, for that matter.

"Your purse," Caleb growled at the squirming youth.

The boy was bleeding, the point of the blade piercing his ear. He tried to demur, but ultimately surrendered a small reticule. Still staring him in the face, Caleb pocketed it. Off in the distance, I heard the sound of a man running in sturdy boots. The sound slapped off the walls on either side of the street. I recognized the sound for what it was, no matter what country or language.

"Police!" I cried.

Suddenly, everyone scattered like mice. My companion let go of the scarf and the youth fled as fast as his broken officer's boots could carry him, clutching his newly pierced ear. He tripped and cried out again. Then he gained his footing and was off.

Too late, a puffing policeman arrived at our feet. He put his hands on his knees and breathed in and out for a moment before speaking.

"*Messieurs,*" he said. "Do you have your papers?"

We gave them to him. He longed to find fault with them, but was defeated.

"Where did this blood come from?" he demanded, pointing at the small crimson pool on the ground.

"From his chin," Caleb told him, nodding at me.

"What happened to it?"

We would do the investigation no good if we spent the night in a Parisian jail. I considered the options and made a decision. Without further ado, I hiccupped and looked bleary-eyed at Barker's brother.

"What happened to it?" I repeated.

"You don't remember? How much wine did you drink? You cut it on a nail."

I turned back to the policeman. "I cut it on a nail. Where are we? Is this the way to the Left Bank?"

"That is a lot of blood for such a small cut."

"Look, Officer," Caleb said. "There is blood, here is a wound. My friend is bleeding and drunk and we are lost. Can you direct us to a proper thoroughfare?"

The gendarme gave me that expression that I had seen on constables' faces all over London: do I arrest this fellow or not? I knew the arrest would involve a lot more paperwork than he was willing to perform. He turned and raised a finger.

"Go down this road to the corner, turn left in the next street, and walk for three blocks. You cannot miss the Rue de Maine."

"*Merci, monsieur.*"

"Take yourselves home as soon as possible, and I don't mean your hotel room."

"*Oui, monsieur.*"

He marched off more sedately than he had arrived.

"Come on," Caleb said. "I came here for more amusement than those insolent tykes. I need some food and some improper entertainment."

"Let's go," I said. "But I'll settle for the food, myself."

We took ourselves to a brasserie a few streets away and ordered beer and a plate of *pommes frites*. The waiter looked at us disapprovingly. Caleb leaned back and stretched, coincidentally showing him the handle of a pistol stuffed into his coat pocket. After that, the service was excellent.

"Where'd you get the revolver?" I asked.

"At the Colt Company merchant in London."

"I thought it was illegal to purchase a firearm if you are foreign."

"It is, but if one is a law officer who had to leave his weapons at home, but still requires protection, one is able to borrow some for a price, while in London."

"And that's legal?"

Caleb looked at me over his beer. "You're really consumed with this 'legal' business."

"I'm an ex-thief," I said. "And I'd prefer to keep it that way."

I reached for my beer and something crinkled in my pocket. I withdrew it.

"What have you got there?"

"It's the list Dacre gave me. The people who visited Perrine in his cell."

"Take a look at it, then."

I did; I unfolded the sheet and looked at it.

"Antoine Mercier visited twice."

"And his wife?" Caleb asked.

"Perrine's daughter." I crushed the paper in my hand.

"What is it?"

"His daughter's name is Camille."

# CHAPTER THIRTEEN

We went to a hotel where I lay on my bed and stared at the ceiling and contemplated all we had learned. Camille Archer was definitely involved in the bombing, as far as I could tell. Her accomplice was likely her husband, Antoine Mercier. We knew Perrine had left the country, and we knew that maddening girl had been to see him before he was released from prison.

This premise was logical. Perrine hated Barker. His daughter would do anything for her father. Mercier would help his wife destroy the man who put her father in prison. She visited him, commiserated with him, and possibly even helped him plan the attack.

Was she French? I wondered. Did she show a trace of an accent? At that hour, one o'clock, one's mind plays tricks. I convinced myself that she had a slight French accent when she spoke, a kind of rhythm to her speech that was not English. Then I convinced myself I was imagining things. Surely, however, it was too much of a coincidence that the woman's name was the same as that of the one who had visited Perrine along with his son-in-law. It all fit together.

I was eager to relate this information to my employer. The only other thing we had learned on this trip was that Les Deux Magots had a fine selection of beer.

There was a knock on the door. Reluctantly, I opened it and looked out. Caleb stood there smartly dressed, with his bowler hat set at a jaunty angle.

"Interested in the night life?"

"No, thank you," I said. "I'm engaged."

"Are you sure your engagement extends all the way to Paris?"

"It does, indeed."

He shrugged. "Suit yourself."

He left and I returned to my bed, where I must have lain deep in thought for half an hour. Finally, I remembered I was in Paris. Of course, I wouldn't follow Caleb Barker, but I could walk along the Pont Neuf, or see the Paris Opera House again, with its golden statues. I could tour the Left Bank or Montmartre, where the artists lived in cold garret rooms and poured out their hearts onto canvas.

It was warm as I walked about the city. I didn't have a particularly good time alone. I wanted Rebecca with me. I watched people drinking and laughing in a small corner café and looked into the windows of brasseries. People walked by with baguettes under their arms or over their shoulders like small rifles. The smell made me hungry, but I could not eat. I just walked from one arrondissement to another.

A nearby cathedral bell was tolling when I returned. It was late for me, but still early for Paris, City of Lights. I went back to the hotel and climbed into a rickety lift, built for no more than a single person. A standing coffin, rising and lowering all day and night. It was only my third or fourth time in one and I didn't care for it. A box suspended by mere rope or cables did not seem safe.

Unlocking my room, I stepped in and took a tumble. My foot

had slid on something. I turned up the gas to see what it was. A slip of paper had been slid under the door, now crumpled by my tread. I reached forward and unfolded it.

It was a cheap sort of paper, the kind with splinters of wood imbedded in it. There was grime along the crease from dirty fingers. A single word was written on the paper, in some kind of dusty graphite or charcoal. One word: "Londres." London. Jacques Perrine had gone to London, where he crawled into our cellars and blew down Barker, like the big bad wolf that huffed and puffed.

It was possible that the note itself was a trap. Someone could be trying to get rid of me, or perhaps they hated Perrine enough to scrawl the word and deliver it to my door. That could be the only explanation, for whoever wrote the note did not receive a sou. There, I thought. The case was solved. So, why did I feel dissatisfied? Because I was here and Rebecca was in London, where Archer and Mercier must be.

Should I leave immediately? Did I need to warn Barker? Were telegrams carried to places as ancient as the Priory of St. John? I decided the Guv was convalescing as safely as anyone anywhere. It would take a small army to push their way in, and no bomb could damage that ancient stone.

Likewise, the house in Lion Street was safe. Jacob Maccabee and I might have our differences, but he had a second sight when it came to danger in his domain. Also, he was very fond of grape-shot in a sawn-down shotgun. The dog named Harm, in his way, was formidable as well, and more than one night visitor had run from his attack.

The offices were surely not a target again. There was little left to bomb. For a moment I thought of Mrs. Ashleigh's London townhome, but it was only a pied-à-terre. She came to town for a reason, and was rarely in the building. Besides, Sarah Fletcher was watching her, armed with her small pistol.

Then something hit me so hard, my legs crumpled beneath me. I had forgotten to secure my own bridge. I had a vision of the house in Camomile Street going up in flames, in pieces, blown to atoms. Before I knew it, I was out the door and slipping clumsily down the stairwell. My feet were so useless I would have thought they belonged to someone else. Finally I reached the lobby, and when I found the desk clerk standing there half asleep, I woke him by throwing franc notes at him.

*"Le télégramme, s'il vous plaît! Le télégramme, monsieur!"*

"The telegram office is two streets from here, sir," he said in better English than my French. "But I regret to inform you they are closed for the night."

"When does it open in the morning?" I asked irritably. Rebecca might be in danger.

"Seven o'clock, sir. Perhaps seven-thirty. Surely it will be open by eight o'clock."

Inwardly, I cursed all Europeans for their lack of interest in times tables. When a sign on the door says they are open at seven, they should not open the door as late as 7:01.

"Thank you, sir," I said, as I began to trudge up the stair.

I went to bed but only succeeded in staring at the cracked ceiling for half an hour. I told myself I should sleep. The chances that Rebecca would be attacked while I was away were remote. Not nearly remote enough for me, however.

The real possibility existed that I had solved the case. Perrine, the only man on the list capable of making a bomb, had been visited by a son-in-law and his wife, Camille. Camille was in London, and Perrine probably was, too, so one could expect that this man, Mercier, was there as well. The two men in the tunnel had been he and his father-in-law.

The next morning, Caleb knocked and came into the room. I had already been to the telegram office the moment it opened and sent a message to Mac to enlist Barker's favorite bodyguard, Bully Boy Briggs, to immediately go to Camomile Street and guard Rebecca. I glanced at the clock and saw that it was already nine o'clock. Caleb looked as if he'd been run over by a cart.

"Where've you been?" I asked.

"Enjoying the bountiful sights of Paris and nursing champagne."

"Are you in any condition to get on a train and go back to London?"

"Yes."

"And the ferry across the Channel?"

"That remains to be seen."

"I'm sure it does. Breakfast?"

He waved a hand at me, as if I'd suggested viewing a postmortem. "Sorry the trip was for naught. For you, I mean: one name on a piece of paper."

"Try two lines on two pieces of paper."

He glanced at me through bloodshot eyes as I handed it to him. He tried to focus. It was not difficult. The one word was two inches tall.

"Someone followed us to the hotel from Perrine's old place," he said. "Aren't we a couple of crack detectives?"

"Enquiry agents."

"Speak for yourself."

"You know investigations," I said. "Sometimes you come up empty-handed. One throws out a line and hopes something nibbles. A full half of an investigation consists of dead ends."

"That's how it works. I haven't figured a way to avoid it. When I first started I figured if I stumbled down the wrong trail, I'd get in trouble back in Chicago. Since then I realized it's just a part of the game."

I pulled on my boots and attached my collar.

"Well, this case is solved. Camille and Antoine Mercier worked with her father to bring down the Guv, and Perrine is in London now with them. I need to get back at once."

We took a cab to the Gare du Nord. Hours later we reached Calais and the ferry. Crossing the Channel I stood and studied the White Cliffs of Dover, a sign that we would soon be in England again. England, with a French bomber threatening our lives, and a young woman who had some imagined need for vengeance against me and mine. Caleb Barker clung to the rail of the ferry deck, looking the worse for wear. I felt a certain satisfaction watching him.

My mind returned to my own problems. I hoped Briggs was already standing in front of Rebecca's house, keeping watch. It depended on how quickly Mac could find him. And while I was at it, I hoped the Guv would be released from the hospital soon. Everything was out of sorts. I began to doubt I would emerge unscathed from this enquiry to stand beside my bride on our wedding day.

In Dover, we climbed aboard the express to St. Pancras Station and all points north. Caleb was silent, his nocturnal escapades no doubt catching up with him. He didn't speak on the train, and he only muttered when we retrieved our luggage at the end of the journey.

We parted company. A cab took me to the City, and in particular to the shadow of the synagogue. I alighted and saw Bully Boy Briggs standing not more than a dozen feet from Rebecca's residence. He is big, lumpy, menacing, and dangerous. He's also a member of an East End chess club.

"Hello, James," I said as I walked up to him. "Thank you for coming on such short notice."

"Any time, Thomas. I appreciate the double rate. Is that girl in there yours?"

"She will be in a week or so."

"Congratulations. She's pretty."

"She is that. How's Minerva?"

"Cracking."

Briggs had married as well. His wife would be delivering a son in a few months, if he was lucky. He had probably walked here from Bethnal Green. No cabs for him. Every sou went for the comfort of his wife and their coming baby. What he had was what all men desire. Myself, included.

# CHAPTER FOURTEEN

I pinched my brim to Bully Boy Briggs and returned to the cab. He nodded solemnly, and turned away, looking solid and menacing to the world at large. She was safe, but I would not tarry. "Clerkenwell!" I cried and was nearly pulled off my feet as the hansom jerked forward. It is not a far distance from the City to St. John's Priory.

"Sir," I said when I entered his hospital room.

He was sitting in a bath chair by the bed, swathed in a large sheet that left one arm uncovered, rather in the manner of a Roman senator. His chest was pale against the swarthy skin of his face and arms. The contraption on his shin was balanced atop a second mechanism to keep it suspended. He looked dejected, but rallied on sight of me, pushing himself higher in his chair with a wince.

"Ah, Thomas, lad," he said. "Good to see you. How was Paris?"

"It was the same as always, sir. But I think I may have solved the case, or at least gained some solid information while I was there."

"Did you?" he asked.

His response was not enthusiastic, nor was it chilled. I knew he always counseled patience, so I tempered my actions accordingly.

"Sit down and give me your report," he said.

I did, telling him everything that had happened from the moment we stepped aboard the express, until we had departed from it the day after. He listened with his arms crossed, concentrating.

"Mrs. Archer is making a nuisance of herself," he finally said when I had finished.

"She is, most decidedly," I agreed.

"The name Mercier is familiar to me, but I cannot remember from where. Perhaps it will come to me later. Perrine has left Paris?"

"Yes, sir. He's here!"

"Thomas, you cannot make that assumption based on an anonymous note."

"Where else would he go?" I asked. "He hates you."

"He hates a number of people. However, he needs to get his materials from Russia. Neither France nor England would allow him to purchase proper equipment. He had to have purchased the devices somewhere."

"Our offices were blown up, sir. It is more than coincidental."

"Perhaps, but you have not convinced me."

"What does he look like, sir? At least we should keep an eye open for him."

"Not an elegant figure. Short, bristly black hair, a broken nose, and a short beard. A very hirsute fellow. Believe it or not, he is an idealist. He wholeheartedly believes that all monarchs should be swept away and replaced with a new order. Anyway, that is his description. He sports the same anarchy tattoo as I, but his is buried 'neath a mat of fur."

"It is good to see you sitting up, sir. Where is Mrs. Ashleigh?"

"I sent Philippa to her town house to get some rest. That chair is akin to a medieval torture device."

"Have they said when you will be released? Mac and I must begin the process of turning the parlor into a convalescing room. I don't believe this chair will fit up the stairwell to your room."

"They will not tell me," he rumbled. "It is maddening! I considered leaving, but Philippa refused to wheel me to the front door!"

Cyrus Barker of Craig's Court, Whitehall, did not like to be at the mercy of someone else's decisions. He is independent, if the word can be used to describe a man for whom other men worked. He preferred to forge his own destiny. That's a positive way of saying that the man was accustomed to getting his way.

"I shall ask Mac to help me as soon as I am home."

"Did Caleb make a nuisance of himself in Paris?"

"Not especially, though he did enjoy some degree of debauchery last night. He was certainly dispirited this morning."

"Mother would pray for his soul," he said, shaking his head.

"That's probably a good idea."

"Did he give any indication of why he was still in Europe?"

"No, sir. I tried pressing."

"Keep an eye on him. Did you account for his movements, save for his visits to the city's dens of iniquity?"

"No, sir, but he arrived late this morning. I can't both work the case and keep track of him."

"Agreed. Perhaps I shall put Miss Fletcher on the task. He didn't see her."

I nodded; it seemed wise. She was working for us, after all.

"She doesn't like me very much," I told him.

Barker gave me one of his wintry smiles. It was the first I'd seen since the bombing. "That's for the best, with your coming nuptials," he said. "Hewitt tells me she finds fault with all of our sex."

"There is certainly enough evidence to warrant that assumption," I said.

Barker winced. I could see it in the skin beneath his round Chinese spectacles.

"What's wrong, sir?"

"A twinge."

I'd like to see what a twinge was to him. No doubt whatever it was would have had me screaming in pain.

"Do you believe you will be able to attend the wedding?"

"Of course I shall attend your wedding!"

I raised my hands. I'd ruffled his feathers. Under the current conditions, he was liable to be moody for some time to come.

"I'm trying to lobby the telephone exchange to install a temporary set here in the hospital," he went on. "I would pay well for the privilege, but the directors of the priory are not happy with the idea. Apparently, telephones are not monastic enough for them."

"Sir, that's not necessary. I can come around more frequently, if you like."

"No," the Guv said. "You shall be far too busy. Now you must go to Newgate Prison to see Mr. Strathmore."

"Why, if I may ask? We already know who is responsible for your injury. It is Jacques Perrine."

His mustache curled up on one side in disappointment. "What are the chances that the first lead you follow will guide you to the right man? Or, in Mrs. Archer's case, the right woman?"

"In theory, it has to happen sometime."

"Let us say it is mathematically unlikely. In either case, it would be worthwhile to proceed with the enquiry and investigate the other men on this list. It might prove instructive, at the very least."

I nodded. "I suppose that makes sense."

"Thank you, Mr. Llewelyn. I am pleased it meets with your approval," he said. There was a layer of frost over that last remark.

"Yes, sir. Shall I visit Burberry Asylum as well?"

"Of course. I am curious as to how Dr. Pritchard is faring."

"Very well."

"Keep your notebook by your side and your pencil sharp. Take down what is said, what is done, your own personal opinions on what you've seen, and anything else that occurs to you. In effect, you are my eyes and ears, while I am stuck in the blasted chair!"

"Yes, sir. Do you still want Caleb to go with me?"

"If he is willing. Have you noted that he has not seen me since our first meeting a few days ago? He can lie to anyone, but I've known him too long to fall for one of his schemes. That brother of mine has plans of his own, something we may know nothing about. Play upon his weaknesses. He has always been vain. He'll believe himself better qualified to run this investigation."

"Oh, he does that," I said. "He's told me several times to rely upon his skills."

"Keep him at your side when possible," the Guv said. "Perhaps he will show his hand and reveal if he keeps any appointments that might indicate he has an accomplice."

"You sound as if you believe he is involved in the bombing."

Barker considered the point. "It is generally wise to accept the probability that Caleb is in some sort of trouble or is keeping something private."

"I'm not surprised."

"Since there has been no other person who can verify or dismiss my brother's words, we must interpret everything he says for ourselves."

I considered what he said, still looking down at my employer in his makeshift toga.

"I suspect there are layers and layers of things we don't know," I said.

"Worse than that, perhaps, is that whatever he says he believes, and he feels justified in whatever he does."

Having agreed, I left as his lunch arrived. Priories are not known for their cookery, but then, neither is Barker a gourmand. He would eat whatever was put in front of him. As far as he was concerned, it was merely fuel. It had been making Etienne apoplectic for two decades.

Back in Whitehall, I considered what to do next, assuming Jacques Perrine was in town, along with his son-in-law and daughter. We must find him as soon as possible, and stop him before he could inflict more damage. But how? There had to be some solution.

The door opened below and I heard an assured tread upon the stair. I did not like these upper offices. There was no escape except those self-same steps. I didn't relish jumping out a window.

There was a flash of blue and I heard a voice asking to speak to me. His English was flat like Caleb's. *Another American,* I thought to myself. A man about my age entered the room and took in everything, myself included. He was nearly as tall as Barker and as deep chested. His face was clean shaven and his square jaw was cleft. I've yet to meet an American who didn't tower over me.

He wore some sort of military uniform, consisting of a blue tunic, lighter-colored trousers with a red stripe, and a peaked cap. His buttons were highly polished.

"Mr. Llewelyn?" he asked.

"I am he."

"I am Captain Yeager of the United States Marine Corps, assigned to the American Legation. I must ask, sir, if you are acquainted with a man named Caleb Barker."

I sighed. "Yes, I am."

"Could you give me his address, or do you know how to locate him?"

"He has not divulged the name of his hotel, nor do I happen to know his exact whereabouts."

"It is vital that I speak to him."

"What has he done now?" I asked.

"There was an incident in Sussex involving three American citizens, all of whom died in a hail of bullets."

"Caleb was involved, I understand."

"Yes, sir. I am to escort him to the embassy and then to a ship bound for the States. He is no longer welcome in this country. I wish your cooperation in apprehending him."

Yeager was an earnest young man who spoke in a clipped monotone.

"I'll certainly cooperate."

"When shall he return?"

"He comes and goes on a whim," I answered. "He is in London visiting his brother, Cyrus Barker. These are his offices and he is my employer."

"This Mr. Barker, is he likely to hide his brother?"

"He is in hospital, so he cannot hide anyone. I suspect even if he could, he would not. The brothers are not particularly close."

"I see," Captain Yeager said, scrutinizing me carefully. "What is a private enquiry agent? Some sort of detective?"

"Yes, but a top-drawer one."

"So, Cyrus Barker is an enquiry agent and Caleb Barker is a Pinkerton agent. Is your boss working for the Pinkertons on a case, or was he?"

"No. There was a bombing down in our regular chambers, which are one floor below. I've been investigating the suspects in the matter."

"Has Caleb Barker been helping you?"

"He has been following me about. I would not exactly call it helping. As I said, he comes and goes as he pleases."

"If the two of them are not close, why would he involve himself in the investigation at all?"

"He considers it a debt of honor to capture the man who almost killed his brother. Some sort of Scottish oath, I believe."

Yeager began to pace, the sound of his heavy boots echoing in the nearly empty room. "Why is your boss willing to allow him to help if he does not trust him?"

"I suppose there are two reasons. First, because he knew Caleb would go after the man himself and ruin our investigation, and second, to keep him close as much as possible to make certain he stays out of trouble."

"I believe it's a bit too late for that. Where does Caleb Barker go when he isn't with you?"

"I confess I don't know, Captain. He keeps saying he is on Pinkerton business. Have you met him?"

"No."

"He is very secretive. He's also irritating, ill-mannered, and moody. Mr. Barker—that is, my Mr. Barker—said he was a 'loose cannon,' whatever that means."

The young officer nodded to himself as he paced. "Has he spoken of the shooting down south?"

"Only once. He claimed that he was purchasing supplies when there was an exchange of gunfire between the agent he was protecting and two Americans from a secret society."

"The Knights of the Golden Circle?"

"That's the name, yes."

"So he did not protect the man, did he?"

"No," I answered. "That's what—"

I stopped myself. I had almost uttered Chief Constable McNaughton's name. I did not want to bring him into this.

"That's what I thought."

"Mr. Llewelyn, I cannot arrest you in this matter, being a British citizen. However, if I feel you are obstructing this investigation, I will turn the matter over to the commissioner of the Metropolitan Police."

I had a sinking feeling. The commissioner of the Met was named Munro. He hated us, both myself and my employer. One cannot get married while in a jail cell. I assume there is a law against it.

"Captain, I have answered each question truthfully. I am cooperating."

"If Caleb Barker appears again, are you willing to send a message to the American Legation?"

"I don't know."

He smote the edge of the desk with a strong hand. "Why do you not know?"

I felt my own temper start to rise. "I don't know because I am merely an employee, and not allowed to make such decisions."

"What hospital is Mr. Barker in?"

"It's a private hospital. St. John's Priory."

He pulled a notebook from his pocket and wrote the name on it with a pencil. "Would you be willing to accompany or follow Caleb Barker to his current residence?"

"If Mr. Barker agrees."

Captain Yeager sighed in frustration. "Do you not understand, sir, that he is precipitating an international incident? He's skulking about London under our very noses and you are abetting him. If he is not captured soon, the American minister will be forced to speak to the prime minister."

"I understand."

"Very well, Mr. Llewelyn. Don't think we shall leave this matter alone."

He turned and left. The very stairs complained about him. I took out my frustrations on the desk as Yeager had. I rued the day Caleb Barker set foot in this country. More than likely, I was not the only one.

As soon as Captain Yeager was gone, I waited a few moments and then hailed a cab and followed him. He was in a closed carriage with an eagle emblazoned on the door. As expected, he led me straight to the priory.

As I rode, I looked out for anyone who might be following or watching me, but I saw no one. I alighted and sauntered up and down the street until I saw the vehicle leave, heading back the way he came. Then I went inside.

Cyrus Barker was resting on his bed.

"Damn and blast!" he said when I came into the room.

"International incident."

"Yes, Mr. Llewelyn. I heard him myself."

"It looks as if we'll have to give your brother over to his government."

"I wish it were that easy," he muttered.

He was sulking again. It took me a minute or two to work out everything that was going on.

"You're not going to turn him in, are you?"

"No."

"Because blood is blood."

The man actually looked guilty.

"Because of an unwritten clan law in Perthshire five hundred years ago. He swore to avenge the attack upon you, and you promised to provide sanctuary."

The Guv continued to look grim and said nothing.

"The two of you haven't been back to Scotland in thirty years."

"That doesn't matter."

"It's not logical. It's not even legal."

"I know it."

"But you won't turn him over to his government."

"No," he said.

I stared at him. At that moment, it was a toss of the coin to decide which was the most exasperating.

"You're right."

"About what, lad?" he asked.

"Damn and blast!"

# CHAPTER FIFTEEN

Caleb appeared in the office when I returned and agreed to join me, but his mood and my own grew more somber and quiet as we reached Newgate Prison to interview Henry Strathmore. I wasn't certain about Barker's brother, but I thought it likely he'd spent some time in jail. It's the price one pays for being an enquiry agent or any other kind of detective. However, jail and prison are two different things entirely. I thought I'd ask.

"Have you ever been in prison?"

"Five months in Mexico in a federale prison. Not my fondest memory. You mentioned something when we were in France?"

"Eight months in Oxford Prison for theft. Unproven, but my accusers had money and a title. I was a collier's brat."

"Hard cheese," he said.

"My sentiments exactly. You'd best be careful. You're picking up English phrases. That won't be helpful in . . . California? Montana? I'm sorry, I've never looked at a map of America."

He nodded, reluctant to discuss the matter further.

I was overdressed for Newgate Prison. Practically anyone was, but I in particular had become a slave to fashion to impress my intended. I was in danger of becoming full of my own pride. It was a jolt to return to a place exactly as I had begun.

Newgate is one of the oldest prisons in the world, having been built in 1166. It wasn't a large prison as prisons go, and was little more than a rectangle in shape. Someone had told me that nearly half of the prison was for upper-class or wealthy felons, men like Henry Strathmore. This was the place where, having been convicted, prisoners can receive rich foods, comfortable furniture, and the like. I'm sure it would be quite a change from the picking oakum I experienced in Oxford Prison.

As one approaches the building, the walls grew taller and taller, and eventually one reached an open gate shaped like a Brobdingnagian keyhole. I imagined a giant key coming down at night to secure the entire prison.

We entered, and met the guard at the gate, while the cabdriver turned and fled the area. Apparently the proceedings were of particular interest to the inmates therein. We were shown into the building by a second guard, who led us through gray, impersonal halls to the warden's office. The latter was built along the lines of a schoolmaster: spare and almost birdlike, with the tail of his coat behind him.

"Oh, yes," the man said when I told him who we wanted to see. "Strathmore. He keeps himself in relative luxury, a wealthy prisoner's prerogative, but otherwise, he is a model prisoner. He's won a small following here, but I have seen no reason for assuming he is involved in anything untoward. I will say that his finances interest me. The government had confiscated his notes, securities, and assets when last I heard. Where is he finding the wherewithal?"

"Perhaps we can ask while we are here," I said. "Tell me, sir. Do you have any record of anyone visiting him here?"

"Mr. Dunning!" he asked a reedy-looking young man sitting behind a desk. "Get me Mr. Strathmore's visitor sheet!"

The clerk looked through some files and came around the desk with a sheet of paper in his hand. "Here it is, Warden Barry."

The warden glanced over the list, after taking it from the clerk's hand.

"There are three names here, gentlemen. Emerson Cullen, a solicitor. Second, George Bryant. Dunning, who is Bryant?"

"A financial advisor, sir."

"And the final name?" I asked.

"It is difficult to read, Mr.—"

"Llewelyn."

"Indeed. It appears to read 'A. Mercer.' Does that name seem familiar, Mr. Dunning?"

"Do you mean Mercier?" I asked.

Barry consulted the paper again. "It says 'Mercer' here."

"Mercer," Dunning nodded. "Tall chap, well built. Small black mustache."

"And what did he do?" Caleb asked. "Why did he want to see Strathmore?"

Dunning shrugged his shoulders. "He didn't say, sir. I assumed he was a business associate. He requested to see Strathmore and signed the visitor's list."

"Where was I?" Barry asked.

"In Exeter, sir. Your mother was ill."

Barry colored a little, slightly embarrassed to have a mother at this stage in life, let alone that such an individual should be so unsolicitous as to be ill.

"Mm, yes."

Barry opened a drawer, took out a small card, signed it, stamped it, and gave it to me. He gave a second to Caleb. Then he had us add our names to the list of visitors.

"Dunning, see that these gentlemen are escorted to ward five."

"Yes, Warden Barry."

Outside of the office, Mr. Dunning visibly relaxed. He accepted my companion's offer of a Sobranie, and sucked in the smoke.

"Tall, thin, mustache?" I asked.

"He was well dressed, too. Fastidious, I'd say. I was impressed by the shiny polish of his shoes. His mustache was waxed to points."

"What did he say?"

"Not much at all. He wasn't communicative, if you know what I mean. Just gave his name and signed the register. He was what you might call a bit of a cold fish."

Dunning gave a loud whistle down the hall, and waved a guard toward us.

"The power behind the throne," Caleb murmured in my ear.

A guard led us down the long hall to a cell. We were taken into the second on the right. The guard there took our identification cards, and scrutinized them as if we would pull pistols from our pockets and attempt to release his charge. Reluctantly, he unlocked the door and allowed us to enter. Inside, I caught a view of a book-lined room with a large desk and some sort of carpet on the floor. Save for the bars, it was better than my rooms in Newington. We saw a figure standing there regarding us.

"Prisoner 54972, you have two visitors!" he announced, as if the man were a hundred yards away.

"Yes?" the man asked. He came forward.

Henry Strathmore was a well-built, good-looking man, with curling hair and bushy side whiskers. The hair on the back of his head was nearly black, which made the gray at his temples resemble wings. His eyes were gray, and his face tanned, no doubt acquired in the Côte d'Azur. His features were fine, even aristocratic. One could see how such a man could dupe so many people. Instead of regulation broad arrows, he wore a suit that probably cost more than mine. Far from being a dispirited and defeated wretch, he looked as hale and robust as anyone I'd ever known. It was nothing like my days in the Oxford Prison.

Strathmore gave us a haughty look, as if he were expecting more highborn visitors.

"Can I help you?" he asked. "You look familiar."

"I work for Cyrus Barker."

"Oh, yes. The little clerk who ferreted out my assets."

I looked around at the comfortable room. "Apparently not all your assets, Mr. Strathmore."

"And who is this fellow?"

"Mr. Barker's brother."

"Charmed," Caleb said, in his most toney aristocratic accent.

"Indeed. I fear the accommodations here are rudimentary. Won't you come in?"

"No, thank you," I answered.

"Suit yourself. Now, what can I do for you, gentlemen?"

"We'd like to know who Mercer is."

"Mercer? Who are you talking about? I know no such person."

"He is listed on the visitor's logbook. Last April thirtieth."

"A visitor for me? Wait. Was he a tall fellow?"

"I could not tell you."

"It appeared he came to the wrong cell. To be frank, I was hungry for some company. We spoke for a few minutes only."

"What prisoner did he come to visit?"

"How should I know?" he asked. "For that matter, why should I tell you?"

"Because you're in a cell," Caleb growled. "Accidents happen in cells."

"Are you threatening me, sir? My barrister is Edward Curzon."

"And mine is Bram Cusp," I said. "I do not believe one shall handily win over the other. What did this visitor look like?"

"Let me think." He closed his eyes, either trying to recall the man's appearance or trying to invent a convincing lie.

"As I said, he was tall, with a small mustache. Thin faced, long nose. Not English-looking, I thought, though he had a little trace of an accent. He wore a nice suit and polished shoes. Yes, very glossy shoes. At the time, I thought him a confidence trickster trying to cheat me out of the last of my resources. Too late, I am afraid. Thanks to you, I am a pauper."

"That hardly concerns me, sir, since you were using other people's money."

"They had no skill with it. I was able to double the income in six months. Then I returned their money."

"Certainly," I said. "After they endured the hardship of no money for half a year."

"Mr.— What is your name again?"

"Llewelyn."

"Ah, yes. How could I forget? Mr. Llewelyn, if you are trying to help me gain a conscience at this late date, I fear your plans are in vain. As far as I am concerned, the amount of work I did to acquire and use that money to my own advantage has convinced me that I earned it."

"That, Mr. Strathmore, is why you are in prison and I am walking about a free man."

"Is there any honor among prisoners? I understand you were once one yourself."

"How come you by your information?" I asked.

"I had my solicitor look into the two of you."

"I'm glad my past has been of such entertainment to you."

"Oh it was, but not as much as your employer's." He smiled coldly. "He is a colorful fellow for one who dresses in black. I saw the newspaper. You had some doings at your office. Your governor was injured in the blast."

"He is recovering well, thank you," I said.

"I won't say I'm overjoyed he lived," he admitted.

"Your solicitor comes quite often, I understand," I noted, trying to resume the questioning.

"Yes. We are appealing the case. It was an appalling miscarriage of justice."

"Does he bring you news of the outside world?"

"How could he not? There are many who feel that I have been unjustly imprisoned, and wish to finance my appeal."

"Since you have no other income now."

"Precisely."

"Since all of your money has been taken away," I said, looking about his cell, a hundred times more opulent than any other.

"Every sou."

"Pity about that," I said, raising an eyebrow. "Losing all that money. Other people's money."

"Are you going to discuss that again? A fellow can only take so much moralizing in one day. What about your partner, here? What have you to say, Mr. Caleb Barker? You've been awfully quiet."

"Our mother taught us to give our full attention to a performance, sir. I find yours very imaginative."

Strathmore gave that demi-smile again. "Thank you, sir. I appreciate the vote of confidence."

I stood. "Mr. Strathmore, I believe we could banter all day and never reach a consensus. I appreciate your willingness to see us."

"Oh, anything in the interest of justice. Tell your employer and his barrister that I was cooperative."

We left the chamber, and waited at the door for the guard to return. I felt a moment of concern as we left that we might not be permitted to leave, but it was merely nerves. Finally, we were released. Even Caleb gave a sigh of relief.

"Thoughts?" I asked, as we walked back to the gate.

"Nobody sells snake oil like a snake."

"Could you translate that from American to English?"

"The man gives every appearance of being helpful, but he'll lie to your face if it suits his interests."

"He was rather rude when we first arrived."

Caleb nodded.

"He was, until he saw a way to use us. During the appeal you might be called upon as a witness to the fact that he was helpful to us, and free with information."

"A paragon of citizenship."

"You do talk posh, Mr. Llewelyn," he said.

# CHAPTER SIXTEEN.

W here are we going next?" Caleb Barker asked at a pub near Newgate, a couple of streets from the prison. We agreed we both needed a pint after our experience.

"Back to Newgate to interview Keller. He's the one who's going to be hanged in a couple of days."

"I know who he is. If you are so fond of this prison, that's your prerogative. However, I've got some work I need to look after. I'll meet you at the office later."

He stood and reached for his coat pocket.

"I'll pay for the meal," I said.

He counted out some coins and tossed them on the table.

"I don't like to be beholden," he said as he left.

*Touchy fellow, that Caleb Barker,* I thought. *Quick to anger, slow to forgive.* When he was gone I relaxed a little. It wasn't merely dawdling. I wasn't looking forward to seeing Keller myself and I wanted to get my thoughts together.

While I was inching forward on the case, somewhere in London

Jacques Perrine was probably lying low and building infernal devices. We had survived his first assault, which must have been a
blow to his reputation. Our being alive was an affront to his abilities as a bomb maker. He would do something about it soon, I
had little doubt.

Idly, I wondered what form his attack would take. Would it be
one of those small black spheres one hears of, that roll under a
European landau, vaporizing it and its royal occupants? Was
it a timed device inside a Gladstone bag? A trip wire outside
our moon gate? A long fuse allowing the anarchist the opportunity to be a half mile away before it detonated? These were
cheery thoughts over lunch. I added my coins to Caleb's and left
the pub.

While Newgate is the best prison in which to be incarcerated if
one is wealthy and willing to pay extra to have plush furnishings
and food hampers carried in, on the other hand, if one owns no
silver spoons or the ability to bribe a guard, it is the very worst of
prisons. Newgate is the hanging prison. All the English prisoners
whose offenses would lead to execution were brought here for
eventual extermination. Here was where they put the dogs down,
the human curs, those who had lost their humanity. Men like
Joseph Keller.

When I saw him shuffling into the interview room, chains about
his ankles, I thought about how he'd butchered his wife and
children in cold blood with the aid of an axe and a wood fire stove.
He was still human like I was, yet he had been capable of atroci-
ties beyond what I could comprehend. Does one cease to be a
human being by committing such an atrocity? The judge had
determined that his crime was to be punished by death.

I had helped in this investigation. In fact, I had been instrumental in his capture and had spoken in court. I had taken work
in Dockland as a navvie alongside him and complained about the
"strain and strife" and how she was always going on about need-
ing this and needing that. I had also told him I was concerned
about whether she was stepping out on me with another man. My

invented tale had cracked him open like a walnut, and he went so far as to tell me the sewer tunnel he'd dropped the bones into. It had not been difficult to locate the pathetic remains of his family and kin.

His wife had been cuckolding him for some time, taking his hard-earned money and even bringing her lovers into their marriage bed. She was brazen about it, so much so that most of the neighbors knew before he did. The real blow was the confession that neither of the children were his, and in fact, they had different fathers altogether.

The neighbors told me they believed she'd gotten what she deserved. They thought him to be a good fellow, hardworking and serious, neither a drunk nor a wife beater, a good provider by East End standards. I suspected the presiding judge felt the same way, but the children were innocent, and though Emma Keller was a libertine and an adulteress, neither marked her for death. His long-suffering temper had finally snapped and he did the horrible deed. The vivisection of the corpses for disposal had unhinged him, I think, and he felt the need for someone to confess to. Unfortunately for him, I was that man.

This was not an interview I wanted to undertake, but some matters about the enquiry business are not pleasant and this was one of them. Still, I squirmed as he was brought in.

"Oh, it's you," he said. He didn't bellow or curse at me. He seemed resigned to see me. "Come to gloat, have you?"

"No," I answered in a low voice.

He sat down in a chair, the chains at his wrists and ankles puddling between his feet.

"What did you come for, then?" he asked. "To be my chum again, bosom comrade-in-arms? Let bygones be bygones?"

"No."

"Seeking absolution? Needing forgiveness?"

"No."

"Good, then. I'm fresh out."

I expected anger from him, but he had become fragile. He

seemed to have shrunk. His head was shaven down to nubs, though it had already been short. They had shorn him of his beard, however, and he looked naked without it. The skin of his face was gray, and his broad arms hung on his frame. I suspected he no longer ate much.

"Well, Alf. Wait, you ain't Alf. What was the name again?"

"Thomas Llewelyn."

"Right. You speak very posh now. You had me fooled. Was you an actor once?"

I knew it would happen, and it did. The guilt set in. She had been poison, Emma Keller, and collecting evidence against him had been my duty. Her family had lost three daughters, a granddaughter, and a grandson. Who should pay the cost for that, other than the man that bashed her skull with an axe?

"No, no actor," I muttered.

Guilt is palpable to me. It's like being engulfed in a wet and heavy blanket. Your tongue cleaves to your mouth and it is difficult to breathe.

"Wad'ge come for, then? Came to say good-bye?"

"I've got some news you might find interesting. The offices of our agency were blown out from under us by a bomb. Mr. Barker is in hospital."

He shrugged his shoulders. "You detectives do have some laughs," he said.

"Is there no gloating on your part, then?"

"Nah. It was a fair cop. You was just doing your duty, though it wasn't the kind of profession I'd take on. Too cold and calculating by half."

It was an absurd position, a multiple murderer lecturing me on ethics, and yet I felt it. He was affable, a natural leader among the navies, uneducated but keen minded. He'd done the best he could with what nature and society had given him until he had been tricked by Emma. She had been rotten to the core.

"Do you have any brothers or sisters?" I asked.

"Two sisters living in the Chapel."

Whitechapel, I thought, the worst district in London, where the Ripper had plied his trade.

"Married?"

"One is. The other, Mary, she's touched in the head. I send them a few shillings now and then. They'll be beneficiaries in a couple of days. After I'm buried, the girls will have something jingling in their pockets for a while."

I watched him carefully. By that time in my employment, I was generally certain when someone was trying to trick me. He wasn't.

"Is your mum alive? Is there anyone to mourn you?"

"No, no one."

"Does the name Camille Archer mean anything to you?"

"No."

"Henry Strathmore?"

"No."

"Jacques Perrine?"

He shook his head.

"Jack Hobson?"

"You reading to me from the Kelley Book Directory?"

"Sorry." I stopped. I had run out of things to say. "Have you had any visitors, in particular, a pretty girl with a snub nose?"

He looked up at me. "Dressed like a lady?"

"Probably."

"She was in widow's weeds. Come to see me. Or rather, had me come out here to see her. First woman I'd set eyes on in a while."

"What did she say?"

"Her mistake. She thought I was another prisoner. She didn't leave, though. What was my sentence, she asked." He went into a falsetto. "'Oh, dear, how tragic! How you must suffer! You will not be forgotten. You will be avenged.'"

"Avenged?"

"S'what she said. Barmy, that one. Jittery eyes. Thought to my-self, I'm in here and she's out there? I asked not to see her again. I can do that, you know. It may be the only power I have left."

I stood, feeling the need to say something, but what? I couldn't apologize for the part I had played in his incarceration.

"Are you coming?" he asked.

It hit me like a jolt what he was speaking of.

"To the hanging?" I asked. "I hadn't thought."

"Come if you like. You was as close a friend as I ever had, even if you went against me. Even if you was false from the very beginning."

"I'll be there."

"Ta, then." He stood. "Guard!"

Five minutes later I was literally pushed out the gate into Old Bailey Street. I was choking as if my mouth were full of cotton wadding. Shaking, I walked into an alley and was sick against the wall.

The first blow swiped across the back of my knees. The second would have shattered my ulna if I hadn't strengthened the muscles around it. The third caught me in the ribs. I pushed off the wall and raised my stick.

The alley was narrow and in near-perfect darkness. I could make out a tall man with a bowler hat and a stick. I had fought with canes for six years and it was my weapon of choice. As I tried to get my bearings, I evaluated what sort of weapon he used. Either his stick was hollow metal or it was some kind of hardwood like maple filled with a rod of steel.

I stepped in, stick raised high over my head with my right hand, my left hand raised forward to counterbalance. It was how Monsieur Vigny had taught us in Barker's bar-jutsu school. The man took the same stance as if it were natural to him, as if he, too, were trained in the art of La Canne.

He swung. I parried and riposted. He parried. My cane shook under the blows. It was stout ash, but it was not metal.

One blow got in and smacked my ear and shoulder. The muscles there protested. I swung, but encountered the wall, spoiling my aim. I had to show this fellow I knew what I was about or he'd be at me harder. I switched from La Canne to Bhatta. The first was French, defending with the point, like fencing. The second was good old Irish shillelagh fighting. I tossed my stick in the air, caught the ferrule, and crumpled the crown of his bowler. A point for the home team. I pressed my advantage, moving in on him. My hand actually caught his stick and I clouted him on the shoulder. Another stick caught me hard in the chest, making my heart skip a beat.

There were two of them there in the shadows. Blows came down like sparks after that, mostly on me, but I gave as well as I could. I aimed where they might be, and kept swinging. The narrowness of the alley was to my advantage, for the second fellow could not circle around and attack from the other side. I was using the first man as a shield, not that he'd stopped putting up a fight. My shoulders had taken most of his blows.

This wouldn't last, I realized. It was two against one, both of them expertly trained, and they had heavy sticks. The odds were not in my favor. But I was holding my own. I caught the first one in the face, and he began spitting blood. I could hear it.

Suddenly, there was a wail from the alleyway, and both of us stiffened. The attacker in front swung, but only took a chip out of the brick wall behind my head. He pulled his battered bowler lower about his ears, brushed past me, and was gone.

I stood for a minute in the heavy shadows, trying to catch my breath. I was panting like a racehorse. I was also waiting for my eyes to adjust to the gloom. It was deathly quiet and the noise of the street sounded far away.

The second attacker lay supine on the ground, not moving, possibly not even breathing. What in the world had happened? To my knowledge, I hadn't brought down a blow on his skull or done anything to stop him. I had barely touched the fellow. My stick wasn't long enough. But he'd been stabbed, I was certain, since there had been no shot. He'd screamed in surprise and in great pain. It was *le cri de mort*. Someone had come from behind and plunged a blade into him without a word and fled. A sword cane, perhaps, or a knife. It had been two against two, only I hadn't realized it.

Taking a breath, I put one hand in my pocket and raised my stick to my shoulder. Then I strolled out of the alley, whistling. I stopped at a shop window and pretended to examine combs and brushes. I required a stout comb to work through my mop of hair, but I did not risk speaking to the shop owner and being recognized. The bookshop beside it had more customers. I stepped inside, moved to a far corner, and found a stool. There, I sat and shook. Everything hurt. I'd have bruises for weeks, but nothing was broken that I could tell. Mac made a fine lineament. I must remember to have him make some when I got home. If I got home, I thought.

After about five minutes I rose, pulled my hat down snugly on my curls, and wandered out of the bookstore. I walked to the corner and looked about. It was a normal day. Hansoms wheeled by, people took in the September sun, and all seemed like any other day.

"What took you so long?" Caleb Barker asked in my ear.

"What?" I said, nearly jumping.

The Guv's brother was standing just behind me, his arms crossed.

"I finished my errand. I've been standing here getting my shoes shined, waiting for you to finish in there. What did that fellow do? Confess to everything but killing Julius Caesar?"

Had he been the silent friend in the alley? He looked as normal as any other day. There was no hard breathing, no knowing look. His boots were highly polished. I looked him in the eye.

"Let's go, then," I said.

# CHAPTER SEVENTEEN

Caleb and I were at St. Pancras again the next morning, bound for New Forest, Hampshire. It was more than two hours of rail travel to reach Burberry Asylum. Even a dedicated enthusiast of rail travel can be bored after such a distance. Caleb took to haunting the corridors, hoping for a glimpse of feminine beauty. Apparently they are in short supply in the rugged landscape where he lives. I merely thought of my Rebecca.

Burberry Asylum, or to give its full name, The Burberry Institution for the Violently Insane, is shaped like a Roman caltrop: three equidistant lengths of buildings, radiating out from a central structure with a tall tower. The tower was full of guards armed with rifles, fine shots one and all. The building is encircled by a tall, square wall with three gates topped with smaller guard towers. It is fortunate that such precautions were taken, since on fine days like the one we had, the patients were allowed out into the sunshine to wander about as they saw fit. Benches were set about to allow these denizens the opportunity to compare notes as to proper methods of murder or other violent crimes. One of the three sections was given over to women, and was separated by iron fences. The women wore plain blue dresses and black bonnets and it would be difficult to tell one from another. Many of the male prisoners stood by the gate passing remarks and flirtations to the other side, which in turn was throwing them back. I would not think there were so many violent women in all the Isles.

Caleb and I were led inside by a guard, for our own protection, but in a moment a man came bustling forward in a morning coat and a top hat.

"How may I help you gentlemen?" he asked, removing his spotless silk hat. He was a little taller than I, with a fan of thin black hair plastered across his bare scalp, a neat mustache, and thick spectacles.

"We are here to see a prisoner and to look at his records," I stated.

"I'll lead you there. And you are . . . ?"

"Thomas Llewelyn, private enquiry agent. My employer was instrumental in capturing one of your inmates. This is Mr. Caleb Barker, a colleague."

He shook my hand with both of his. Barker's brother did not offer his.

"I'm Dr. Anderson, at your service."

"Pleased to meet you."

"What patient are you here to see?" he asked, clasping his hands behind his back as we walked along.

"Henry Thayer Pritchard."

"I might have known. He's one of our more illustrious residents. Has his name come up in any enquiry? I assure you he has been a model prisoner since his arrival."

"Hello, Doctor!" an inmate called as we passed. The man's head was shaved and he wore a nightshirt made of canvas.

"Hello, John!" he called, then turned to us. "They try to curry favor, you see."

"How can the violently insane be allowed to walk about freely on the grounds?" I asked. "This seems more a sanatorium than an asylum."

"That is the attempt. We had a black reputation for several years and there was the threat of closure. Instead, we went to a more humanitarian method pioneered by the Swiss. We have had much less trouble since we have implemented it. Of course, one must realize that the inmates are and shall probably remain criminally insane despite their treatment. Nonetheless, we hold interviews with our more docile inmates and in some cases we have had some success. Watch your head here."

The latter was for Caleb's benefit. If he hadn't ducked, the doorway might have struck him on the forehead.

We stepped through the front door into an open room with a small library on one side and a dining hall on the other. A number of the inmates were within view. Some of them were not physically acceptable to modern society and others chattered or screamed. It was unsettling to watch, even for Caleb Barker.

"A model prisoner, you say?" I repeated.

"Within bounds, of course. He has a macabre sense of humor, one must understand, and he happens to be one of the most dangerous inmates in this facility."

"What is he in for?" Caleb asked.

"He drowned three consecutive wives after having them make their wills in his name," Dr. Anderson replied, shaking his head. "They were drowned in a local bog, one by one. He could have escaped to the continent if he did not have a certain kind of mania. For some reason known only to him, he polished their shoes and left them displayed near the bogs where the bodies were discovered."

"He's mad," Caleb muttered.

"That's not a word we use here, Mr. Barker, but if we did it would have been apt. Here is the main office."

He led us into a round room bisected by a long desk. Clerks were seated at tables behind the desk with their paperwork scattered before them.

"We have a couple of visitors here, Mr. Clement."

"Thank you, sir."

"I must get back to my charges, gentlemen. Again, it was a pleasure to meet you."

He shook my hand and went on his way.

"What can I do for you, sirs?" one of the clerks said.

"We are here to interview Henry Thayer Pritchard, regarding an ongoing enquiry."

The clerk raised a brow as if something had finally broken through his blanket of boredom. "Pritchard?"

"Yes, sir."

"It was Dr. Pritchard who just led you here."

Suddenly, I felt a tingling in my hand. I lifted it. A pin had been neatly inserted through the epidermal layer of my palm. Skewered through the top of the pin was a bottlenose fly. I cried out in surprise. All the clerks chuckled.

"You have to be careful, gentlemen," Clement said. "The doctor likes to play his little tricks."

I looked over my shoulder. As I expected, Caleb Barker was laughing harder than the rest.

Once the pin had been removed and I had washed my hands a dozen times, we learned that the number of people who had come to visit Dr. Pritchard were naught. According to his visiting sheet, he wasn't popular outside of these walls. Women have opinions on men who drown their wives. It is an affront to all of them. Many of them must have drawn the line as far as their husbands visiting him were concerned, as well, or surely some journalist or novelist would have visited one of England's most notorious multiple murderers.

Two guards led us to Pritchard's cell half an hour later. He was seated in a chair in the center of the room and he had been chained to a link in the floor. The walls were lined with buttoned padding and there were mats at his feet. Everything was pristine, as if it had been freshly cleaned. However, the dark gray walls above the six-foot-high padding were covered in chalk marks. Mathematical formulas, anatomy lessons, poetry, sketches, snippets of Latin and German; all showed that Pritchard had received a classical education. He must have stood on a chair in order to reach the upper wall. The lettering stopped at nearly eight feet. Two feet in which to express one's existence, even if it were a twisted one. Some of the art would shock any man at its depravity.

"Hello, gentlemen!" he hailed as we entered, as if we were boon companions. "How good to see you again."

"That was a nice trick, Doctor," I said.

"Did you like that? I've had that bottlenose fly in my pocket for simply ages, hoping to find just the right person to give it to. I'm so glad you came along."

"I'm surprised your cell is so spare, Dr. Pritchard," I said. "I assumed your status would have afforded you sumptuous furnishings. I've seen some cells that look like club rooms."

"Yes," he said, looking down sadly. "I had such a cell for a while. Unfortunately, I have a gift for making small weapons from just about anything. Even now they search my cell at night. But I am not cast down. Far from it. These furnishings chain me to the earth, but my soul flies to the heavens every night."

"Nice drawings," Caleb said, pointing at one with his thumb.

"Do you like them? I am absurdly proud of them. My cell is a tabula rasa every morning. I no longer require any stimulation to produce them. If anything, I must sketch quickly or lose a thought to the following one. All I need are a bit of chalk and an old rag and I am deeply content."

"Very nice," I said.

"So, what did you want to see me about, Mr.—"

"Llewelyn. I've come to ask you about Cyrus Barker."

He smiled benignly at me. "Who? I'm afraid I can't place the name."

"Cyrus Barker, the man who committed you here."

"Mr.—I'm sorry, I have had several types of therapies. I vaguely remember them now. Water and electricity and batteries in jars. Anyway, I'm afraid some portions of my brain, my history, for example, have gone missing, as if they had fallen down a hole. I am told I killed three women, though I cannot recall doing so. I cannot even place their faces. Of course, it was terrible what I did, and I accept the fact that I committed those acts, but for whatever reason, I am as much in the dark as anyone else."

"You remember nothing?"

"I do not. As far as I'm concerned, I awaken here every morning as if freshly born and have spent the duration of my life here in this cell. Sometimes I chafe at the restraint, but I am not mistreated. As I said, the warden has embraced a new type of therapy that I find much more pleasant. I have heard tales of the outside world and let me assure you, sir, I have no interest in going there. It must be a perfectly wretched place."

"It has its moments," I said.

"I am sheltered here, fed, clothed, left alone as I desire, and have freedom to think. I miss tobacco, I must admit. The guards tell me I am a danger with a box of lucifers, and apparently I jammed the stem of a pipe down a fellow inmate's throat. Of course, I don't recall doing it, which only makes it that much worse that I lost that pipe. It was one of my favorites, a straight-stemmed briar. It smoked sweet every time. I'm on my best behavior, hoping they will return it."

"Putting that pin through my hand was not exactly good behavior," I said.

He grinned. "I didn't say it was good behavior, merely the best behavior for me. I am an evil man."

"Are you?"

"So the doctors tell me. I seduced a wealthy widow, convinced her to marry me, forced her to sign away her fortune over to me, and then drowned her in a bog. Then I moved to another location far away and began the process all over again. Depraved, sir. I don't recall anything beyond what my doctors tell me, but only a depraved, evil man could do such things. It is best that I am here, but having my pipe would make it all the better. Oh, and slippers. I had slippers once. Opera slippers. They were so pretty."

He was quite pathetic, this man with half his brain erased, living only in the present, hoping merely to enjoy a pipeful and a pair of slippers. These places are hard for the casual visitor, as I have said before. One isn't prepared for the stories and encounters, or the tragedy on each face.

I turned to Caleb. He'd pushed his hat back on his head and was looking distinctly uncomfortable. I didn't blame him.

"So you remember nothing of Mr. Barker?" I asked.

"Mr. Barker? Is this man here not Mr. Barker?"

"No, I meant Mr. Cyrus Barker."

Pritchard's eyes moved back and forth, trying to remember the Guv, the man who locked him away here, but not succeeding.

"Would you call the orderly? I want to lie down now."

"Dr. Pritchard, I assure you—"

"The orderly!" he shouted. "I want to lie down, please!"

"I'll get him," Caleb drawled, as if dealing with a petulant child. He took himself off on his bowed limbs.

Pritchard put his face into his hands and sat for perhaps a full minute.

"I'm sorry, sir," he finally said. "I am subject to fits of temper, a result of my treatment. I am embarrassed by my behavior."

"Not at all," I replied. "So, you recall nothing of my employer, Cyrus Barker? Nothing at all?"

"I remember nothing earlier than the electric therapy that I had six months ago. At least, I think it was six months ago. I'm not very good with time these days. Things seem to get away from me when one day is the same as another."

He said nothing for a moment and then his face went slack. His eyes half closed in their sockets and his jaw became loose. Slowly he sagged forward like a marionette when its strings have been loosed. I jumped as he fell forward and hit the flagstones with a thump.

"Orderly! Orderly, come quickly!" I called.

The response was not immediate. I rolled Pritchard onto his back. His mouth was bleeding where he'd bitten his tongue, but he had not swallowed it, which would have been far more dangerous. I called his name once or twice but received no response. Eventually, Caleb and the orderly entered and immediately began to lift him. I saw froth at the corners of his mouth. The orderly listened to his heartbeat.

"Is he often like this?" I asked. "He was all energy when we met him, then he grew maudlin, then his mind seemed to shut itself down."

"He goes through cycles like this, sir," the man said. "Two or three times a day. Chances are by dinner he won't remember you were here."

"How long has he been this way?"

"Close on half a year, sir. Maybe more."

"Has he had electric therapy?"

"Yes. Dr. Cannon prescribed it. Not a pretty sight. A bucket of water, then a jolt from a battery to terminals in a cap on his head."

"That sounds barbaric," I observed.

"I assure you, Dr. Cannon is a pioneer in his field," he said.

"How long do his lucid moments last?"

"An hour or so. You came at the right time."

"And his low moments?"

"Sometimes all day. Mostly two or three hours."

"You don't think his damage was a result of the doctor's experiments?"

The man shrugged. "I dunno, but this chap used to kill women and now he can't hurt anyone ever again."

Half an hour later we left Burberry Asylum. It felt good to be out of that oppressive and depressive atmosphere, even if we were being led by a guard and could not speak freely.

At the gate, we signed a piece of paper identifying ourselves again, and finally left the horror behind us. I knew I would have nightmares that evening, and I was correct.

"So, no visitors, then," I said to Caleb once we were free.

"No, and it seems obvious they keep very close records of the comings and goings."

"Let's find a public house. I need a drink."

"One? I think I need about five."

# CHAPTER EIGHTEEN

few hours later we were back in Craig's Court. I was in the room where we kept bits of clothing and oddments, in case we needed to disguise ourselves. We were going to the East End to find Jack Hobson. Caleb Barker poured some flakes of tobacco into a rolling paper, ran his tongue along the edge, and twisted it. He stuffed it under one end of his mustache and lit the end with a vesta. He pondered it for a moment, removed a flake from his tongue, and then considered himself satisfied.

"Mr. Llewelyn, I can almost hear the gears clanking in your head. You've been silent since we returned, which is about as unnatural as feathers on a camel. I reckon you've either run out of things to do, in which case, I'll be off, or you have something that doesn't satisfy you and are trying to minimize the risk. Which is it?"

"The latter," I admitted.

"Everything looks straightforward to me except the Hobson brothers. There are six of them, and probably more of the gang, as well."

"It would take Scotland Yard to rush them all at once, and even then a few would escape. Neither of us can walk in and ask to join the gang, and above all we can't mention your brother's name. I don't see a reasonable solution."

Caleb was busy trying to blow one smoke ring through a larger one. He was not successful. Nettled, he looked at me.

"Perhaps there isn't one. Just because you reason something doesn't mean there is a solution. Look at cats. There's no reasoning about cats. They serve practically no purpose, but they're everywhere."

I tried to take in the opinion but it only gave me a headache. "Do you have a point?"

"I do. You're thinking too much. You're stuffing your head with too many solutions and chances that won't pan out. Let's just go and see. We're seasoned. We'll figure out what to do when we get there."

I looked at him and shook my head. "Your plan, then, is to have no plan at all. We walk into a pub or stable filled with gang members, most of them armed, and decide what to do on the spur of the moment. No planning, no consideration of the dangers."

He frowned for a moment, then brightened. "Yep."

"I suspect you cut a broad swath wherever you go and you're not usually there to pick up the pieces afterward."

"I've got too many things to do on this earth and too few hours to cram them into. What do you think?"

"I think your plan is the equivalent of jumping into a pool of water without knowing the depth."

"Are you ready?"

"This evening would be best, after dinner, when things are happening there. Let me change into something appropriate for the East End and we'll have a decent meal before visiting Hobson's territory."

"I'll need a few drinks before we meet the Hobson brothers. You don't want to go into this kind of thing cold sober."

"Caleb," I said. "Just once I'd like to hear you say something that makes me feel encouraged instead of worried."

Barker's brother finally wafted a smaller smoke ring through a larger one.

"Never give up hope," he said.

The Guv doesn't care for elaborate disguises. I donned a ragged jacket and a leather peaked cap, changed my striped trousers for a sooty and oversize pair, and laced some out-at-heel shoes on my feet.

I looked in the mirror. I was a disaster. After tying a decayed neckerchief around my neck and smearing a little coal on my chin, I was ready to go.

East Ferry Road is hard by the East India Docks and the rancid public house the gang frequented was called the Clove Hitch. If I called it unpresentable, it would be a compliment. It needed a wipe round with a rag soaked in kerosene. I slouched in behind Caleb and ordered a beer. I took a sip and shuddered.

"Strychnine and Thames sewage," I pronounced, after spitting it on the filthy floor.

"Oy!" a harridan behind the bar called.

I pointed a thumb at her over my shoulder. "Whose bag is this?"

A chair scraped in the back of the room, drawing attention to a dozen or more men ringed around a large table. One, obviously the leader, sauntered forward. He was tall, about five and thirty, and unshaven save at the sides of his head, below the donkey fringe he wore. He had a silver ring in one ear, a pugnacious jaw, and bleared eyes from a diet of the aforementioned beer.

"What's your name, larrikin?" he demanded.

"Snuff," I told him.

"And what's your business here?"

"Showing this Yank around the East End," I said, nodding at Caleb.

"Oh, and what brings him here?"

"He's scouting a patch, I think."

The men sitting behind Hobson had been muttering and jesting, but suddenly the room went silent.

"Hunting a patch? Here?" Hobson growled.

"Just showing him about," I answered. "Didn't come here especially. Thirsty work trodding the streets of London Town, so we stopped. I'm not so thirsty after tasting this swill."

"You look familiar," he said.

"I remember you from when I was with Hooligan's gang. Did six months with him before he died. Went to Liverpool after that."

He grunted as if he accepted my story but reserved the right to change his mind.

"Can he talk, this American of yours?" Hobson asked.

"'Course he can talk."

"Make him talk, then. He's making me jumpy."

Caleb had been leaning over the bar, nursing his villainous beer, and as all eyes in the room turned to him, he hooked the side of his suit jacket behind the holstered pistol. A dozen chairs squeaked on the sawdust.

"Afternoon, gents," he said. "Beautiful day."

"What's your name, stranger?"

"Sir, you are awfully concerned with people's names for a man in your line of work."

"Name. Name!"

"Touchy fella. Driscoll. Diamond Joe Driscoll."

"What's this about a patch?" Hobson pressed, coming close enough so they were nearly nose to nose.

"I was looking to open a saloon and a faro parlor in London. Maybe more than one."

"And you thought you'd come here, did you?"

"Mr. . . . Sorry. You wanted my name, but you never offered yours."

"Hobson. Jack Hobson."

"Mr. Hobson, there is money to be made north of the Thames. If you want some of it, you might consider letting us go about our business. However, we could use a gentleman of your talents. There may be a local gang who would want some spondulix for the privilege of opening on their patch."

Although I was standing behind Caleb with my head down, I was watching the gang. Half of them were standing, the others sitting, but all were watching us carefully, waiting for the nod from their leader to attack like so many hounds. Surveying the room, my eyes lit on a scuffed bit of planking on the floor. I whispered into Caleb's ear and he nodded and went on his way.

"You've got some brass ones if you think you can swan in here with your schemes without some sort of payment. If you choose to stay, if we let you, those payments will have to be regular."

Caleb shrugged. "Well, Mr. Hobson, we haven't decided yet where the first faro parlor will settle, but how about this? I challenge you to a friendly game of arm wrestling, and we lose, I'll buy everyone in this house a drink. Not beer. A proper drink, if you have enough whiskey here."

"We do," Hobson said. "And if I lose?"

"You'll set some up for Snuff and me. Win or lose, we shall decide about a possible business arrangement. Of course, the choice is yours."

There was some clapping and whistles from the back of the room. The crew was looking forward to seeing this rube from the West get the punishment he deserved. Hobson outweighed Caleb, but only by about two stone, and some of it damaged by heavy drinking and whatever other weaknesses in which he indulged.

Jack Hobson nodded. Caleb unbuckled his gun belt and handed his pistols to me.

"Hold this for me, Snuff. Try not to shoot anybody. Especially not yourself."

Both men stripped to their singlets and trousers. Caleb was around fifty, but he appeared to be in fine sharp: hard, tanned, and wiry. Like his brother, he had various souvenirs of a hard life. There was a poorly executed eagle tattooed on one forearm, a brand mark burned into the other bicep, and what appeared to be an old rope burn around his throat. Hobson was ten years his junior, but much of his physique had gone to seed.

Hobson's gang was excited by the diversion and the chance for a good drink afterward. Some cleared the area around the scuffed spot on the floor, while others ran outside to inform everyone about the impromptu event. In the West End, there are plays, concerts, balls, and dinner parties. Here in the hardscrabble East End one cobbles together whatever entertainment one can find.

Both men came forward and faced each other. Each put out his right hand, hooked their thumbs together, and seized the fleshy part of the hand below the thumb. They stepped forward with one foot and placed it inside the other's space so that the left ankles rested against each other. I noticed no judge had been chosen.

"Go!" I cried.

I had never attended a standing arm-wrestling match before, so I was unprepared for the sound as every muscle of both their bodies strained at once. I can compare it to a half-dozen ropes being suddenly pulled and twisted. Each muscle engaged with or against its neighbor. The tendons that held each to its corresponding bone were drawn taut. Each was nearly twice my weight, so to me they were like bulls locking horns. If I were so unwise as to step between them and try to stop the match I would have been trodden underfoot. Not that I intended to. In any case, it was preferable to the two of us fighting several dozen of them, even if they understood the Marquis of Queensbury Rules, and were willing to put down the knives, knuckle dusters, life preservers, and cudgels they carried. Which they did and were not.

They grasped each other's hand so tightly that I thought it possible bones would be broken. Both strained in a way I could not even comprehend. Their hearts must have been pounding in their chests. The only part of their bodies holding them to the ground were their booted feet, locked ankle to ankle. Cyrus Barker had pointed out the marks to me in various East End public houses, but I had never actually witnessed a match before.

"Take him down!" a man beside me called, but I wasn't sure for which combatant he was rooting.

Caleb Barker began to overtake his opponent and might have won handily, but then Hobson's bulk came into play and we lost whatever ground we had gained. Both were perspiring freely and the fronts of their singlets were sodden.

Just when I thought Caleb's arm would give out, he dug his back foot into the floor and began to press forward again. Both men were closer matched than I had realized. The men in the room began to chant a word. One single word.

"Jack! Jack! Jack! Jack!"

Men, women, and even a few children hurried into the Clove Hitch, having heard of the fight and the chance of a free drink. The room, if possible, began to stink even worse, a combination of bad beer, unwashed humanity, too many people, and the duo in the center of the room, struggling like titans. The atmosphere was heavy and I wanted to be outside breathing the cool air, or better yet, standing in Hampstead Heath, inhaling fresh air untainted by factories and sewage.

"Come on, Caleb!" someone yelled, and then I realized it was me.

He had taken command, and Hobson's idle ways were getting the best of him. It would not be long now, I told myself. Caleb Barker was definitely in control of the match. And then he wasn't.

I thought the match all over, but there was a sudden movement and the next I knew, Barker's brother was falling, his feet in the air. He thumped hard against the sawdust-covered floor, and the entire room burst into cheering. Men were jumping up and down and low women were looking about for companionship. Dirty children danced on tables or stole watches and handkerchiefs. I could not hide my disappointment. Standing, I crossed over to Caleb and helped him up. He was soaked and his newly cut hair was spiked about his head. He was totally spent. I would have to help him home.

"Publican!" he called. "Whiskeys all around!"

Another cheer went up. Everyone pounded Jack Hobson on the shoulders. Someone had draped a towel around his neck. Awkwardly, he made his way over to the table I had seated Caleb in and gave him a flaccid hug. Then each man was given a full pewter mug of Irish whiskey.

A tumbler was put in my hands.

"How are you?" I asked in a low voice.

"A bit rough," he said.

"I was afraid you were going to win."

"I had to make it interesting."

"Here's your gun belt. I'm going to find a pigeon."

It took me no more than a moment to find the weak link, a young gang member not celebrating with the others. I took a tumbler from the bar and set it down beside him. He smiled and nodded, anxious for the company as well as the drink.

"Your boss looks in solid shape. I hear he got out of prison recently."

"Three months ago," he answered. He was a slope-shouldered adenoidal youth, of little use to the gang.

"What was the name of that detective who got him convicted?"

"Barker," he replied, his voice brimming with disgust. "Cyrus Barker."

"That's the bastard. So, is your boss going to go after him now that he's free?"

"Believe it, Mr. Snuff. I've heard him say he'll take the man apart piece by piece until there's nothing left of him."

"He should!" I insisted.

I looked up. The harridan was standing over me, grinning at me through a picket fence of dirty teeth.

"Mr. Driscoll says you is the one to pay," she stated.

She set a dirty slip of paper on the table, where it began to soak up spilled beer and spirits. I leaned forward and read the billet.

"As much as that?" I asked.

# CHAPTER NINETEEN

There was an unusual sight awaiting me when I reached the Priory of St. John the following day just after noon. Cyrus Barker was seated in a bath chair with a sort of plank attached to it for his injured limb. He was in a respectable shirt and tie, collar and cuffs, over which he wore his favorite black-and-gold Asian dressing gown. His lower limbs were covered in a discreet heavy blanket; his dark hair had been combed and his chin freshly shaven. He was in a foul mood, still weighed down with the gall caused by not anticipating a move from an unannounced opponent. He was not accustomed to being taken unaware.

Philippa Ashleigh stood beside him in a dress the color of pale butter, with embroidered roses. She patted his shoulder, trying to soothe him, and looked at me expectantly.

"Is everything well?" I asked.

"Of course everything is well," the Guv replied. "Why shouldn't it be? We are awaiting word as to whether I can leave today. It's infuriating having one's fate in the hands of a physician."

"Is it too soon to be leaving?" I asked.

It had only been a few days and he was barely sitting up on his own.

"No," he growled. "On the contrary. It is nearly too late."

This was obviously not the convalescent patient speaking. This was Cyrus Barker, the protean Cyrus Barker. One mentioned weakness at one's peril.

Barker frowned as I explained what had occurred both at Newgate Prison and Burberry Asylum. He leaned forward as far as he could when I talked of the fight in the alleyway, then spat questions at me like bullets from a Gatling gun, trying to place all the people and events in his mind.

I expected most of the questions, of course. Part of my occupation is to anticipate such things. So I contrived to answer them, but as I did, I observed my employer closely, making mental observations of my own.

The first thing I noticed was a muscle in his neck as taut as a violin string. His forehead was shiny as well, and it wasn't the treatment of brilliantine Mrs. Ashleigh had put in his hair. His left hand was clenched in a tight fist.

I glanced at Mrs. Ashleigh again. Was she conspiring to free him? I assumed she would be the first to insist he stay until he was well enough to go home. Perhaps being in this room, dealing with his stoic silence, had worn down her resolve. The only way to deal with Cyrus Barker is to give him what he wants.

There was that look again. I had no idea what it meant. Perhaps she was less worn down than I believed.

"Are you well today, Mrs. Ashleigh?" I asked.

"Never better, Thomas. Thank you for asking."

I glanced at Barker. Something was happening, but I didn't know what it was, and by the look on my employer's face, he was unaware of it, as well.

*She's up to some mischief,* I thought. Perhaps even now two burly orderlies were coming down the hall with restraints, to tie Barker to his bed. If so, they'd need four of them. Possibly even six.

"Thomas?"

I turned when I heard a mellifluous voice at the door. My heart skipped a beat as it did whenever I saw her.

"Rebecca?" I exclaimed. "What are you doing here?"

She lifted her veil and folded it back from her face. She was in widow's black but it somehow became her, the kind of simple black dress that made Lily Langtry famous, or infamous, if you prefer.

"Mrs. Ashleigh was kind enough to invite me here to meet Mr. Barker," she replied, looking at me warmly. "I understand he is to be released today. Mrs. Ashleigh, it was so kind of you."

"Not at all, Mrs. Cowan. And I insist you call me Philippa. What a beauty you are. Thomas claimed you were, but we assumed it was bias on his part."

My fiancée stepped forward, toward my employer. "Mr. Barker, I'm very pleased to make your acquaintance."

She raised her gloved hand to him, much in the way a circus performer would put theirs into a lion's maw. The lion, in this case my employer, took her petite hand in his oversize one and nodded his head.

"Mrs. Cowan, I don't know what you see in this rascal, but you're free to have him. Certainly, I can't teach him. I suspect he is untrainable. I fear your decision was rash and not fully considered."

Philippa Ashleigh laughed and shook her head. "I can't believe it. You and Thomas come from two completely different backgrounds, yet you appear a matched set: curly hair, dark eyes. A matched pair."

"Thank you," Rebecca said, breaking into one of those smiles that will illuminate a room. It was her. She was here. She and Barker had finally met. And I had Mrs. Ashleigh to thank for it.

"Mr. Barker, my father still sings your praises," Rebecca continued. "He claims you saved the East End from a pogrom entirely by yourself."

"He gives me too much credit. The citizens protected the community themselves. I merely found myself in the thick of it."

Something was wrong with Barker. He was being brusque. I have seen him charm women when he wanted to, so it was not that. I wondered if his concerns about our marriage had overcome his civility.

"Tell me," Philippa asked, "would you care to dine with us in a few days' time, after Mr. Barker has been installed in the house once more?"

"My dear Philippa," Rebecca said, "I would be delighted to dine with you whichever day is convenient."

"I will let you know when things are settled."

Barker gave a quiet grunt. Dining with guests meant that he would have to eat later than he preferred and he would spend an evening entertaining a guest when he would rather be reading. He's not what one might call a bon vivant.

"Do you have any dietary restrictions?" Philippa asked.

"No pork, if I may ask."

"Certainly not."

There was an awkward silence. Barker brooded, Rebecca stood awkwardly, and Philippa looked for anything that might lighten the conversation.

"I'm sorry about your injuries, sir," Rebecca said.

"I've had many before and doubtless there will be more to come. Thomas here was set upon just yesterday."

"What?" she asked, turning to look at me. "I heard nothing about it."

"I have not had the chance to speak with you," I answered. "It was a trifling matter. A couple of men with sticks."

"Two men?" she repeated, clutching her throat.

"I'm fine," I assured her.

I noted Philippa giving the Guv a sharp look, which he ignored. He was also ignoring mine. This was not the time to discuss the dangers of being an enquiry agent. I was hoping to gloss over that particular subject for some time to come.

"Cyrus is anxious to get home," Philippa said, trying to apologize for his behavior. "It's been very trying here since the accident."

"It was not an accident, my dear," he said.

I watched a trickle of sweat roll down his temple. Only Philippa and I knew him well enough to read him. He was in pain and finding it difficult to be gracious. The man was not himself. I knew that, and yet I was becoming angrier by the minute.

"It's been a difficult case, Rebecca, but it is nearly over," I assured her.

There was a tear gleaming at the corner of Rebecca's eye. She had not anticipated that there would be parts of my life that I might not want to share with her, for fear of burdening her or causing her alarm.

Philippa smiled at Rebecca. "You and I must have tea after the two of you return."

"I'd like that."

There was another moment of silence, save for a shift in the bath chair and a groan.

Rebecca's face brightened. "You must be proud of Bok Fu Ying's baby. She brought her to Camomile Street just the other day. Such a little beauty."

"Oh, you're so fortunate!" Philippa cried. "I wanted to have them to my home in Sussex, but they are not yet traveling."

"It has been a sore trial for her this year," my employer remarked. "Her husband has been weaning himself off of opium."

Rebecca sputtered and I bristled. I didn't care how much pain he was in. He must be polite to my fiancée. Philippa saw how angry I was becoming, but the Guv was oblivious.

"Mr. Barker has a dog," I said, hoping to turn the conversation to a safe channel.

"Oh," she said. "What kind is it?"

"A Pekingese."

"One of those little Chinese dogs? They're so delightful."

Barker said nothing. I even wondered if he had fainted from the pain.

Rebecca took matters into her own hands. "It was so nice to meet you both. Thomas has spoken so warmly about you. Mrs. Ashleigh, I hope we shall have tea very soon."

She took Philippa's hand briefly and curtsied to my employer. Then she turned and left. I followed her, taking a moment to look back at the two of them and shake my head. Then I hurried to Rebecca's side. She had her handkerchief to her face.

"He hates me!" she murmured in the hall. "The man is terrifying. How can you work for such a horrible person? Tell me he won't be your best man. Tell me he will not come to our wedding!"

"Cyrus!" I heard Philippa bellow through the halls as we stepped out into the morning sunshine.

Outside, I dared take Rebecca into my arms. She shook as she cried against my chest.

"I don't understand," I said. "I've never seen him be so rude. He's usually very kind to women."

"Are you defending him?" she asked.

"Certainly not. His behavior was unconscionable."

"Take me home. I want to go home!"

I hailed a cab and helped her up when one pulled to the curb. Then I climbed in beside her.

"The City," I told the cabman.

"Am I so unsuitable?" she continued, once the carriage had begun to move. "Does he not want you to marry? Are you to be his servant forever?"

"No, dear, no," I murmured.

"Resign! Take the offer of a position in the City. We'll find a nice home. It doesn't have to be the one I live in now. I'd live anywhere with you!"

"And I with you. My head is in a whirl. I can't believe his behavior."

"He is even more frightening than Israel said. But Mrs. Ashleigh was so kind. It doesn't make sense!"

"I'm sorry," I replied.

The truth was, I didn't know what to say. I may have understood some of the reasons he was in such a foul mood, but I could not defend him to her. She was distraught, and rightfully so. If it became a choice between my position and the woman I loved, there was no contest.

I tried to touch her gloved hand, but she pulled away, as if for that moment she feared all men. She retreated to the farthest corner of the cab and grew silent.

After an interminable journey, we reached Camomile Street. She hurried to the house and by the time I had paid the cabman and returned, she had gone inside. Through the window, I saw the maid's face giving me a stern look. I reached for the knob and found it locked.

That was how it was. I lifted the gold knocker and lowered it again.

"Bad luck," James Briggs said at my elbow. I hadn't seen him when we'd arrived. "Should I leave off guarding the house?"

"No," I answered. "Her safety is my only concern. It is not based on how she might feel about me at any given moment."

I returned to the office and sat to think. Jenkins knew something was wrong, but did not know what precisely. He kept looking at me, asking me a question by not asking it.

Lifting the Hammond typing machine, I put a piece of paper in it and typed my resignation letter. When it was done, I folded it in thirds and put it in an envelope. I felt better having written it.

The Guv had presented all of his faults to her at once, and at the same time given her cause to believe I was in constant danger if I kept my position. I understood that Barker was in a great deal of pain and wanted to leave the priory because there was a madman or madwoman somewhere in London trying to destroy his entire life. Philippa had good intentions trying to broker a meeting between her intended and mine, but it had been a complete disaster. I even wondered if she were speaking to him now.

"Is there anything I can get you, Mr. L.?" Jenkins asked, looking at the envelope on my desk. "A cup of tea or something?"

"No, thank you," I replied.

172 • WILL THOMAS

He went back to his desk, but every sound rankled on my nerves, from the flap of his newspaper to the squeak of his chair. I hesitated with the envelope in my hand, then I stood and placed it in the center of Barker's desk.

"Good-bye, Jeremy," I said, taking his hand before he had even offered it. "It was a pleasure working with you. Take care of yourself."

It was worth it to see him with his mouth open, gaping at me as I took my hat, which had miraculously reappeared on the hat-stand, and walked out the door. At the bottom of the stair, I stepped outside and pulled the door to. There was a plaque in the gate with my name upon it. I'd have to remove it later.

"So, out of work again," I remarked to myself.

The position Rabbi Mocatta had arranged for me could vanish as quickly as it had been offered. I felt like the acrobat who leaps from the trapeze hoping beyond hope that someone will catch me from the other side.

"Where to now?" I muttered.

It isn't every day one resigns, or if it is, I feel sorry for the fellow. I put my hands on my hips in Whitehall Street and looked south toward the Houses of Parliament, then north toward Nelson's Column. Where should I go? I wondered. I stopped a cab as it came by.

"Cornhill Street," I told the driver.

My favorite spot in all London is in what is known as St. Michael's Alley. It is a small terra-cotta building called the Barbados, a coffeehouse which some say is the oldest in London. Here men puzzled over the strong new bitter drink brought to the Old World in hopes of competing with the tea trade. In my opinion, it won.

Once inside, I breathed in the earthy aroma, sloughed off the horrible day, and gave a sigh as if expelling evil humors. I sat down in a booth constructed of old pews, and enjoyed the near darkness, which was comforting in comparison with the bright sun outside.

"Black Apollo," I told the waiter. "And a barrister's torte."

I was indulging a fondness for sweets. First half a pie and now a torte. In my defense, it is a good torte, chocolate on the outside and coffee cream inside, plundered from the Americas. I drank innumerable cups of strong black coffee and ate the torte, which was gone too quickly. Then I had them bring my own church-warden pipe and smoked some of that Virginia tobacco that Caleb extolled. I wondered what he was doing at the moment, but no matter. He wasn't my concern any longer.

Between the tobacco and the caffeine, I was jittery after an hour and feeling sorry for myself. I cursed Barker for a while, then grew tired of it and turned my attention to Rebecca. Had she recovered from the ordeal that morning enough to accept a late call from someone who cared for her very much, or was it still too soon? One does not want to subject a woman to one's attentions too early. On the other hand, one does not want her to think you complacent, either. I decided to go after I finished my cup. Then I decided to go after the last bowlful of tobacco. After I read *The Times,* and possibly *Blackwood's.* Anything but stand between warring factions.

Five o'clock came around by the quaint bells of St. Mary-le-Bow. By then the wooden pew was as hard as a rock. I took myself off, the idea occurring to me that I was walking to my doom. How readily would Rebecca forgive me for not standing up to my employer and for not defending her? Perhaps my resignation would be a peace offering of sorts.

Cornhill became Leadenhall Street. Leadenhall led to St. Mary Axe, and there it was: Camomile Street. Such a gentle name. Nothing bad, nothing coarse, nothing dangerous could ever happen in a place called Camomile.

Or could it?

# CHAPTER TWENTY

A n hour later I stood in front of Rebecca's house, thinking of a plan and looking for any possible loopholes.
Barker called it "testing the knots," a nautical term. I had
a plan. I didn't know if it was a good one, but I had a plan, the
only thing I could do: I must throw myself upon the mercy of the
court.

I crossed the square to Bully Boy Briggs, who was standing
across the street, leaning against a lamppost. His cap was pulled
down low over his head, making him look half asleep, although I
knew he was nothing if not vigilant.

"Hello, Jim," I said.

"Thomas."

"Quiet tonight?"

"Like a graveyard."

The truth was, I was nervous to speak to Rebecca. She had been
put in an uncomfortable position on my account, while hoping to
make a good impression on Barker and Philippa. I had hoped my-

self that the first time they met, it would be a wonderful occasion, the Guv slapping me on the back and Rebecca realizing she had never had any reason to worry on that score. Instead, all had gone as bad as, or worse than, she had feared. Now I lurked about her residence, afraid to go inside.

"Has anyone come or gone since I was here last?" I asked Briggs.

"A brougham arrived. Older woman, black hair, rather severe-looking."

"Her mother."

"Come and gone."

"Excellent."

Things had not been difficult enough; now her mother had been brought into it. Her mother, who despised me. I almost re-thought going in to speak to Rebecca.

"How'd you like a little exercise?" I asked.

He gave me a gap-toothed grin. "Now you've caught my interest. I'm your man. What do I have to do?"

"Not much. I thought we might take down the Hobson gang."

Briggs whistled. "That's a tall order. When do you want me to do it?"

"Now."

He grinned again. "You've become much more impatient since you met this bit of fluff."

"She's not a bit of fluff!" I said, my dander up.

"There, you see?" he replied, as if I'd fallen in his trap. "You're going off half-cocked."

I thought about it. "Very well. Perhaps not tonight. Would you consider reconnoitering around the docks?"

"That would depend on what that was," he said.

"A look-see," I replied. "A walk around. I'd like to know what the boys are up to this evening."

"That I can do, but who will guard the missus?"

The missus. I liked that.

"I will."

He shrugged his mountainous shoulders. "Suit yourself, if you think you're up to it."

"Who says I'm not up to it?" I said, stepping toward him.

He raised his hands in front of him. "Not me. I'll leave you to it. They're over by the East India Docks, right? Or have they moved?"

"They're still there, or were last night."

"I'll take myself off, then. Cheerio."

"Cheerio."

I turned and walked toward the door, looking overhead. It was growing dark. The clouds were like soot against the iron sky. I took hold of the knocker and banged it. The sound reverberated in the quietness of the neighborhood. One thing I knew: by dismissing Briggs, I was letting myself off the hook of having to have a talk with Rebecca tonight, although if she wished to speak to me, I was available. It wasn't the bravest thing I'd ever done, but there you are.

Half a minute later the maid answered the door, looking disappointed that it was only me. I suspected she had never particularly cared for me, and now that Rebecca's feelings had been hurt, I was the most convenient one to blame.

"Come in, sir," she said. "I'll tell Mistress you're here."

"There's no need. Merely inform her that I shall be guarding the house myself for a while, so Mr. Briggs can run an errand."

"Yes, sir," she said, before shutting the door in my face.

I am of the opinion that young maids should not give themselves airs. Merely because they work in a certain residence does not make them members of the family. Rebecca thought her loyal, but privately, I believed she was a spy for her mother.

Turning, I went to stand at Jim's post and looked about. A mist was falling, so fine it merely beaded on my bowler hat. I watched it swirl about the gas lamps like will-o'-the-wisps or fairies. It was beautiful, as though God were presenting an entire performance for me alone.

"Thomas!"

I turned as I heard that voice that always put a catch in my throat. She was coming out of the house, buttoning a cloak about her.

"Rebecca, go back inside," I said. "It isn't safe."

"Not safe, with you here? Don't be silly. Now what is this nonsense about you standing out here all night?"

"Not all night," I argued. "Merely until Mr. Briggs returns. It shouldn't be more than an hour."

"Come in, then. You'll catch your death, love, and we have much to discuss."

She called me "love." That went straight to my heart.

"I can't be protection for you if I'm inside the house."

"Surely you can watch from a window or something. You cannot protect me with a cold, and you know how they can quickly slide into something more serious. I prefer to stand at our wedding, not your funeral."

I couldn't help smiling.

"My dear," I said. "Aren't you being a touch melodramatic?"

She looked at me solemnly, and then the facade cracked as she gave me a crooked smile. "Perhaps a touch."

The door opened behind her and an ochre light spilled onto the flagstones. Silhouetted against it was the trim figure of Aunt Lydia.

"Is he being recalcitrant?" she asked.

"Of course he is," came the reply. "He is a man."

I crossed my arms. "I will not allow my entire sex to be disparaged."

"Make him come in," Lydia called. "He'll catch his death."

"My words exactly," Rebecca said.

"He should have some tea!"

"No!" I said. "No tea!"

"Duty?" Aunt Lydia asked. "Thought as much. Men are so impractical."

"I was not aware that women were so free with their opinions lately."

Both of them erupted into laughter.

"I didn't say anything funny."

Rebecca put her arm under mine and led me to the door. Once there, Aunt Lydia seized my other arm, and that was it.

"I apologize for the way my employer acted today, since he is not here to apologize for himself. Neither Mr. Barker nor I were aware you were coming. I assume Mrs. Ashleigh considered it a surprise for all of us, never imagining that it might not go well."

Rebecca grew solemn. "It was not the meeting I had envisioned."

"Mr. Barker did not find you lacking in any way. He was just feeling unwell and anxious to leave the hospital. Nothing you said or did affected his ill mood."

"I understand."

I wasn't so certain she did. I had been so accustomed to living in a bachelor household for years that I had never considered how much effort would be put into addressing the sensibilities of a woman on a daily basis. In our house, Etienne threw pans out the window or Mac got into an uproar over how I left my shirt on the floor on a daily basis. All of us scattered when the Guv was in a mood, but we thought little of it, knowing it would blow over like a summer storm in a short while. This husbanding business was going to be harder than I thought.

In spite of the fact that she was still smarting from my employer's sharp words, she was not one to bear a grudge. Soon I was sitting with a cup of tea and some kind of round powdery biscuit with candied fruit in the center. I was trying my hardest not to get powdered sugar on my suit, and to balance my cup without rattling it. To be honest, I was still nervous about being there. I felt that it was still possible to find myself on the other side of that locked door again. Aunt Lydia liked me, but there were limits to her largesse.

"Really, I need to be outside, watching the house," I said.

"To stand in the rain in a quiet neighborhood, staring into the street?" Rebecca asked, more for my welfare than in argument.

"Mr. Briggs, who is far gentler than his appearance might lead one to believe, has stood there every night for a week, drinking cold tea from a ginger beer bottle, because you've hired him for no good reason."

"Camille Archer was here, posing as my sister," I pointed out.

"It was a practical joke. I don't believe she meant any real harm. Do you know for a fact that she is dangerous?"

"She disappeared quickly from a hotel after she left our offices. A woman of the same name visited a criminal in Paris."

"That sounds frightfully circumstantial," Rebecca said. "Perhaps the poor dear is merely eccentric."

"She may be a great number of things," I said, "but one of them is certainly not a 'poor dear.' I suspect her of being connected to the bombing of our offices."

"Do you think a young woman is capable of building a bomb?" Rebecca's aunt asked. "I've never heard of such a thing."

"I've known one who did, but then one meets many kinds of people in my situation."

"I'm sure," Aunt Lydia said, looking unsettled.

"I apologize, ma'am," I said. "I did not intend to alarm you."

She regained her composure as quickly as if I had flipped an electric switch.

"Of course not, Thomas. What a thought."

"This is excellent tea," I said. "Darjeeling is so refreshing."

"This is Assam."

I lied. I hate tea. I'm strictly a coffee drinker myself, but I understand tea is more than a drink. Tea is a language. It soothed rough nerves and restored order to one's world during difficult circumstances.

Rebecca poured another cup. Aunt Lydia set another biscuit on the edge of my saucer. I tried to protest, but one man is no match for two women. He had best get used to it or retire from the field. It was comforting, I must confess. I had never been fussed over by a woman in my entire life. To find one at each elbow was a unique experience.

"Did Ivy not take your coat?" our chaperone asked. "That girl is no use at all."

"No, ma'am," I said. "I retained my coat intentionally. I must leave in just a minute or two."

I didn't want to tell them that I carried a Webley in each pocket and did not like to hand it to a maid unaware of what was inside.

"Rebecca, surely you can talk Thomas into removing his overcoat."

"Really, I need to go—"

"But, surely—"

They were trying to remove my coat when we were interrupted by men bursting through the front and the back doors simultaneously. I recognized those low-crowned bowlers and donkey-fringed haircuts. It was the Hobson boys. Somehow, they had got around Briggs's dragnet.

There were three or four at each entrance. They held axe handles and sailor's hooks and staves of wood. They charged in through the doors, and came at us standing in the center of the room.

The woman screamed. I dropped the biscuit and the delicate teacup and saucer. My free hands slid into my coat, crossed-armed, and seized the grips of my Webley revolvers. I withdrew them and swung my arms out, a pistol in each hand, as the china crashed at my feet. Jack Hobson and a couple of his men coming forward saw the weapons I brandished. Some slowed or stopped in their tracks. Others did not.

It is in my nature to hesitate, to ponder, to make calculated decisions. However, I had not been affianced before. The wide circle ended with my arms straight across from each other, pointed east and west. Simultaneously, I pulled both triggers. Barker had overruled my request to carry the weapons uncocked.

The first bullet caught a man high in the chest, probably piercing his lung and breaking his clavicle. He moaned and fell into the arms of one of his comrades.

The second fellow, Jack Hobson himself, I shot between the

eyes. He was dead before his body even started to crumple and fall.

The acrid smell of gunpowder was in the air. All of us stared blankly at each other. Rebecca and Lydia had just discovered what sort of monster had been sitting in their house, drinking tea with engines of destruction in his pockets. The Hobson gang was coming to terms with the fact that their leader was dead and a man was brandishing revolvers at them. At such a time, a belaying pin or a length of wood was of very little value.

# CHAPTER TWENTY-ONE

Rebecca and Aunt Lydia were still screaming. I suppose they had reason to. Of all the scenarios of which I could conceive, this was by far the worst: killing a man in front of my own bride mere days before our wedding. The fact that I was defending them was of little concern when there were bodies crumpled on kilim rugs.

There was a commotion at the front door and Briggs burst in, momentarily filling the doorway. He passed through the knot of men, his wide shoulders pushing them out of the way. Silently he regarded the injured man and the dead one and then he nodded as if he now understood.

"Hop it!" he ordered the Hobson gang. "Take these boys with you."

He shook an arm and a long pipe of lead slid into his hand from inside his sleeve. I'd seen it before. He knew how to use it very well.

The gang immediately retreated, lifting their fallen comrades, living and dead, and removing them from the room. One hooligan actually bent down and wiped a gout of blood on the parquet with his sleeve, although it was impossible to get it all. Within a minute both doors were closed and we were alone again.

Briggs turned to me. "What are you carrying?"

"Webleys."

"Give them here."

I did, watching as he stuffed both into one pocket.

"Clear out," he ordered before turning to Lydia and Rebecca. "Ladies, Mr. Llewelyn was not here tonight. Have the maid mop this floor."

I turned to say something to Rebecca, but she stepped away from me, as if she were afraid. It felt as if someone had poured a bucket of cold water down my back. I looked at her and she frowned. I looked at Aunt Lydia and realized the chances of her becoming my aunt Lydia had become exceedingly small.

"Thomas, get out of my house," Rebecca said in a low voice. "I never want to see you again."

My shoulders slumped and I shuffled out the front door. Outside in Camomile Street, the rain suited my mood. I began to walk away from the house, my thoughts as dark as a man's can get.

There was one last tough nearby, perhaps keeping an eye out for the gang. I crossed the street, reaching into my coat. He backed away and beat a hasty retreat.

*Devil take all Mondays,* I said to myself. I'd ruined my life rather effectively. What was I thinking, that something might go according to plan? I was bitter. I wanted to kick things. I wanted to knock people's hats off, as the author Mr. Melville said.

Gradually I calmed myself, but then the realization hit me that I had killed a man. Me, Thomas Llewelyn. What had I been thinking? Why had I taken the guns into the house? That, I supposed, was the problem. I had not thought. I had pulled the pistols purely out of instinct, feeling the need to protect my own. There had been entirely too much interest in Camomile Street, and my personal life. When the time came, I didn't hesitate. I reacted instinctively. What happened was bad enough. What could have happened if I had failed to act, or acted too slowly, would have been worse. Perhaps far worse.

I found Liverpool Street Station and took the Underground to the Elephant and Castle, feeling as low as a fellow can feel. The rain was pouring down then, and it battered my leather coat and my waterproof bowler. For once, the Universe was in sympathy with me. Finally, I reached Barker's home. I heard the argument before I opened the door.

"Are you going to tell me what you're really doing in London?" Barker demanded inside the front room.

"I'm not doing anything!" Caleb shouted back. "I concluded a case and I thought I might take some time to visit my only living relative. That decision may have well been a mistake!"

"You're gone at odd hours and reticent about your activities."

"I'm in the greatest capital city in the entire world. Forgive me if I take in some of the sights. What's the matter, brother dear, do you miss me when I'm gone? I have a life apart from you. I've had it for twenty years. Besides, I have an employer to serve."

"Aha! So you admit you are working for your employer. What kind of case is it? Will it interfere with this one?"

"Cyrus, I did not claim I was on a case for the Pinkerton Agency. You inferred it, and the inference happens to be wrong. I'm not on a case, and I chose to help you with yours, simply because you are injured, and Mr. Llewelyn here might require another trained detective who happens to be free in London with little to do."

I came closer, leaning against the doorframe, feeling all in. So far the night had been a disaster and there was more to come.

"The reason is my problem, Caleb. It's not as if you wish us to bond again as brothers. You have visited me only twice since you arrived. That is hardly solicitous."

"Oh, I didn't realize your pride was hurt. No one told me that I needed to visit you every day. Should I bring flowers?"

"That is not what I meant. Just let me know what you are about. We might need your help on the case."

"I'm not your lapdog, Cyrus."

He pointed at Harm, who was sitting on the rug, shivering. We didn't raise our voices in this house and the dog was unprepared for it. I wanted to reach down and pet him, but to do so I would need to pass Caleb, who was pacing. I'd soothe Harm's ruffled fur when it was over, aware that there was no one to soothe mine.

I heard a short cough and stepped back. Mac was near the back door, looking as concerned as Harm. Behind him I heard the soft hush of the rain, and thunder rumbling overhead. He shook his head, as if he had no idea what to do. I nodded in return.

"I didn't ask you to be my lapdog," Barker went on. "I assumed you volunteered, unless you wish to present a bill later."

"I am paid well by the Pinkerton Agency, thank you. This is a private matter. Unless you prefer I quit and move on."

"You are free to come and go as you like," the Guv barked. "Thank you for your help in the case so far. It was decent of you."

Caleb looked at him as if it were some kind of a trick. He sighted down his nose, his eyes mere slits in his face.

"Not at all," he said cautiously.

They both looked away, embarrassed. Shouting is perfectly acceptable behavior, but thanking someone, or accepting thanks, is practically a sign of weakness.

My employer fixed his spectacled gaze on me, as if looking for someone else to harass. "Well, lad, why are you holding up the wall and looking so glum?"

I pulled away from the wall. He considers leaning to be indolent, as if one could not be bothered to use the two feet God gave you.

"The wedding will be canceled, sir," I said. "There was a fracas at Mrs. Cowan's home tonight."

"Was there, by Jove?" Barker asked, sitting up in his bed. "What happened?"

"I killed Jack Hobson."

Both men looked at me, turned to look at each other, and then returned their gazes to me. I wasn't sure whether they were concerned or impressed. Possibly both. Ours is a very strange occupation.

"Report," Barker growled, sitting back in the nest of pillows Mac had placed there, which I knew he did not want. The Guv is an ascetic at heart. Pillows are frippery.

I told him all that had occurred, from my arrival and talk with Jim Briggs to him sending me out into the night. I omitted my feelings. They were not germane to the conversation.

"Was anyone else injured?" the Guv asked.

"I shot another in the chest. I did not recognize him. He was young."

"So, one of our suspects is dead."

"Yes, sir."

"You shot two men at once?" Caleb asked. "Are you pulling my leg?"

"No. Two at once. They were advancing on me in a group from both sides, and I shot into both. I did not expect to kill anybody, let alone Hobson himself."

"And you shot them in front of Mrs. Cowan?" Caleb asked.

"And her aunt."

"So the wedding—"

"Is off. Most brides are not tolerant of having their grooms kill men in their own house. Rebecca and her aunt were hysterical when I left. She ordered me from the house and said she never wanted to see me again."

"Where are your pistols?" the Guv asked.

"Briggs took them," I said.

"Good. No doubt he will toss them in the river. I shall order a new brace of snub-nosed Webleys for you."

Ordinarily I would have thanked him, but at that moment I didn't want to see another gun as long as I lived.

"I suspect Hobson's body will be found floating in the Thames near Wapping in a day or so," he continued. "Convenient. Did Briggs tell them to remove the bodies?"

"He did."

Barker smiled. That is, his mustache bowed.

"He's a good man. I suggest you double his wages for the service he performed tonight."

"I will, sir."

Both brothers went silent. I believe they each wanted to give me comfort about killing a man and losing a fiancée in the same minute, but were unable to find the words. It wasn't in either's vocabulary.

"Mac!" I called.

"Yes, Mr. Llewelyn!"

"Is the bathwater still hot?"

"I shut down the boiler but half an hour ago. It should be steaming."

"Gentlemen, I'm going to have a bath."

I turned to leave, and as I headed toward the door I noticed my hands were violently shaking. I'd killed a man. A moment before he was making plans, and the next he was standing with a hole in his cranium and a trickle of blood sliding down his nose. He was a common street hooligan, but still, he was a human being, scrabbling to survive as I was. It didn't happen this time.

Five minutes later I was in the bath, steaming as Mac had said, with a wet cloth on my head, staring at nothing. My brain had ceased to function after functioning overmuch. The shaking had stopped and all was still.

The door opened suddenly, and Mac entered with a tray. He set a glass of brandy by the edge of the bath and turned to leave. It was a nerve cure for our occupation.

"How are you faring?" he asked, still looking away. Men cannot look at each other in situations such as this.

"Not well," I said.

"I could speak to Rebecca, if you like."

I had forgotten Mac had been a classmate of Rebecca's in Hebrew school at the synagogue and had known her since she was a small girl.

"Thank you," I replied. "I believe that ship has sailed, old boy."

Mac put the tray under his arm, and beat a hasty retreat. I took a sip of the brandy, which was dreadful, but it was called for in such circumstances.

Gone, I thought, my brain slowly beginning to run like a clock mechanism after winding. Rebecca was gone. No more soothing evenings in her garden, no being fussed over and cossetted by her and her aunt, no more needling of the ill-mannered maid. I was persona non grata in the Cowan household.

I'd met her more than five years ago but her parents had chased me off. I'd watched her carriage go by several times over the years without having the courage to stop it. I was anguished when she married, but secretly elated when her husband had died, though I bore him no personal ill will. I had proposed, and been accepted, after a year's courtship. That year was almost up. Now—pop!— the bubble had burst.

I should have known better than to think this would come easily. In twenty-six years I had not had a single plan come to fruition, save my employment with Cyrus Barker, Esq., which I had blundered into. It had been both a blessing and a curse. Tonight it was a curse.

I tossed off the end of the brandy as a kind of punishment. The heat rose up my throat and through my nose. I shook my head as it burned.

I stood, dried myself, and put on one of the thick, white robes. Then I sat on the stool one uses to wash one's self prior to bathing, and put my palms to my eyes.

God's whipping boy.

# CHAPTER TWENTY-TWO

The telephone set in the hall jangled twenty minutes later, making Mac and I jump. Caleb Barker gave us a withering stare as Mac picked up the instrument from the alcove in the hall.

"Ahoy? Yes, this is the Barker residence. What?" He paused, looking at me. "What? Are you certain? Give me the address. Yes, that is the one. Would you be willing to give me your name if we promised never to use it? Very well. Thank you for the information, sir."

He put the receiver back on its hook and looked at us. All three of us were on tenterhooks. What could possibly have happened now that might be worse than the attack in Camomile Street?

"Mrs. Ashleigh has been taken, sir, from her private residence here in town. It happened not much more than an hour ago."

I suspected the attack in Camomile Street was a diversion. The Hobson gang would have split into two parties. One had set upon us and retreated under withering fire, while the second burst in upon Philippa and found only Frost, the butler, for protection, who was growing rather long in the tooth.

"Confound it!" Barker roared. "Get me my clothes!"

"You're in no shape—"

"Don't say it!" he demanded.

"We'll go," Caleb said, being of a like mind in the matter. "We shall call as soon as we learn what happened."

"I'm going, damn and blast! Mac, my clothes!"

"No, sir."

"You are sacked!"

"Yes, sir."

I'll say this for Jacob Maccabee. The fellow has sand.

"Sir," I said.

"Do you wish to join him?"

"No, sir."

"Then bring me my clothes!"

Just then there was a thump on the knocker of the front door and everyone froze. There was another thump. Behind it, we could hear the peal of thunder and the windows by the entrance illuminated in the hall by lightning.

As one, we responded. I pulled a stick out of the stand by the front door while Caleb loosed a peacemaker from the waistband of his trousers and Mac, who technically had no say in this fight, came out of his butler's pantry-cum-bedroom armed with his sawn-down shotgun.

He was the first to step forward and open the door.

The rain was falling in a torrent. A man stood upon the sill, barely sheltered by the lintel over the entrance. He wore a shiny mackintosh and a bowler hat, clutching his lapel about his throat. Scotland Yard, I thought. Too late to inform us that Barker's lady friend had been taken.

We brought him into the room, where he stamped his feet on the mat and removed his bowler. A cascade of russet tresses fell about the shoulders of her coat.

"Philippa!" I exclaimed.

"Please help me out of this coat. It's waterlogged," she said. "It was beastly finding a cab. Now I understand how you men must feel—practically invisible in foul weather."

"How did you get here?" I insisted.

"No!" Mac cried. "She should have the opportunity to change and refresh herself before being called upon to speak."

We couldn't argue with that, of course. In fact, we felt like cads for not suggesting it ourselves. I led her upstairs and showed her the amenities, although she had been in the room before. Then I left her.

Coming downstairs, I heard the front door close. I was shy about sounds at the moment, and went to investigate. Caleb was leaning against the doorframe, facing out of Barker's room. The Guv was sitting in his makeshift bed with a hand in his hair. It had been a trying day for everyone.

"Did someone just leave?" I asked.

Caleb nodded.

"Mac?"

Another nod.

"Is he getting something?"

"A new job," he answered. "It's what you do when you get sacked."

"But, Mr. Barker was just joking. And Mrs. Ashleigh is now safe!"

"Sensitive fellow, your butler."

"He's a factotum. He does everything."

"Sounds like he was lucky to get out, then."

"Sir!" I called to his brother. "Mac has left."

"Has he?" Barker asked. "Go after him. Mrs. Ashleigh is my first concern."

My Macintosh was in the butler's pantry. I stepped inside the room, Jacob's sanctum sanctorum. It was quiet, however, and when I looked about, I saw chaos there. Mac is as neat as a pin. Even his private room is never out of place. That is, until today. His bed had been mussed by what I could only assume was a valise. Shoes spilled out of his wardrobe. A lone stocking garter lay on the floor.

I threw on my coat and my stoutest bowler hat, then seized the brolly and ran out the front door into a cascade of water. The air was so moist one could choke upon it like a consumptive patient. I put up my umbrella, and looked for any sign of Jacob in the streets. London looked deserted. A man or woman with any sense would be inside by a warm fire.

My errand was unsuccessful. Mac must have found the one hansom in the district and was on his way to the City, where his parents lived in Aldgate. I turned and made my way back to our front door. As I entered, Mrs. Ashleigh came down the stair. Caleb stopped leaning on the doorframe and even bowed to her. Barker sat up on his pillow. I nodded, dripping a flood of rain on the parquet floor. Mac would have jumped up and down for the state of it.

"Tell me, Philippa," Barker insisted. "How came you to be here? We were informed you had been taken."

"I very nearly was," she answered. "My butler, Frost, that dear old fellow, put his own coat and hat on me and thrust me out of the kitchen entrance. Then I came out into an alley and crossed to the other side of the street under a low-hanging oak and watched as the door was burst open. Frost attempted to stop them but they dealt him a strong blow. From where I stood, I saw him fall. A moment later, they dragged her from the house and forced her into a covered brougham. They took her away to who knows where."

"I don't understand," I interjected. "Who? Whom did they take?"

"My bodyguard, Miss Fletcher."

"Presumably, they did not have a physical description of her," Barker rumbled.

"From the conversation I had with Miss Fletcher, I think it likely that she claimed to be Mrs. Ashleigh," I told him.

"I have little doubt," Barker said, bedridden but very much in control.

"Will she be harmed?" I asked.

"Or worse."

"Oh, god," I said. "I hired her."

"If you recall, Thomas, you just shot and killed Jack Hobson. These were likely the same men, looking for revenge."

Just then the hall clock tolled once. Another day had begun. Monday was over. I hoped Tuesday wouldn't be as bad as the day before. All of us stared at each other, nonplussed.

"Go to bed, everyone," Barker ordered. "I can make no promises about what the new day might bring."

"But what about Miss Fletcher?" I asked. "Shouldn't we try to find her?"

"We have no idea where they are going, Thomas. We can't search randomly all night. We'll have to wait until morning."

We climbed the stair, each to his own room. Mac had moved Caleb to his brother's rooms at the top of the house before he left, leaving Mrs. Ashleigh in possession of the rooms which in fact had been decorated for her, though she seldom used them. Caleb would be much more comfortable in Barker's bachelor domain, with the leather wingback chairs, the old Georgian cabinet bed, and the walls of weapons.

I changed into my nightshirt and crawled into bed. Then it all caved in upon me.

It was the look of horror Rebecca gave me when I shot those men, as if I were a creature no better than the ruffians who had burst into her house. Now she would never speak to me again. I'd wanted Rebecca for so long, only to lose her now. She seemed tailor-made for me. I was entranced within a few minutes of our meeting and was in love within a day. There was a quote I'd had in my mind from *Far from the Madding Crowd*, my favorite book by Thomas Hardy. His character, Gabriel Oak, says to young Bathsheba Everdene, "Whenever you look up, there I shall be— and whenever I look up, there will be you." There was something so peaceful in that sentiment. I longed for it. Alas, all that was over now.

There was a rasp beside me and a bright light that made me jump. Caleb Barker had pulled up a chair to my bed silently and was applying a vesta to his hand-rolled cigarette.

"Here's Mr. Thomas Llewelyn feeling sorry for himself," he said, blowing smoke in my face.

"Men cannot do that, even in the privacy of their own bedroom?"

"It's been my experience that women go all over peculiar when someone is shot. It's in their nature to rush to someone's aid, to show solace and caring. You can imagine how upsetting it must be to have the one doing the shooting be yours."

I sat up and scratched my head. "What would you know about women's natures?"

"Experience over four continents. No, five! I was in Australia for a week once."

"Not respectable women," I countered.

"Of course not. Would a respectable woman associate with a cowboy detective?"

"I suppose not," I said. "Ever been married?"

"Once, for about a week. I don't care for staying on one piece of land for too long. Turned out she wanted a garden and chickens. Chickens, by God! Nasty creatures."

I stopped to ponder the matter, Caleb Barker being domesticated.

"Tell me," he asked. "When do you carry a pistol?"

"Only when I fear for my life or your brother's."

"How often is that? How often have you carried it?"

"Hundreds of times, I suppose," I said.

"And how often have you used it?"

"Rarely. Three or four times, at most."

"You carried it to protect yourself. That's its purpose."

"That is correct."

"And you used it to protect Mrs. Cowan."

"I did."

"Then you used it for the purpose for which it was intended. You don't carry it around as jewelry, do you? An ornament?"

"Of course not," I agreed. "It's heavy and cumbersome."

He smoothed his thick mustache with his hand and tweaked one corner. "Is Mrs. Cowan aware that you sometimes carry a pistol, and need to?"

"I suppose she is," I answered. "We've never discussed it."

"You do realize that most peacekeepers are unmarried."

"Yes, I realize that. Mrs. Ashleigh is similarly troubled."

"Where I come from, most every man carries a pistol on his hip, well displayed, and believe me, Thomas, I've protected myself more than just three or four times. The U.S. west of the Mississippi isn't civilized, like London."

"So, what's your prescription, Doctor, for a woman who has just seen you shoot someone?"

"Show some brass. Act like it didn't happen. Don't apologize until you feel the need to. Don't bring flowers. Don't appear frightened. She has a decision to make, and you won't win her over by going on about how sorry you are. A woman prefers a man who is confident."

"I hadn't considered that."

"And when she talks, listen, by god. She feels she has important things to say. Maybe she does and maybe she doesn't, but listen anyway. Like I said, she has a decision to make. Can she stand to be the wife of a man who's in your line of work? What do you call it again?"

"Private enquiry agent."

"As you say. From what I hear, she is a fine little lady. Possibly too fine for the likes of you. Be prepared to be refused."

"Have you had experience in this, as well?"

"No, I've never been up this alley before."

"Yet you feel comfortable dispensing advice."

He smiled. The man smiled far more than his brother. I did not completely trust it. It came to him too easily.

"I always feel comfortable giving advice," he said. "I enjoy giving it, and watching fools brought low when they choose to ignore it."

He puffed on the last of his cigarette and stamped it out on the floor. I shot him a look of disbelief.

"A fag end on Mac's floor?"

"I've been torturing your butler since I arrived. He has practically nothing to do here, he is so well organized. I thought I'd give him something to do. I've been leaving cigarette ash all over the house."

"In case you haven't noticed, Mac is gone."

"He'll be back. He cares too much about this place and his position here. Oh, he'll sulk for a while, but he'll come back. When he does, my dear brother, who already regrets sacking him, will welcome him back with open arms."

"Your brother has never welcomed anyone with open arms."

"I see that. He sure didn't welcome me. However, I doubt the clocks will run with Maccabee gone, especially with Cyrus forced to stay abed. I take it he is not a man who cares to lie about."

"Not in the slightest," I said.

"Perhaps he will appreciate what the boy does around here."

"How did you learn so much about Mac in so short a time?" I asked.

He pointed to his face with two fingers.

"Eyes," he said. "Observation and ratiocination. I've got a fresh pair of peepers here, and training. I could tell right off your butler understands what he's about."

I hated to admit it, but Caleb was correct. For all our squabbling, I couldn't imagine a life without Jacob Maccabee.

# CHAPTER TWENTY-THREE

There is a schedule of sorts in Lion Street each morning, and it begins with Mac coming into my room and drawing the blinds. All creation began with Mac drawing the blinds, but now he was not here to let in the sun, to air the house, to beeswax the floors, or to sigh over what an oaf I was. Without Jacob Maccabee, there was no one to hold me to a times table, to get me up and out the door by a certain hour. I reached for my watch and opened it. It was fifty minutes after seven. On normal days we arrived by seven thirty. We didn't have normal days anymore.

I had blown out a man's brains as easily as if I had swatted a fly with a rolled-up edition of the *Sporting News*. Rebecca had been there to see it all. Once seen, such things cannot be unseen. Jack Hobson, for all his faults, had been a living, breathing human being until I blew a steel bullet through his skull. One second he was alive thinking thoughts, making plans, and the next all thought ceased, and for a brief moment he was literally dead on his feet. Then he fell, right there on my fiancée's marble hall floor, brains and all.

There seemed no reason to get out of bed that morning, to wriggle my way into a suit of clothes, or comb my hair, and act as if nothing had happened. Something had happened all right, something momentous, and it was possible nothing would ever be the same again.

I struggled from under the counterpane and donned my slippers and dressing gown and went downstairs to see if everyone was about. The house seemed deathly quiet. I heard the oddly comforting sound of Barker snoring in the front room. Most days he is up at five, toiling in his garden like a farmer. Here he was sleeping past eight o'clock. No doubt his body was full of tincture of opium. Two ounces left him flat upon his back.

Harm came waddling down the hall to me, looking perturbed. The whites of his eyes were showing, as if they were straining harder than usual to start out of his head. He sniffed something on the floor, and then sneezed because of it. Coming closer, he twitched his tail, as if he were making an effort to be civil under the circumstances. Mac was gone and we were here, and the schedule had gone right out the window into the koi pond with the copper pot. It was enough to give a dog apoplexy.

I wandered into the kitchen and found our guest in attendance, and our cook, Etienne Dummolard, gone. Mrs. Ashleigh was sitting in front of the remains of an omelet, holding a delicate cup of coffee in her hand. My immediate concern was my state of toilet. I would have withdrawn, but her eye caught me from her peripheral vision.

"Good morning, Thomas," she said, staring into the back garden. The glaziers had come and installed a new and very expensive pane of glass.

"Morning, ma'am."

"I'm sorry to hear about your loss. I cannot assure you that Rebecca will come round in time for your wedding."

"If ever," I said.

"As you say, if ever."

"I don't know why I supposed my luck would be any different now than it has been for the last twenty-six years, ma'am."

"You're being maudlin," Philippa said.

"I think I've earned that right."

I crossed and poured myself coffee from the pot on the Aga.

"Etienne has been here," I said.

"Yes, and he left as soon as he saw the changes."

"He doesn't like changes, does Etienne?"

"*Non.*"

I rarely got Mrs. Ashleigh to myself, but after seven years we had grown less reserved around each other. She had sense and offered good advice. She was the kind of woman that I hoped Rebecca would become in fifteen years.

"How are you, Thomas?"

"Beastly. I reacted, just as Mr. Barker trained me. I shot two men at once. The Guv would have been proud of my marksman-ship. He's always after me to practice. I needn't worry about need-ing skill with a revolver anymore. But it cost me the hand of the woman I love."

"You don't know that yet, Thomas," Philippa said.

"You should have seen her eyes, ma'am."

"I'm sure, were Cyrus to kill someone in front of me, I'd be equally dismayed."

"Even after years of being together?"

I needed to be careful when describing their relationship. They were neither married nor unmarried. They were not affianced. She was not a mistress. I didn't know what they were, and I sup-posed neither did anyone else. She had many social engagements in Sussex. I wondered how her friends described her relationship with a rough-hewn enquiry agent.

"Yes, I'd be dismayed. But I wouldn't leave him. However, Rebecca has not known you as long, and is not prepared for this."

"Mrs. Ashleigh, you are not reassuring me."

"Thomas, how long have you known me?"

"It must be six, maybe seven years now," I said.

"I think it high time you call me Philippa."

"M-ma'am, I don't think I can now."

She smiled. Her teeth were perfect, a rare thing in England.

"You must. I have asked. As a gentleman you cannot refuse."

She was correct.

"Very well . . . Philippa."

"That's better. What do you intend to do about Rebecca?"

"I thought I would try to see her in a day or so, and find out how she felt about what occurred. The wedding will be postponed for a month or two, but . . ."

Our guest reached up and pinched the bridge of her nose.

"It's a wonder men get anything done, Thomas. Leave this to me. I'll do what I can, but I make no promises. Perhaps she'll take pity on a scapegrace like you."

"You don't think letting her contemplate a day or so—"

She shook her head.

"Her family shall retrench. They never found you suitable. Two days from now and they will have convinced her."

"But I have duties today. Mr. Barker will have orders."

"Thomas, go. Change. Don't shave; it shall make you look desperate. She'll complain, but she'll like that. Give her all the control."

I stared into my coffee and didn't move.

"You're frightened, aren't you?" she asked.

"Philippa, I am quaking in my boots."

"Excellent. It will enhance your plea. Go tonight after work. Give me time to think."

I walked through the hall to the front door and turned toward my employer, who had awakened. His crisp hair was now disarranged and he was frowning. Everything was going to hell.

"I'm sorry I am late this morning, sir."

"That is understandable, given the events of last night. Keep me informed of your progress. Mac will answer the telephone if it rings."

"Sir, Mac is gone. You sacked him."

Barker had a fit of temper. I'd seen it building since last night.

"Damn and blast! One would think that a man who had worked for me for ten years would understand when I was merely venting my spleen."

He was going to go on, but there was a sudden knock at the door, almost beside my head. We looked at each other, wondering what would happen now. I opened it to find Captain Yeager on the other side, accompanied by two large marines armed with rifles.

"Mr. Llewelyn," he said.

"As you see. Come in," I said. "This is my employer, Mr. Barker. Mr. Barker, this is Captain Yeager of the U.S. Marine Corps."

My employer nodded. "What can I do for you and the U.S. government?"

"Sir, Mr. Llewelyn has been seen in the company of Caleb Barker on several occasions."

"True," I said.

"He promised to notify us when your brother returned."

"Not true," I argued. "I don't believe I made a promise. I tend to shy away from promises. They only get one in trouble."

"Mr. Llewelyn, you are already in trouble."

"Captain," Mr. Barker said, trying to sound patient. "What would you ask of us? We told him you are looking for him and that he should turn himself over to you. Neither of us can make him come. We cannot make him do anything."

"That man is becoming an embarrassment to the United States of America. It is high time he was on a boat bound for New York."

"I completely agree with you," the Guv said. "He is rather headstrong. It is a family trait. I do not envy you your duty."

"Help us, then."

"I'm already helping you. Neither of us trusts Caleb, but come, he is my brother. What can one do?"

"Get him safely back to where he came from, that's what one can do. Do I need to bring the ambassador himself here? Or a man from the foreign office? Need we call the prime minister himself to settle the matter?"

"No," I interjected. "He might learn that I didn't vote for him."

"Caleb comes and goes," Barker said. "He lives on his own schedule and has duties to perform for the Pinkerton Agency. If I ask him to meet me, it is likely he won't come. If I tell him to stay, well, what can one do?"

Captain Yeager crossed his arms and looked hard at him. "Mr. Barker, I know we are merely a legation and not an actual embassy, but we can make things difficult for your agency. We provide goods and services to your country: beef and tobacco, timber and furs. I do not wish to have you arrested by Scotland Yard, but I can."

"I'm confined to this bed with a serious injury," my employer replied. "I think even Scotland Yard will find that I have been in no condition to confine my brother."

"Yet, you sent Mr. Llewelyn with him to Paris."

"You make it sound like a holiday," I said. "My employer was nearly killed and I've been following leads to discover who did it. Caleb came along because he also wanted his brother's injuries avenged."

"Avenged how, Mr. Llewelyn?" he asked.

"We're not in America. There are laws here, Captain. You've been talking to Scotland Yard."

"We have mutual respect. It might interest you to know that there are many who are not particularly impressed with your agency."

"As a rule, police forces do not get along with private agents. Or soldiers, for that matter."

He turned to my employer. "Sir, give up your brother and nothing will happen to your agency. Continue to harbor him, how-ever, and we'll make a formal charge against you. Both of you."

"A formal charge?" I asked. "Is that the best you can do?"

"In public, Mr. Llewelyn. You best watch your step. London is a dangerous city."

The guards behind him grinned.

# CHAPTER TWENTY-FOUR

The sky wept the next morning, as if ashamed of some private indiscretion she dared not voice. There are a dozen types of rain in London: the wall of mist, which soaks your clothing in spite of your umbrella; the hard, vertical rain that attacks the cobblestones and anyone standing on them; the gentle rain one doesn't mind walking about in. During one storm alone one might experience six or seven kinds of rain.

It was a desultory rain that morning, as if it couldn't really decide what to be, but felt apathetic to the question. I made my way to the Elephant and Castle station, and after a change or two reached Charing Cross, near our offices. Working my way out of the bowels of the earth, I stopped and watched a sleek, apple-green express getting ready to depart for Dover. Then I unfurled my umbrella before stepping up into rain again at the entrance to the Underground.

I needed to find Miss Fletcher. She had been working for me when she was put in harm's way and I felt responsible for her safety, even though I knew if I had spent the night in the rain searching for her, I would have failed. I should have tried, anyway.

Now it was daylight, such as it was, and I was on the trail again. I decided to start at the East India Docks, looking for any sign of the Hobson gang. That was my plan as I splashed through the flooded streets and came upon the scene unfolding in Craig's Court.

The court was fully congested, a clogged artery of commerce. Despite the rain, and the difficulty of lifting an umbrella in so narrow a confine, men and even women stood peering at the back of the court, raindrops drumming on their hats. Ours is a quiet street, the odd explosion notwithstanding, and finding dozens of people here gave me a turn. What had happened now? I wondered.

"What's all this, then?" I asked a tall fellow peering over other people's shoulders.

"Someone's been hurt. A woman, I think. Two constables just rolled a hand litter up the street there. That's all I know."

My hand was on the door of number 5, but I took it off again.

"Make way," I shouted. "Make way!"

I began to push through the crowd, none too gently. If one moved authoritatively enough, people assumed one was official. Most of the people gave way. The rest I gave what they deserved.

I saw the hand litter coming toward me, led by a constable in an opalescent oilskin. As he hurried past me with the litter, I looked down on the still form. It was as I feared. It was Sarah Fletcher.

Her nose had been broken, and the blood, currently being washed away by the rain, drenched her chin and collar. It was swollen and her eyes blackened. A bruise on her cheek distended it, as if she had a toothache. I suspected there were many more bruises and possible broken bones about her person. She was unconscious, mercifully so. I did not envy her when she awoke. It was part and parcel of being an enquiry agent.

An ambulance arrived and Miss Fletcher was loaded into it. There was a commotion for a moment as someone tried to get into the vehicle but was expelled. The court was full of onlookers by that time and I began questioning witnesses about what had happened.

No one knew when or how she had arrived at that spot. Her clothes were wet, but not overly so. She must have been dry when her body was left there in the street.

"When did anyone first see her?" I asked a young man who worked in the telephone exchange.

"One of our linemen came in a bit after seven, saying a woman was lying in the street outside our offices. He didn't know if she was injured or drunk. We went out to help the poor woman. I bet it was her fella."

Just then a hand seized me by the shoulder and I was dragged by the arm across the street and into an office. J. M. Hewitt's office, to be precise. His normally placid features were frantic and angry. His hair was plastered to his head and his clothing drenched. It had been he who had caused the commotion at the ambulance, trying to climb aboard. He shook me by the collar and pushed me against the filing cabinet. I never thought I would have to defend myself against a friend.

"What in hell kind of assignment did you send her to?" he bellowed. I could see that he was at his wits' end.

"It was routine," I said. "She was merely to follow after a young woman to learn where she went. Then she was to stay with Mrs. Ashleigh to protect her. It should have been an easy assignment."

"Well, it wasn't, was it?" he shouted. "You nearly got her killed!"

"Hewitt, you know this work is dangerous. You yourself have the scars to prove it. Miss Fletcher knows it as well. This is the work she chose. I asked her to handle a simple assignment. There was no reason to think she would be injured, but ours is an unpredictable profession. Any assignment she undertakes may become dangerous. If you have private reasons for wishing her to stay out of danger, you must discuss that with her. I asked you to recommend a female operative, not a lady friend."

"She's not a lady friend!" he insisted.

"May I assume that you want her to be?"

"That's beside the point. I'll not recommend people to you anymore. You may have the wealthiest agency in the court, but you're often the most violent."

"We've just had our floor blown out from under us. Obviously our search for the perpetrators has been met by a second attack on their part. I believe she was taken by members of the Hobson gang. Jack Hobson himself was just killed."

I didn't tell him that I was the one who had killed him. There was no need to tell him everything.

"You believe they were Hobson's men, then? Why was she taken?"

"She was mistaken for Mrs. Ashleigh and abducted from her residence. We have to follow this line of enquiry to find out if they are the ones responsible."

"When did this happen?"

"Late last evening."

"Why didn't you go after her?"

"We had no idea until Mrs. Ashleigh appeared at our door after midnight, and by then they were long gone from her residence."

"I'm going after her," he said. "I want to be there when she wakes up. And never ask for a female operative ever again."

"I'm sorry about what happened. I'm going to find who did this or die trying."

"You said it, not I. I wish you luck finding the Hobsons, but don't expect Miss Fletcher to help you any further with this case."

"That's fair enough, J.M. I hope she recovers quickly."

I nodded and walked back to our chambers. In number 7, several pieces of furniture had been reclaimed or replaced, and it was starting to look like an office. The old carpets had been cleaned, looking good as new, and Barker's tall leather chair had been re-upholstered in that shade of green he preferred. The desk would be replaced as soon as it was finished. His old one was beyond repair, and I'm sure Cyrus Barker would not want old memories of how the desk had crushed his limbs.

I picked up the telephone set to call the house, but no one answered. Barker couldn't get to the telephone in his condition, and Mac had left, which left Caleb Barker. Had he left his brother alone in his condition?

It never occurred to me that Barker might be both injured and alone. What if he were attacked? Philippa had returned to her town house to nurse poor Frost, who had been knocked about by Hobson's boys. She told me that morning she would talk Scotland Yard into sending a constable to stand outside her door. No one would dare attack her now. Had I the foresight, I'd have done the same for Barker.

We could rest easy knowing she was safe, but Barker was another matter. He could not walk, or prepare his own food, or defend his home. I suspected he would not ask Caleb for help, and it was doubtful Barker's brother would offer it. Therefore, I was left with one conclusion. Mac would have to come back, and it was my duty to convince him to do so.

"Jeremy, have you seen the agency address book lately?" I asked. "I'm looking for the street where Mac's parents live."

"I have it here, Mr. L. Mr. and Mrs. Ezekiel Maccabee, 29 Watling Street, Cheapside."

I wrote the address on my cuff. Then I tore my resignation letter in half.

"Thank you," I said. "I shall be out hunting for Mac for a while. Could you do something for me while I'm gone? Lock the front door and don't let anyone in you do not fully trust."

"What about Mr. B.'s brother? I guess that would make him the other Mr. B."

"Tell him that I'm out and you don't know when I'll be back."

"Right."

"Lock up," I told him. "Stay safe. Good clerks are hard to find in this day and age. Not to mention good forgers."

Watling Street was a trim residential street, a row of attached houses alike in size and shape but dissimilar in brick front or trim.

Some of the residences were centuries old, but others had been built in this century and were cleverly designed to fit among their elder sisters. Jacob's parents lived in one of these. I looked about, since the rain had finally passed, and had to admit that having a residence in the City was not so bad a thing. I stepped forward and knocked on the door. A maid answered.

"Good morning. I wish to speak to Mr. Jacob Maccabee, please. My name is Thomas Llewelyn."

She disappeared for five minutes or so, long enough for me to begin to suspect I'd been forgotten. The door finally opened and Mac stood there, wearing a brown cardigan over a soft collared shirt. Instead of his highly polished shoes, he wore a pair of slippers.

"Oh, it's you," he said, looking at me over a pair of half-lensed spectacles.

"Mac, you need to come back."

"As you saw," he said, "I was sacked last night."

"It was a rash act and the Guv regrets it. He wants you to come home. You are sorely needed, as you are no doubt aware."

We were still standing in the doorway, and it seemed obvious he had no intention of inviting me in.

"Thank you," he said. "It's nice to be appreciated. However, I have not had a holiday in over five years and I thought I might take one before applying elsewhere."

That was it, then. This was to be a negotiation.

"Certainly you deserve one, Jacob. You overwork yourself every day. I understand how you feel. But, think of the Guv! The man is in pain and lashing out at anything and anyone. He is a bear in a den with a wound he might or might not recover from. He spoke to you without thinking. He was rude, but then you've heard how he treated Rebecca."

"I have, indeed," he answered. He was being at his most priggish, I thought.

"The man's under a good bit of pressure. After all, his offices were dynamited. His bank account was ransacked. Mrs. Ashleigh was nearly kidnapped. His assistant was getting married, which might be the most alarming catastrophe. Now, because of a few poorly chosen words, the last prop has just been removed. No, it was ripped from under him, unprepared."

Mac crossed his arms and leaned against the door frame, twirling his spectacles in his hand. "He should have thought of that before he sacked me."

I listed to the left and tried to peer inside. He listed to the right to stop me. I told myself if I could get him to invite me in, I would have won.

"Yes, but this gives you the moral high ground. If you act the better man, he shall note and appreciate it for years. There is no telling what good shall come of it."

"Thank you for your concern, Thomas. I appreciate it," he said, sounding almost sincere. "But, you know, I've looked at everyone around me. You're getting married, everyone's lives are changing, yet here I am in the same position and the same life I had ten years ago. I'd like to get married myself, perhaps work in a larger house, with servants to work under me. I'm not five and twenty anymore."

Mac was a strategist. I reminded myself never to play chess with him.

"You won't believe what happened this morning. I called home to tell the Guv that Miss Fletcher was found beaten, and do you know what happened? No one answered the call. You were on holiday, apparently. I was trying to find Miss Fletcher. Etienne had gone to his restaurant. Caleb has disappeared again. The Guv was alone. Completely alone. There is no one to bring him a glass of water. He is completely defenseless. A street Arab could beat him in a fair fight. If he choked there is no one to slap his back. No one to see if he's taking his medicine. It is a sad state of affairs."

"That is a great pity," he replied. "He should have thought of that before."

*Think, Thomas, think,* I told myself. Strategy, flattery, irony, empathy, whatever would work. I hung my head, defeated.

"Very well, if I can't change your mind, I'll leave you to your reading. Let's have a cup of coffee sometime, after you've settled in to your new position. I would like to see you again soon."

"Certainly. Thank you."

"Good, then. I've got to get back. That American is mad. He burned a hole in the carpet with one of his blasted cigarettes."

"A hole?" he asked.

"A scorch mark, or perhaps a hole. I'm not certain."

"Which carpet?"

"The runner in the front hall. He must have mashed the lit cigarette into it as he was leaving."

"That was ordered special. It extends from the front to the back door exactly!" he exclaimed.

"Does it? I hadn't noticed."

"Did you tell the Guv?"

"Of course I did. He said this case was too critical to 'waste time on a rug.' Those were his words, not mine."

Mac bit his lip, deep in thought. Then he opened the door wider.

"You'd better come in."

# CHAPTER TWENTY-FIVE

That evening Cyrus Barker was ensconced in his castle, the shutters bolted, the drawbridge raised. He was garrulous because he could not wish away his injury, and there was no magic wand one could wave so he could track the man who bombed his offices. In his mind, I think he could forgive a fellow for coming at him, even in an underhanded way, but one did not interfere with the agency, or his working chambers. Then one incurred his wrath, which was terrible to behold.

We were at dinner. Mac had returned and cooked it for us. It was near seven o'clock, and the sun was setting slowly out our front windows, dawdling among the branches across the street, as if looking for a place to roost. Caleb and I were seated at one corner of the table to vex Mac, who would have set us at either end with six feet of empty space between. The Guv was in bed with a tray of soup and a glass of water. Philippa had forbade him beer while he was recuperating, and he was limited to two bowls of tobacco per day. He had cut up rough about that, but then it was

Philippa, and she always got her way. He argued merely to make his position known.

We were having tournedos of beef in a mustard and wine sauce, with mushrooms and Brussels sprouts. Caleb was being his usual laconic self. He held up a sprout skewered on the end of his fork.

"Beef and sprouts," he said. "I came all the way across the ocean for this?"

"If Etienne was here, you'd better be at least mid-ocean on your journey home, or he would cut your throat."

"How does Cyrus rate his own chef? Two, including ol' Mac here. He'll eat practically anything. I've never known a man so uninterested in food."

Barker intoned from the other room.

"'Put ye on the Lord Jesus Christ, and make not provision for the flesh, to fulfill the lusts thereof.' Romans thirteen, verse fourteen."

"Amen, Brother Cyrus!" Caleb called. "Mac, pour me another pint of this wonderful ale. I think I'll roll myself a cigarette, having no good woman who gives two damns about my health."

Like all brothers, Caleb knew just how to vex the Guv. Having several brothers of my own, I understood perfectly. They will be the first to call you an idiot and the last to pat you on the back, but your successes and failures matter to them very much in the end. *It is a complicated and delicate relationship,* I thought to myself as I watched Caleb deliberately blow smoke in his brother's direction.

"Would you care for some poker after dinner?" he asked me.

"Poker is a card game, is it not?"

"It is. I could teach you how to play. Penny a point."

"The Devil's pastime!" Barker warned from the other room. Caleb raised his eyes to the ceiling, pleading for divine aid.

"Mac," he said. "Would I insult your ale if I decided to go over to the Elephant and Castle public house? Y'all are handsome men, I'm sure, but I'd like a little feminine company."

He stood, but Harm jumped from his place near the table and

ran to the front door, beginning what I consider his alarm call. The dog circled and scratched at the door, making enough sound for an entire kennel, as we stared at him blankly. There was something wrong, but I couldn't tell what it was. Just as I detected an odd odor, Barker let out a bellow.

"The house is on fire!"

We followed Harm into the hall, where I lifted him from in front of the door before we ran outside. In the gloaming, I saw bright yellow flames licking the front of the house, and ivy curling from the heat. The fire was reflected in the panes of the Guv's beautiful Georgian windows. We had very little time before the fire attached itself to the building.

"There he is!" Caleb cried, pointing to a man in the street, visible because of the bottle in his hand, jammed with a burning cloth in the neck of it.

Harm chose that moment to dig his nails into my ribs just enough to squeeze out of my arms. He pushed off from my chest, springing forward like an acrobat, and once he reached the grass he charged at the intruder.

"No, Harm! No!" I called, but it was wasted breath.

As straight as a plumb line he flew, and when he reached our attacker he clamped jaws upon his ankle. He has a trick where he bites and then throws his back limbs around, savaging the flesh. He did this now, rending the man's leg above his low boot. Surprised by an as-yet-unidentified attacker, the stranger cried out and dropped the burning bottle. There was a tinkle of glass, and then dog and man went up in a ball of flame.

"Harm!" Mac and I cried.

A minute before, we had been sitting at the table, bantering, and now our beloved dog could be dead any moment.

Our attacker wailed in pain as the flames engulfed him, and at the last minute Harm separated himself with a screech and circled the lawn with his tail on fire. Not certain whether our duty was to save the man, catch the dog, or stop the fire, the three of us managed to do absolutely nothing.

Harm rolled across the damp grass and smothered his own fire without our aid. Our neighbors in Lion Street ran out of their homes to help, and prevent injury to their own families and property. We could do nothing for the fellow who had come to destroy our home.

"Jacques Perrine," I said, looking at the burnt remains in the middle of the street. I recognized his burly frame and thick beard.

"Of all the ways to die," Caleb muttered. "Burning is the worst. But he meant it for us, so I don't feel particularly sympathetic."

Mac hurried out into the street. "I've called the Southwark Fire Brigade. They're on their way. If we use Etienne's pots we can carry water from the stream to the fire!"

Mac seized me by the shoulders and turned me around. The fire had reached the roof and many of the bushes in front were aflame. Fortunately, the building was made of stout Georgian brick. We ran through the house, each taking a pan, pitcher, or other vessel, plunged them into the stream, ran around to the front, and threw the water on the roof and the burning embers of the bushes.

The firemen arrived on their pumper, and began spraying an unending stream of water onto the roof. Meanwhile, the rest of us drowned every last ember with unending buckets of water. The fire was contained within a quarter of an hour.

After it had been quenched, I sat down on the grass beside Harm. He was alternately licking his paw and sniffing at his tail. He was very proud of that tail, and now he looked more like a rat. At least one pail of water had been thrown on him. He was panting, and possibly in pain, but he was the savior of the hour, and I think he knew it.

"Thomas!" a voice bellowed from within the house. Mac and I turned.

"We forgot the Guv," we both said at once.

A good deal occurred within the next half hour. Having completed their work, and assured themselves by the small plaque by our front door that we were insured by them, the firemen were able to fill their tank again with a hose stretching all the way to our stream. A group of constables arrived, led by an inspector I had never seen before. We answered questions truthfully. It was always easiest to tell the truth.

A blanket had been thrown over the smoldering corpse, which was then rolled into it before being placed in the Black Maria. I didn't know how the constables would get back to the station. However, there were more important and immediate things to do, such as placating my employer, so I left them to work out the conundrum for themselves. I carried my employer's dog, still smoldering and reeking of singed hair, into the house.

The Guv does explode every now and again, over a boneheaded mistake I have made, but once or twice I had seen him in the very worst of situations adopt a patient, Buddha-like calm which I found unnerving. I almost wanted him to scream about his home nearly burning down and his dog catching fire.

"What's happened to you, laddie?" Barker asked, taking the wet and stinking Pekingese onto his lap and patting his head. "Och, they've ruined your pretty tail, haven't they?"

Harm is not above theatrics. He snuggled closer to Barker and shivered, all the while casting glances at me with those goggly eyes of his, as if I were the offending party.

"How is the roof?" the Guv asked.

"The front edge shall need to be reshingled and we'll need a new shutter on one side of the southeast window. The brick will have to be scrubbed."

"Did I hear you say Perrine's name?"

"Jacques Perrine, yes, sir," I answered. "He finally came after you. The man must have hated you. He blew up our offices, he stole money from your account, and then he tried to burn down your house. What raised such ire in one man?"

"I stopped his plan to assassinate all the royalty of Europe. He didn't know I was working with the Sûreté."

"He certainly had reason to hate you, then," I said.

"Aye, but the Cox and Co. business wasn't his method. For one thing, the man could not have been the one to impersonate me. Perrine was a short man."

"Yes," I said, looking out the window behind my employer's head at Caleb talking to a fireman. "But Jack Hobson wasn't."

"You think the two were working together?"

"It is one possible theory. He could have joined forces with him to destroy you."

"I'll agree that it is possible, but I doubt they would work well together. Both are lone wolves, and have a tendency to snap."

"Well, then why did Hobson's gang attack Rebecca's and Philippa's homes, if Perrine is the one who bombed the offices?"

"We can't ask either one," the Guv intoned. "They're both dead."

The Black Maria rolled off with Perrine's body. The firemen took their leave, as well. Scotland Yard questioned us thoroughly about the incident. I was not impressed by the newly minted inspector they sent. At length, the constables finished their investigation, hailed cabs, and took themselves off.

I looked up to see Mac muttering over the sorry state of affairs of his house and garden. The lawn was trampled. The roof had been burned. The brick front was blackened, the hall had been marked by firemen in hobnailed boots. It was more than one highly strung Jewish factotum could stand. Then I noticed Caleb was missing.

"Sir," I said to Barker. "Your brother seems to have slipped off again."

"That does not surprise me."

"He is not a very social fellow, is he?" I asked.

"You have a gift for understatement, Thomas."

"Shall I make a telephone call to have Harm looked after?"

Bok Fu Ying, Barker's ward, generally arrived once a week to groom and bathe the prized Pekingese. She would know best how to care for him in his injured state.

"You do that, lad. Poor wee dog. He's miserable."

I looked at the "wee dog." I'd never seen him so sad-looking, nor so filthy. He was getting soot all over the Guv's bedding.

"He acquitted himself well, sir, I have to admit. He really does have no fear. I think he'd attack a bear if it came lumbering down the street."

I sat on a chair near the bed and retrieved the notebook from my pocket, thinking about what had happened.

"Obviously, it was Perrine," I said to the Guv. "He couldn't get his bombs from Saint Petersburg, so he filled bottles with kerosene to try to burn down the house. But as you said, he doesn't match the description of the man who stole the money from your bank account."

"A paltry five thousand pounds."

"Spoken like a rich man, sir. It's far more than some people shall earn in their entire lives." I pulled my handkerchief from my pocket to rub the soot from my face. "There can't be a connection, but Hobson was an unlikely candidate to go to the bank. It would have been a man like Strathmore who would have known the limit at which the bank would question a withdrawal."

The Guv snorted. "I would expect a man like Strathmore to withdraw the entire deposit, with aid from his financial associates. Also, he'd have to find a man meeting my general description. Wait."

"What, sir?"

"Did you investigate all my other accounts?"

"I did."

My employer looked relieved.

"Sir, it might be in your best interests to visit your banking institutions once in a while, and make yourself visible to the clerks. I don't think the man who stole your money needed to resemble you very closely."

Barker put down Harm, and then tried unsuccessfully to brush away the mud and dampness from his linens.

"You're thinking of my brother," he said.

"All the man would require was a pair of dark spectacles."

Barker leaned back into his pillows and frowned. "I don't disagree. But what would be his motive?"

"Who can say?" I answered, closing the notebook. "A badge does not prove that your brother is a Pinkerton agent. We have no idea what he has done all these years, whom his associates were, or whether or not he had been in trouble with the law. It could all be bluff. I'm sure lying comes easily to him."

"It always has," the Guv answered. "The man's a rascal, no mistake. But he's my brother. What can one do?"

"He seems to feel the same about you, which I suppose is a good sign. At least I certainly hope it is."

"Perhaps, but one cannot rely upon it. He's reserved. He will not reveal his plans to anyone whom he does not trust, and he trusts very few."

"Not unlike you, sir," I said.

He grunted. It was all the response I would receive.

"Is he merely secretive," I went on, "or does he have something to be secretive about?"

"Who can say?"

Barker crossed his arms and continued. "Don't try to best him as far as thinking is concerned. I suspect he is very canny. However, don't let him hamper you as you go about your business. The important thing is finding who is coming after us."

"Do you suppose that Camille Archer is the killer? We have gentle opinions of women, but really, they are no less capable of killing than a man."

"That is true, Thomas."

He reached for his heavily carved meerschaum pipe, and opened the sealskin pouch full of tobacco. Then he recalled that Philippa had restricted its use.

"Blast," he muttered to himself, tossing both onto the table by his bed, a fine way to treat a work of art.

I didn't imagine that the next two or three weeks would be easy in this household, between him and Mac.

"Sir, if I may say it, you are not being very helpful in winnowing suspects."

"Mr. Llewelyn," he said, switching to the more formal and somewhat colder address, "do you require help?"

It would have been easier to admit it and ask, but I understood if I did I would not have assured him that I knew what I was about. Let us face it, I had been in his employ for six years, and should have been able to solve such matters on my own.

I was not going to fail in front of Cyrus Barker and make a fool of myself. The man had put a roof over my head, and it would all be for naught if I could not bring one criminal to justice. I could not hold my head up in front of Mac or Jenkins, or any of our watchers who provided us with information. Miss Fletcher's words about the circumstances of my employment cut sharply. Worse, if I failed, what did that say to Rebecca's relatives about me, or for that matter, to Rebecca herself?

"No, sir," I told my employer. "I do not require help at all."

# CHAPTER TWENTY-SIX

From time to time I wake in the morning with the feeling that something will happen that day, but it takes a minute or two for the mind to work out exactly what. My brain sifted through the case for a good minute or two before it bubbled to the surface like a bloated corpse: today was to be the hanging of Joseph Keller.

As I recalled, the hanging was to occur late that afternoon at Newgate Prison. My first order of business was to telegraph the prison in Barker's name to inform them he was sending a person to represent him. I was willing to set out on my journey with no acknowledgment or response to my telegraph, thus putting the burden upon their shoulders.

At our chambers, Caleb Barker was buzzing about like a blue-bottle trapped in the room, bouncing off windows with little to do. He was free to disappear at a moment's notice, stay out all day, and return without an explanation, but heaven help us if we should inconvenience him. I began to pity the late Mrs. Barker for having not one but two exasperating sons. They became two men absolutely certain that they are correct, with little or no proof, or need for it. Somehow, I was the one to fill the slack between them, despite the fact that each had gotten along without the other for twenty years. Agree or disagree, but do not expect me to play counselor or alienist.

"Would you care to attend a hanging?" I asked Caleb.

He squinted his steely gray eyes. "I've seen plenty of them. They don't bother me, but they aren't my favorite form of entertainment. What poor soul will breathe his last day today?"

"Joseph Keller. He's one of the fellows whom your brother caught and turned over to CID. He vowed vengeance on the Guv. He killed his family and he has shown remorse, but he's still dangerous, although I'm not convinced he was involved in the bombing. He asked me to attend."

"It isn't a public hanging, is it?"

"No, they've done away with that years ago. No speeches on the wages of sin, no broadsheets, no one selling tea and pasties."

"Seen one in Fort Smith once. They hanged four men on one platform. People brought their children like it was a fair. Hotels were full, saloons full, and the hangman practiced with feed bags the day before. It was ghoulish, but I reckon towns have the right to engage in commerce as best they can."

"Are you coming? My request for attendance was for your brother and myself. You are a Barker."

"Do you think he is involved? Did he hire someone to kill Cyrus? How does he have any connection to that madwoman? I just don't see it."

"Nor do I, but I can't leave this stone unturned, being the man's last breath. He might confess. Asking him tomorrow won't do us much good."

"True."

Once we arrived at Newgate, we entered through the large wooden gates at the front and explained to the guard our identity and purpose for being there. Caleb gave his real name, but accepted the name Cyrus on his clipboard as a clerical error. Inside, the rough stone blocks and flagstones were worn smooth and shiny underfoot by a million treads. It was impossible to come inside and not feel as if one were a prisoner. The sense of oppression was palpable.

"I'd rather be hanged than to be here for any length of time," Caleb muttered, and I nodded in agreement. "What did this fellow do again to get himself hanged?"

"He killed his wife and children with an axe."

"That would do it."

"Keller was being cuckolded by his wife. He discovered too late the children were not his own. He butchered them and then simply disappeared. Barker finally tracked him to a garret in Poplar and I worked alongside him to get evidence against him."

"So, why did he ask you to attend?"

"Because his whole family was dead. He wanted someone to stand there."

We approached a knot of guards and officials in a hallway and introduced ourselves. We milled about for a while, waiting to be ushered inside the chamber.

"How long has this Keller fellow been waiting to have his neck stretched?"

"Three weeks since the judge found him guilty."

"And they're hanging him already? What about the appeal? Even Hanging Judge Parker didn't hang them that fast."

"The solicitor has three weeks to find suitable evidence to justify an appeal. It's considered cruel to keep a man month after month, knowing he is to be executed."

"Very civilized, I'm sure, but if I ever get in such a situation I hope the government will give me plenty of time. I'll need to write my memoirs."

"How long would that take?"

"No more than four or five years. You cannot rush the muse."

The door opened and we were ushered into a small room and

lined up along the wall like an identity parade. The room was spartan, and there was a raised dais with a long noose. Below it, I noticed the trap door and a handle near the wall, much like the brake handle on a steam engine.

"What's with the noose?" Caleb said. "It looks strange. There's no knot."

"That's a Marwood ring," I explained. "He was an executioner a few decades ago. He'd had too many prisoners asphyxiate and kick, thanks to a short rope. He came up with a longer one and that metal ring that the rope is threaded though."

"Let me guess. More humane."

"Well, I don't know about that, but it breaks their neck every time."

"Efficient. I notice the chamber is in the middle of the prison. No chance his pals can break in with some pistols, and rescue him."

I tried to imagine such a thing happening in England. It was possible in the days of Dick Turpin, I supposed, but not now.

"None."

"Aww, you don't even give the poor man a chance."

I shrugged my shoulders. I wasn't responsible for the form of punishment Her Majesty's government meted out.

"I suppose . . ."

There was a clang overhead, like the ringing of bells in a tower. A door immediately opened in the wall behind the dais, presenting the tableau of two guards doing their very best to clap darbies and leg irons on a struggling prisoner. That is, on Joseph Keller.

He was spitting and snarling, his face red from the exertion. The bell continued to toll overhead as he was shuffled forward in his chains, protesting all the while. Beside me a man began to quote scripture, but I was too mesmerized by the struggling man in front of me to listen to what verses he quoted. Barker would know if he were here. The other one, at least.

Five bells. They dragged him to the position over the trap. A third guard fitted a small black cloth bag over his head, barely coming to his chin. The man's screams and curses were muffled.

Six bells. The same guard, whom I assumed was the executioner, settled the rope around Keller's neck, and adjusted the ring up behind his left ear.

Seven bells. The guards holding him let go and jumped back. The executioner crossed quickly, and without preamble pulled on the lever.

Eight bells. Keller's body fell through the trap. There was a sound like laundry being snapped in the breeze, and then a second one, like a bass cello being plucked, as the rope went taut. Slowly, the rope swung to and fro.

"Jesus!" Caleb nearly bellowed, drawing all eyes to him.

He pushed his way to the door and beat on it until a guard outside unlocked it. I followed him out into the hall.

Caleb leaned against a window, hands on either side of the glass, breathing like a thoroughbred.

"Humane, my arse!" he growled.

"The Marwood method," I explained. "Eight seconds from when the prisoner discovers he's about to be hanged until his final breath."

"No chance to say anything? No confession? No last words for his ma or his sweetheart?"

"Eight seconds."

"You can keep your so-called British justice system and your goddamned Marwood ring! Even the worst vigilante hanging I ever saw took place on the back of a horse. The man had a chance to get out some final words!"

"I wished he had," I admitted. "Perhaps he would have said something to incriminate himself in the bombing. I had to come in the off chance he said something."

"When? What can you say in just eight seconds? Get me out of here, Mr. Llewelyn. I need whiskey, and lots of it!"

As little ceremony as there had been on entry, there was none upon leaving. The hanging was over and nearly forgotten. As we

230 • WILL THOMAS

left, a clerk ticked our name on a list. Within five minutes Caleb was pouring whiskey from a bottle into a tumbler in the same public house we'd visited that Sunday.

"You might have warned me."

"You said you'd seen hangings before."

He poured the entire contents of the glass down his throat and poured another. "How many of these things have you witnessed?"

"This was my first," I admitted.

"You are one cold-hearted old son."

I poured myself a temperate glass of the spirits. "I knew what to expect. Besides, I have no time for sentiment."

He drank down a second glass, his Adam's apple bobbing. "So, this got us nothing. No clue whether Keller was out to get my brother or not."

"That's right," I said. "Not every lead will take us to the killer. Your brother always says to have patience."

"S'cuse me if I'm not so civilized as I once was. I've seen men with their scalps cut and ripped off, and I've seen Indian women and children slaughtered by federal soldiers on horseback. However, I've never seen a man get his neck snapped like a chicken in the hands of a farmer's wife."

I sipped the whiskey and set it down again. Despite the reputation of detectives in the penny press, I do not care for strong spirits, although a pint of stout or porter with a meal is perfectly acceptable, in my opinion. If one has tasted the water in our fair city one will understand. There is a reason we overboil water for tea or coffee.

Caleb poured my glass full, despite my protest.

"I'm not drinking alone," he said.

I thought of my Methodist mother, the look on her face if she saw me drinking Jameson whiskey a few steps from a prison. Then I thought of Rebecca. I was certainly doing my best to impress her these days. I unbent and swallowed a little. Meanwhile, Caleb poured the last of the bottle into his tumbler. Promptly, the publican brought a second. Barker's brother waved it away.

"I need to keep a clear head."

"Clear head?" I demanded. "You just drank an entire bottle of whiskey!"

"Thomas, you're what we in the Territories call a tenderfoot."

Outside, Caleb crawled into a hansom as if he'd had nothing stronger to drink than ginger beer. Meanwhile, the one and a half tumblers I drank bounced about in my head as we rode. Eventually we drifted into Whitehall and stopped in Craig's Court.

"Are you coming up?" I asked.

"No, I think I'll wander about awhile. I could use some air after that experience."

I nodded and trudged up the stair.

"Good afternoon, Jeremy," I said as I went into number 5.

"Afternoon, Mr. L. Celebrating early, are we?"

How did he know? I thought I was acting in my usual manner, or at least I was doing my best. Could he smell the alcohol on my breath from across the room? I wasn't even close to him. I suspected that Jenkins and alcohol had some kind of mystical union only they understood.

"We've just attended a hanging," I said. "Caleb and I were in need of a drink."

"No doubt," Jenkins agreed. I supposed in his mind he was always in need of a drink.

"Did any visitors come in our absence?"

"No, sir, not a one."

"What about messages?"

"One from the priory. Miss Fletcher wishes to speak with you at your convenience."

"Do you have any idea what about?"

"How should I know, sir? I only work here."

"I'll visit her later," I said. "I've just come from a hanging. I need some time to think."

# CHAPTER TWENTY-SEVEN

I had promised Scotland Yard under some unnamed penalty that I would communicate with them on the case with pertinent information, though not necessarily my opinions. I had received no such promise from them in return. With so many inspectors and chief inspectors running hither and yon, it is a wonder that even they can communicate information between themselves.

I had once worked temporarily for the Metropolitan Detective Police Force. Therefore, I understood how they work. Each inspector is buried beneath a mountain of cases, some recent and some not. The latter must be investigated in perpetuity, even if, as Dickens said, the case was dead as a doornail. Therefore, they are constantly harried, working sixteen-hour days, though paid for ten, and develop ulcers from food served in low public houses eaten at irregular hours. I genuinely feel for them, and I thoroughly understand why they are prone to declare the most obvious suspect as the killer. That being said, sometimes the Yard will surprise you. There is a reason why the Metropolitan is considered the best police force in the world.

I couldn't shake the feeling that the case was stalling. The files were spread across my desk, and on a table nearby was a tall stack of papers that had separated themselves from other files, or which had lost their folders, so that no one knew where one began and another ended.

Jenkins had retrieved for each of us a particularly potent and nearly undrinkable cup of coffee from the Silver Cross at the corner of the court, while I stared at a map of London in between the daunting, teetering tower of papers.

"This is hideous," I told him, putting down the cup.

"It is, but it will keep you awake."

I took about an inch worth of papers and took them over to his desk.

"Jeremy, I want you to go through these papers and make whatever order you can of them. If you find a connection to this case, put them in a new folder. If not, start a second pile."

Jenkins raised an eyebrow. He rarely received such a specific and complicated task. He was no Percival and required no quests, thank you.

"All right, Mr. L.," he said with a world-weary air. Like me, like all of us on this revolving sphere, he wanted to be left in peace. I was out much of the time, however, and I wasn't going to make life too easy for him. He was already leaving early most days, as it was.

"Have you ordered a new filing cabinet?" I asked.

"I have. It's due tomorrow, I think."

"Is it a copy of the original?"

"It's coming from the same factory."

I looked at him. At times he can be highly organized. When he's sober, at least.

"How do you know it is the same manufacturer?" I asked.

"I keep an inventory of the furnishings, of course."

*Hidden depths,* I thought. *We all have them.* I patted him on the shoulder.

"Good work, old man."

He brightened a little and we set to work. If I leafed through an inch of papers per day, I would be through by the new century. Some of them made no sense whatsoever. Others were like an adventure tale without an ending. Still others I read were as dull as a chancery suit. There were photographs with no notation of who was pictured, sketches, and Bertillon forms, with the criminal carefully measured.

Then the telephone set jangled, an unwelcome interruption. Even Jenkins looked at the candlestick base with a baleful glance. I reached out and lifted the receiver.

"Ahoy?"

"I have an incoming call for you, sir," the operator said, as he put me through.

"Llewelyn?" a male voice said. "This is McNaughton. You said you would share information, did you not?"

"I did."

"Can you come over in, say, ten minutes? There is something here you will find very interesting. I'm sure you have something in return for me, as well. I heard you have been busy."

"I have, at that. Ten minutes, then."

"Nine, now."

I set the receiver back in its cradle. There is something satisfying about hanging up on a chief constable.

"They want me over at 'A' Division."

"Permanently or temporarily?" Jenkins asked.

"Don't you start."

I walked over to Scotland Yard and found McNaughton lounging in the hall on the ground floor, waiting for me. We went into his office and without much fanfare, I told him what had happened since last we spoke.

"This Mrs. Archer. Is she a looker?" he asked.

"In an East End sort of way."

"Someone's left-handed wife?" he asked.

"Possibly."

"Is Barker's brother staying out of trouble?"

There was a photograph on his desk in a standing frame, a woman looking stiff and formal. It was a professional portrait of McNaughton's wife. Suddenly I wanted one of Rebecca for my own desk, but I knew it would never happen.

"I assume he's off doing Pinkerton work," I continued. "He won't tell us what he is up to."

"That's not a bad way to work. Has he been assisting you with the case?"

"On and off," I said.

"Do you trust him?"

"Do I have the word 'idiot' stamped on my forehead?"

He put up his hands in apology. "No offense intended. Anything else?"

We spoke for a few more minutes. I told him as much as I thought the Guv would allow me to reveal. Yes, we wanted to help the Yard, but we still wanted to win the race ourselves.

"So," I finally said. "You have some information that might be of interest to me?"

"I do, indeed," he answered, rising from his chair. "Follow me."

We went down the hall, then took a set of stairs to the basement. There were offices below, just like the ones above. I realized where he was taking me. A sign directed us to the end of the hall that read "Body Room." It was the new Scotland Yard's postmortem office. I began to wonder who might be in there.

"You don't go all weak-kneed, do you?" he asked.

"No, I don't."

He led me inside. A body was on a hand litter in the back, covered in a sheet. Another corpse on the main table was only partially covered.

"Strathmore!" I cried.

The financier's body was already turning an unhealthy purple along his neck and shoulders. His skin looked sallow. The tip of his tongue protruded from his lips, equally dark. There were rough marks around his neck.

"Strangled?" I asked.

"No. Hanged."

"He topped himself?"

"We thought so, but there is a problem. Presumably he stepped off the bed. But the rope is too short for his feet to reach it."

"Could he have stepped off the bars of the cell?"

McNaughton shook his head. "Too far."

"Did he share a cell?"

"No."

I thought for a moment. "So someone, presumably, came in and hanged him."

"Two people, I'd say."

I thought some more. The brain is a marvelous thing when one exercises it now and again. "Was he widely disliked?"

"Not especially."

"Would they have access to a key?"

"The guards would."

Of course, I realized. The guards would have a key. He was pushing me toward a conclusion.

"It was a prison for small crimes, as I recall," I said. "Or those like Strathmore, who dealt with the wealthy. Such men would not be acquainted with how to pick a lock or hang a fellow. Bribing a guard is another matter. Strathmore himself probably bribed people on a daily basis, I'm certain. Have the guards been questioned thoroughly?"

McNaughton snorted. "Of course they have. They're being questioned right now."

"Guards are not well paid, are they?"

"Not even as well as a constable, which is to say almost nothing."

"They work in a facility with men who possibly have a cache of bonds or notes hidden away somewhere."

"Or several somewheres," he said.

"Ipso facto, it was a guard. Tell me, honestly, how thoroughly can a guard be questioned?"

"Generally speaking, as thoroughly as it takes. Confessions in such cases are very high. It is not worth their while to remain silent."

I bent over the table and regarded Strathmore again. He looked older than he had when he was alive. His eyebrows were shaggy, and he had needed to shave when he was burst in upon and murdered.

"You say it would take two guards?"

"Yes, I'd think so, at least."

"So each might fear the others would confess, and hope that by doing so first, he'd receive a lighter sentence."

"That's how I read it."

I leaned against a chest of instruments, thinking. I liked McNaughton. I had encountered him a year ago, although so far Barker had not met him. I was developing a few associates of my own. Watchers. Soon I would have my own network of people upon which I could rely.

McNaughton cleared his throat.

"I'm sorry. You're busy. Did you call me to inform me or to ask for an alibi?"

"Both, I suppose."

"If it was last night, I was at Barker's residence. We had a fire, and the Southwark Fire Brigade will vouch for my presence."

I looked down on the mortal remains of Edward Strathmore. Because of the lividity, his pallor was almost ghostlike. I had been speaking to this man, face-to-face, but a few days ago.

"Do you recall the first body you saw as a constable?" I asked.

"Of course," McNaughton said, crossing his arms and leaning against the wall.

"Did you get weak-kneed? I know I did my first time."

"Passed right out. Took a ribbing from my superiors for a month. Why? Do you need a chair?"

"No," I said. "Perhaps that's the problem. This fellow, for whatever reason, is dead. He was murdered. This is perhaps the third corpse I've had to look at this month. You've probably seen more. I don't want this to become routine. I don't want to give up my outrage over a person's murder."

He shook his head and tried to sweep a smile under his mustache.

"What now?" I asked.

"Most of us want to just go home to the missus at the end of the day. Bounce little Jenny on our knee. Have a warm pint at the corner pub. We're not tortured souls like you."

"I was told last week, in confidence I suppose, that when I was first hired, most of the people who worked with Mr. Barker thought he'd made a tragic mistake. Even I wasn't sure I could do the work."

"And you're still here six years later. Where are the naysayers? They gave up harping on you and went on to another subject, haven't they?"

"I suppose."

"Look, if you're wanting for absolution, find a priest. If you had wanted to fit in, you'd have cut your hair, grown a mustache, and stopped buying ties from Saville Row."

"I like Saville Row ties," I said.

"Mr. Llewelyn, you are one of a kind. Now will you kindly vacate our body room, and let me get on to my next case?"

I was in the hall trying to gather my aplomb when McNaughton called me back.

"Oy!"

I turned around and looked at him. I'm not one of his constables to be ordered about.

"What is it?" I asked.

"Don't get shirty. There's something else I wanted you to see."

He lifted the sheet from the face of the other body. It was a male, perhaps forty, more decomposed than the newly murdered Mr. Strathmore. He was a solid-looking man, over six foot. He had a fussy little mustache, waxed to points, which was very un-English.

"Do you know him?"

"No, I don't recognize him. What's his name?"

"Anatole Mercier, a French national. We are applying to the Sûreté for information about him."

"How did he get here?" I asked.

"He was stabbed in the back in an alleyway a few days ago."

"There was a Mercier connected with Jacques Perrine's case," I told him. "His son-in-law, the record said."

"You don't know how he came to be dead in an alley, do you?"

"Sorry, Chief Constable," I said. "I can't help you."

"Perhaps you can. Look again. He's about the same height and build as your employer. I wondered if he could impersonate him well enough in a bank."

"Perhaps," I said, still unconvinced.

"Llewelyn," McNaughton said. "I am off duty after a thirty-six-hour shift. Come have a pint with me."

I sighed and consulted my pocket watch. "It's barely noon."

"It is midnight as far as I am concerned."

"Very well. Where shall we go?"

"My favorite is near the Houses of Parliament. The Red Lion."

We made our way down Whitehall Street and eventually came upon the pub. There was a long queue at the bar, but we managed to find a table and sat.

"How is the investigation going?" he asked, wiping the foam from his mustache with a finger after our stouts had arrived. I'd always wanted to do that. I thought of growing one, but knew Rebecca would object. Then I remembered, she wasn't mine anymore, and it hurt all over again.

"Tolerably," I said. "There is a lot of information to digest, but I feel like I'm getting close. I don't know why, I just feel it."

"Good. I've got some welcome news for you. A present from the Met, so to speak."

"I've always liked good news," I told him. "What is it?"

"We arrested the Hobson clan last night. Every last one of them."

"Really? On what charge?"

"Being a public nuisance. Actually, being an accessory to murder."

"What? Of their own brother?"

"He didn't jump into Limehouse Reach of his own accord. By the way, you wouldn't know anything about that, would you?"

"Me?" I asked, feeling uncomfortable. This may seem strange coming from an enquiry agent, but I didn't like to lie. "No, not at all."

"We found your man Briggs in Aldgate, guarding a house. Brought him in for questioning. He didn't carry a pistol, just that metal-tipped truncheon of his, and no one has heard of him ever carrying a firearm. But you do."

"I do, but I wouldn't carry one in front of my fiancée."

There it went. One lie leads to two, as Barker often said. I qualified it by thinking she was no longer my fiancée.

"Perhaps not," he said.

"Anyway, why would I need a revolver with Bully Boy Briggs around? He'd make short work of them."

"Perhaps," he repeated, still unconvinced.

"What about the elusive Mrs. Archer?"

"We almost had her yesterday near the train station, but she disappeared, her and another man with her."

I stared at him, my pint ignored. I rarely ignore a pint.

"I thought she was with Mercier."

"No, that was Anatole, who was murdered. This is Alphonse."

"That's right, there were two of them in the tunnel! Two bombers who smoked French cigarettes."

He smiled, and set his own pint down on the ringed table.

"You've been a busy little fellow, Thomas Llewelyn. According to one witness, you were seen, you and that American, not two streets away from where the Frenchman was stabbed."

"Have you been following me?"

McNaughton sipped his ale. The foam had dissipated. "We were following Caleb Barker. As you recall, the American government is very interested in his whereabouts. He's a very interesting chap. He led a few plainclothesmen on a merry chase. And of course, we'll follow anything named Barker. Something is bound to happen."

"I confess I've been going about London asking questions. In fact, I'm paid for it. You may clap the darbies on me, Chief Constable."

"Sarcastic little fellow, aren't you? I have half a mind—" He stopped, waiting for me to step in and make some remark. For once I remained silent. Wisdom comes with experience. "I could bring you in on a number of minor charges. However, since we are both working on the same case, I thought we would give it to you. After all, it was your offices they bombed, not ours, thank god. Good luck to you."

"Thank you," I said.

He lifted his pint and clinked it against mine on the table.

"You're welcome."

"I've got work to do," I said, rising.

"Stay out of trouble."

"I'll try."

"Try harder."

I walked back and entered our office, still thinking about lying. How can one love a profession that causes one to go against one's own principles?

Jenkins eyed me critically when I returned even more dazed than when I left. He placed a salver beside me with an envelope on it almost as soon as I sat in my chair. I glanced at it, thinking that I wasn't Barker, and did not deserve the salver. I am a humble workingman. However, I lifted it and cut it open with the Italian dagger the Guv kept on his desk, which survived the bombing. I pulled out the telegram. It read:

> Dr Nevil Lewis
> Burberry Institution for the Criminally Insane
> Matley Bog
> Hampshire
> Wish to inform you that Dr Pritchard found hanged in his cell this morning STOP Local police are investigating the matter STOP N Lewis
> END

I scratched my head. It's hard to run an enquiry when your suspects are dying one by one.

# CHAPTER TWENTY-EIGHT

I bought flowers in Covent Garden. They were not for Rebecca. After the dozen or so bouquets I had sent her it ceased to become a novelty, and she told me to save my money. This bouquet was for Sarah Fletcher, the woman who had nearly lost her life doing what I had asked of her. It was a wonder that I did not have to buy lilies.

She was still in a private room in the Priory of St. John, having been taken there at Barker's request. Once inside, I sat in a chair near her room and waited for a nurse to come by. When one finally did, I asked if Miss Fletcher was able to receive a visitor. A few minutes later I was invited in.

Both of her eyes were black and the bridge of her nose was swollen. One arm was wrapped in gauze, and the other in a sling. Her hair was combed back severely and looked damp. There was a bottle of laudanum in the nurse's hand. I suspected they did not keep it within reach of the patient.

"Good morning," I said, giving the flowers to the nurse, who left to get a vase. "I'm so sorry you were hurt."

"Don't," she answered, waspish to the last. "If you in any way claim that I should not have been where I was, or have done what I did, I shall ask you to leave."

"I'm sorry that I have not had the opportunity to visit earlier. There have been several developments with the case."

She closed her eyes and sunk into her pillow. I began to wonder if the laudanum was taking effect. "Tell me all of it. Tell me everything. This place is deadly dull. I cannot hold a book. I am trapped in my own thoughts."

"Very well," I answered, settling back in the hard chair, exactly like the one Mrs. Ashleigh had endured for many days. "I would like to consult you, as a colleague. I should like your opinion. I have formed my own, but it is subject to change. Mr. Barker has given me his, but that does not mean that I would find yours less valid."

"I appreciate that," she murmured.

I cleared my throat and began to inform her of some of the facts of the case. It took nearly a quarter hour. My natural inclination would have been to make my efforts sound heroic and my deductions sage, but she would have seen through that. When I finished, there was silence in the room for nearly half a minute.

"You've had a narrow scrape," she finally said.

"The beating in the alley?"

"No, with your fiancée when Camille Archer went to her home. For the briefest of minutes she was in real danger. It was a mercy this was Mrs. Archer's first salvo, or there would be no wedding at all. As for the second event in her home, if she cannot forgive you, she doesn't deserve you, not that you are a prize. She knew she was about to become an enquiry agent's wife. She now knows what it is you do as a profession; the worst of it anyway."

Miss Fletcher was a kind of loofah sponge, rubbing the epidermal layers until one was raw, but the better for the rubbing.

"You would have shielded her from that. Confess."

"Yes, I would have," I admitted.

"Don't. She needs to know. She has a right to know. Mrs. Cowan has a decision to make."

I considered the matter, and could find no fault with what she said, at least to a point.

"And furthermore, Mr. Barker was right to warn you about his brother," she continued. "Do not trust him. There's something going on there that bears investigation. He has no valid reason for following you about. You are not that entertaining."

I laughed, and a slight smile came to her thin lips.

"Granted," I said. "Continue."

"This entire business could be at his instigation."

"Perhaps, but to what end?"

"We don't know. It's possible we may never know. I'm sure he would never tell you. I approve of Mr. Pinkerton's methods. He has great respect for female operatives, and has made fine use of them. However, he must work with what he has, and some of his agents are or were cattle thieves and train robbers."

"They are desperate men, but Pinkerton cannot afford to be particular."

"Precisely."

"And what of Mrs. Archer?" I asked.

She shifted on her pillow, still in pain.

"Either she is well organized or someone is giving her orders. She changes hotels every morning, always with one of the men along as a bodyguard: a tall fellow with an absurd mustache."

"Mercier. Yes. There are, or were, two of them. Anatole is dead, not Alphonse. That's one fewer person helping her. One of them posed as Barker to withdraw from an account."

"She's young," Miss Fletcher said. "That isn't to say she is incapable of plotting all these machinations."

"But more likely she's following after a man, someone like Caleb Barker."

"Yes."

"Tell me of your work," I said. "What happened when you followed Mrs. Archer?"

"I observed her for a few days. Do you know what she was doing?"

"No," I said. "What?"

"She was buying a trousseau!"

"What are you talking about?"

"She was preparing for a wedding."

"I know what a trousseau is, Miss Fletcher. The question is why would she prepare for a wedding?"

"You are the enquiry agent, Mr. Llewelyn, not I."

"There isn't a possibility that she believes she is going to marry me, is there?" I asked, incredulous.

"She did sign the register 'Camille Llewelyn.' Who knows what's happening in that mind of hers. I don't know if you noticed it but there is something in her eyes. Dangerous. Possibly even mad. But I digress. She was buying clothes."

"And she didn't notice you?"

"No," she went on, "and that was the problem, you see. Men don't notice other men, but women notice everything. I suspected she knew she was being followed. I left and went to Mrs. Ashleigh's house, where, as you know, there was an altercation and I sent Mrs. Ashleigh out the back to go to Mr. Barker's. I don't know if the attack I suffered was a result of following Camille Archer or not."

"What do you remember about the attack, if you are able to talk about it?"

"I was pulled into an alley and set upon."

"How many men?"

"Two."

I leaned forward in my chair. "What did they look like?"

"East Enders, rough-looking men. Donkey-fringe haircuts."

"Part of the Hobson gang, sure enough."

"And then?"

"I woke up several hours later in the rain, unable to move."

She closed her eyes again.

The nurse came in with the flowers in a vase and gave me a look, like a constable does when he tells one to move along. She set the vase on a table beside a more lavish arrangement.

"That's from John," she said.

"John?"

"Hewitt."

"Oh, J.M."

"He's angry with you, for letting me be injured. He has proposed, you know."

"Has he?" I asked.

"There are entirely too many weddings afoot. I have no intention of marrying him, but he doesn't seem to notice. He's out there somewhere trying to solve your case for you in order to 'get the blighters that did this.' Mr. Llewelyn, do you think I could have a drink of that water, please?"

I poured water from a glass pitcher into a tumbler, and raised it to her lips carefully. She sat back again and I returned to my chair.

"He wants me to give up my detective work, as if it were a hobby, like collecting paperweights. He does not believe a woman should be in this profession."

"He means well," I said. "He just doesn't understand you."

"Mr. Llewelyn, there may be hope for you yet."

"So what else have you gleaned about Mrs. Archer? What impressions and facts have you collected?"

Miss Fletcher sat up in bed, warming quickly to her subject. "She is a very interesting study. First of all, as you must know, her name is not Archer. I am certain that is an alias."

"What of her character?"

"She is erratic, self-indulgent, and manic. Quite the flibbertigibbet, and very spoiled. I would say she is on a spree with someone else's money."

"I believe I know whose money," I remarked. "Continue."

"She flits from hotel to hotel. It took a few days to find her trail, but I have been able to follow her because she sends her growing luggage to each new hotel."

"Ah."

"She gorges on sweets. I've rarely seen her have an actual meal. She buys herself trinkets and visits old curio shops. She went to a merchant who deals in medical supplies once. I saw her speaking at length to a corset maker. She is quite a spendthrift."

"Thank you for following her and getting this information. It may prove to be useful."

"Mr. Llewelyn, there is more. She was in a tearoom stuffing herself with cakes. I was near a window watching her. A waitress dropped a spoon and she practically screamed at her. Everyone in the room reacted to the loss of decorum. She had the poor girl in tears. And then she returned to her tea cakes as if nothing had happened."

"Do you get the impression that she herself is capable of violence? Was the waitress in any danger, for example? Apart from her being very spoiled, that is?"

"Oh, decidedly. She acts as if she were sweet, but there is something alarming about her, and if she isn't dangerous, her companion is."

"Tell me about him. I assume we're talking about Mr. Mercier."

"Yes. I've tried to decide whether he is her bodyguard or her handler. He watches everyone around her. He's kept me at my best this week. He's not a brute. In fact, he's elegant, but I think he would kill without a moment's hesitation or concern. He carries a black walking stick that is heavy. I heard it fall and clang once."

"Yes, I am familiar with it. Excuse me, Miss Fletcher. May I bring you more water or get you anything?"

"No, sir," she answered, pulling the blanket up to her chin. "But could you do a favor for me?"

"Anything."

"Could you address me as Fletcher? Think of me as just another detective. I do not wish to be treated differently than anyone else merely because I am a woman."

"I'll try. Fletcher. I'm sorry, I interrupted you. Continue your narrative. It's very interesting."

"That's all I have to say about Mr. Mercier, or should I call him Monsieur?"

"What is his Christian name? Anatole?" I asked.

"Alphonse. I heard her call him that. Why?"

"Because his brother, Anatole, is lying in the morgue at Scotland Yard. He was killed in an alleyway by Newgate Prison. I saw the corpse in the body room myself."

"Are you joking?" she asked, sitting up straighter. "No, you're not, are you? Were they twins?"

"I'm not sure, but I suspect they resembled each other enough to fool people. One was able to move about as he pleased, as long as the other one stayed behind to maintain an alibi."

"Very clever," she said.

If I was going to treat her as a colleague, I would begin by not standing around. I dropped into a chair beside her bed.

"Tell me about Mrs. Ashleigh."

"We created a schedule between us," she began. "I arrived at dinner and she fed me. It was a wonderful meal. I stayed dressed and armed all night."

"Fletcher, I didn't expect you to work round the clock."

"I'm a light sleeper, but I returned early to the front room. They came on the third night."

"What happened, precisely?"

"I was in the front of the house and Mrs. Ashleigh was in the back, talking to the cook about the next day's meal. When the ruffians burst through the front door, I hid my pistol and confronted them to give Frost enough time to help her out the back entrance. I told them I was Philippa Ashleigh and they believed me. Obviously, they were sent by someone, possibly Mrs. Archer herself."

"Tell me what happened next."

"There isn't much to tell. I didn't like the look of the fellows, so I started a fight."

"You started a fight?"

She tried to grin, but her lip was split and swollen. "It was preferable to what I suspect they had in mind."

I had to smile. "There's a question Barker always asks me. 'Gave as well as got?'"

"Oh, rather!"

"Good, then."

Her smile faded.

"Listen," she said. "I'm sorry for what I said to you the day I was hired. It was rude. I suppose I was jealous. The nice office, the mansion, the training under a first-class detective. I live in a flat with three other women."

"The fault was mine," I told her. "This case was more difficult than I'd anticipated and I suppose I've been a bit ill-tempered."

"I don't think Mr. Barker made the wrong decision."

We paused and looked at each other.

"Thank you," I said. "Thank you very much."

I returned to the office and sat in the chair, or tried to. Jenkins delivered another letter on the salver. This was growing tiresome. I took the envelope and cut it open. The message was written in a feminine hand. It said, "Go."

# CHAPTER TWENTY-NINE

I offered the cabman double the fare if he would take me to Camomile Street as swiftly as possible. Mercury he wasn't, but we arrived soon enough for him to earn his fare. Once on the ground again, I shook out my suit, shot my cuffs, and tried to beat down my tangle of curls. Then I swallowed, said a prayer, and knocked on the door.

Aunt Lydia answered it at once. The maid had been put off, I think. She arched a brow in my direction and I wondered if my actions had made her friend or foe.

"Come inside, young man," she said, waving me into the house. "You have a good deal to answer for."

The atmosphere inside seemed oppressive. When invited into the sitting room, I avoided the spot where I had shot two men on that very rug. I removed my hat, and began turning it in my hand, a habit I reveal when I am nervous.

"How is Rebecca?" I asked.

"Do you mean Mrs. Cowan? You shall see for yourself presently."

My Adam's apple suddenly felt like a bone lodged in my throat. I did my best to swallow, but coughed instead. She took pity on me and unbent a little.

"What a to-do," Lydia said, putting a hand lightly on my arm. "None of us slept a wink since it happened. I still cannot believe it."

"I would take it back if I could," I assured her. "I was merely trying to defend you both. It was instinct."

"Thomas, you killed a man!"

"It wasn't my intent. I was firing in two directions at once. But watching him die at my hand was appalling."

"Are you involved in such altercations often?"

"No, not often, but occasionally," I admitted. There was nothing for it but to tell the truth. "I knew that your lives were in danger. That's why I sent Mr. Briggs on an errand, to watch the very men who burst through the door."

She looked away, deep in thought. Again I saw Rebecca's looks in hers.

"Save the rest of your explanation for Rebecca," she said. "Don't think I am unsympathetic, Thomas, but it was a blow."

"Is the wedding canceled, then?"

"It teeters on the brink. What you say in the next half hour shall probably determine it. And you aren't making matters better by appearing unshaven at the door."

"My hand was shaking, ma'am. I did not trust myself with a sharp instrument."

"Thomas," Rebecca said, coming down the stair.

I looked up at her. She was in her widow's weeds again, black as a funeral. She was a forbidding sight for so small a creature. I'd forgotten how beautiful she was. A Rose of Sharon; a rose no longer meant for me.

"Shall we go into the parlor?" she asked, her voice cold.

"As you wish."

I followed her into the room.

"Sit."

"I fear I cannot," I said.

"You know that you owe this visit completely to Mrs. Ashleigh's persuasion. She would not stop hounding me until I agreed to hear you. Sit!"

"I cannot," I replied. "Mrs. Ashleigh said little to me of this visit. I have nothing that requires hearing."

"Nothing?" she demanded.

I bowed. I, too, was astonishingly formal, all of a sudden.

"Nothing prepared, I mean. You know everything in my heart, and it is unchanged. I regret you having seen what occurred that night, but if given the chance, I would do it again to defend you."

"Please sit," she pleaded.

I sat.

"I wish you would quit that terrible profession, and find a reasonable situation in the City. My father knows almost everyone."

"Very well. I've written a letter of resignation. I can deliver it in the morning."

I noticed her hands were shaking. She hadn't anticipated it would be so easy. "That's settled, then."

"Of course. I'll tender my resignation, and then I'll pack. Perhaps I'll find a hotel here in the City. It shall be difficult to inform Mr. Barker that he is no longer invited to be my best man, but I'm sure he'll understand. When he is well again he can gather the scraps of the case I've left behind and solve it himself. After we are wed, I'll move here and establish myself as a clerk or a junior stockbroker. Something like that."

I stopped speaking and looked at her. Her eyes were large and brown, like velvet.

"You would absolutely hate that, wouldn't you?" she murmured.

"But I'd be willing to try. For you."

She'd been sitting up, a model of deportment, but her shoulders slumped a little and she sighed. "You'd be miserable. You can't hide it, Thomas. I know you too well. Oh, what are we going to do?"

She leaned forward and put her face in her hands.

"Perhaps I am a mistake after all," I said gently. "Your mother thinks so, and your father, and your sister. Your entire social class, your crowd, would be so much happier if the earth opened and swallowed me up. You can send back the gifts, if you wish. I fear Mrs. Ashleigh has overstepped her bounds."

"Thomas, stop being so agreeable and listen. And sit!"

I had stood at the last words, preparing to depart for good. I sat again.

"Have you entered my house armed before?" she asked.

"No," I said.

"Do you often carry . . . what are they called? Pistols? Revolvers?"

"Sometimes. My profession is occasionally dangerous."

"How dangerous?"

"Very, at times. My predecessor was killed while performing his duties."

"Do you understand in what a position that places me?"

"Yes, I do."

"You did not sufficiently warn me, Thomas."

"I'm sorry," I murmured. "I did not."

"You should be. Firearms in my house! In the very shadow of my own synagogue, no less. This goes far beyond sorry."

"True."

"You haven't shaved this morning," she remarked. "You look terrible."

"I feel terrible. Can you possibly forgive me?"

She put her hand out, warning me back. "I don't know. I haven't considered the matter thoroughly."

"Does your family know?" I asked.

"I don't see a reason to tell them. Not yet, anyway."

"Has the wedding been postponed? Or even canceled?"

"The time grows short, but I have not decided. Nothing has been canceled. It can, should I choose, but I have not."

"Certainly."

"You are fortunate to have friends willing to work in your favor."

"I know Mrs. Ashleigh has spoken to you."

"And your advocate, as well. Your barrister, if you prefer."

"Who are you talking about?"

"You're being uncommonly thick this morning, Thomas," she said, smoothing her skirt. "I'm talking about Jacob."

"Jacob who?"

"Jacob Maccabee. Your butler, silly."

"Mac was here?"

"Yes, on your behalf. And doing rather well, I might add. Aunt Lydia and I were fully convinced I should refuse you, but he almost changed our minds."

"He left in a hurry after Mr. Barker sacked him."

"Mr. Barker sacked Jacob?" Rebecca asked, shocked.

"It was only temporary. A fit of pique on our employer's part, I suppose. He regretted it after a minute, but Mac had already gone. He must have just heard what happened between us before he left."

"You're lucky to have him as a friend, my old classmate from Hebrew school."

I blinked. Not only were he and I not friends, we were very nearly enemies. He barely suffered my presence, while I managed to thwart his every attempt at keeping the house running smoothly. There was mutual disdain on both sides.

"Of course," I told her. "He's quite a fellow."

"He stayed until nearly midnight."

"I owe him more than I can say. I should hate to lose you."

The last thing I wanted was to owe Mac a huge debt of gratitude. He would hold it over my head for years, against any infraction on my part. He would use it again and again, without actually using it at all. Mac was clever that way.

What was his plan now? I wondered. Why did it matter to him whether Rebecca and I should wed? One would think as a successful member of the Jewish community he would be against our union. Men outnumbered women here. They didn't require any competition. Despite Mac's good looks, he was among this group of men all jockeying for the same few women. Why help a goyim take a Jewish beauty out of such a small market? It was a mystery, if there ever was one.

"Let's not talk about what I want, Rebecca," I said. "What do you want?"

"I want you, Thomas. I want to have a last name no one can spell. I want us to love each other and get married. I want to have children. Your children."

I frowned and looked at her. "I assumed the wedding was over."

"You assumed too much. I haven't canceled anything, not even your precious baby's breath. Oh, I am angry, of course. After all, you shot people in my home, right in front of me. Shooting them was not your decision to make, it was mine."

"Rebecca," I said, "the moment they kicked in the door, the decision was made. I work by instinct."

"You were a very good shot," she sniffed.

The tears came then, silent but plentiful, a cascade dripping from her lashes, dripping off her chin. Propriety be damned. I pulled the handkerchief from my pocket and took her into my arms as gently as if she were a plover's egg. Her thin fingers seized my lapels so tightly I feared she would rend the satin. Even the forbearing Aunt Lydia would be scandalized.

"What are we to do? How are we going to fix this?"

"We might give optimism a try first, I suppose," I said.

She sniffed, hiccupped once, and tried to smile. "What am I going to do with you, Thomas? My mother was right. All men are beasts."

"Far be it from me to disagree with your mother, since we are as one in all other matters."

"Stop making me laugh when I'm angry with you."

"Sorry," I said.

"I shouldn't have listened to Jacob. You're much more trouble than you're worth."

I nodded. "There's that."

"Be serious!" she exclaimed, clouding like a sudden squall. "There's so much we haven't even decided. Where are we going to live? How are you going to support us? Where will we worship? What friends will we have?"

"Do you mean Jew or Gentile?"

She ran a hand across her forehead. "I don't know. Either, I suppose."

"Look, I don't care what religion a person belongs to. I care about the person themselves. Are they kind? Do they have character? You've known Israel Zangwill since childhood. He's the best friend a man could have. He doesn't care if I'm Gentile and I don't care if he's a Jew."

"But doors will be slammed in our faces," she continued, cradled in my arms. "Some will shun us."

"Then that is their loss. If they turn us away, we shall shake the dirt from our sandals and go our way."

"Is that a Gentile reference?"

"Yes," I admitted. "From Matthew, I think."

"There, you see? I don't even know who Matthew is."

I took her hands in mine. "Darling, we don't have to decide everything now. That's what marriage is for. Everything shall work itself out in the fullness of time."

"Do you promise?"

In answer, I kissed her; a real kiss, the kind that left both of us breathless.

She pushed me away and stood. "Oh, good heavens! Thomas, you must leave now. Send in Aunt Lydia. We have a wedding to prepare! You'll be underfoot!"

The next I knew I was standing on the porch with my bowler in my hand again. It had become dented during our kiss and I pushed it back into shape. The rain had returned and I had no umbrella with me, and there was no cab in sight. So why did I click my heels together as I stepped off the curb?

The wedding plans had never been canceled. I walked through the gentle rain and touched the brim of my hat to a pair of women huddling under an umbrella. This gave me a brief few days to solve the case, I thought. Perhaps not plenty of time, but at least it was possible. I touched my brim as I passed a man in a top hat. He pinched his, as well. Too late, I noticed the absurd little mustache. His cane swung hard against the back of my neck and I remember nothing else.

# CHAPTER THIRTY

I awoke to the requisite throbbing head. My shoulders were aching and there seemed to be little circulation in my arms. My head was hanging down, held by no more than my spinal column, and I was seated in a chair. Rather, I was tied to it with stout hemp.

Raising my head on my aching neck, I looked about. I was in some kind of empty house. I could see doorways leading to other doorways, and light streaming in from outside. The sound of a clopping horse could be heard in the street, accompanied by the jingle of a harness. The chances were good I was still in London. As for the house, I doubted anyone owned it. It was no doubt awaiting a sale. I reasoned I must be in the center of the house, since there were no windows visible. The crown molding and a view of several feet of staircase informed me I was in an affluent neighborhood.

I inhaled, preparing to cry out, when I caught a scent in the air. My captor was behind me. I felt warm breath on the back of my ear, and a voice spoke in my ear, triggering a nerve that ran down my body like an electrical charge.

"Hello, Mr. Llewelyn. So happy to see you again."

Camille Archer circled around me, and I heard a sound like drapes being dragged across the floor. I jumped at her appearance and she seemed pleased by my reaction.

She wore a serpentine corset, a sort I had only heard about. It constricted her bosom fully and shifted her hips backward then down, so that her position resembled a standing cobra. It must have been painful to wear. She wore a scale-like green dress made from anodyne dye, very bright. It, too, came to the top of her bosom, leaving her arms free, revealing a spray of freckles across her shoulders. The dress pooled on the floor behind her. Her hair was thick and loosened down her back. Her nose was upturned as always, but her eyes were black with mascara.

She clapped her hands in delight. "Oh, we're going to have such fun."

I turned my aching head and looked at her from under my brow.

"*Bonjour, mademoiselle,*" I said.

"How clever of you, Thomas. I may call you Thomas, may I not? How did you realize I was French?"

"Your cadence is not that of an Englishwoman, although you sounded thoroughly English in our offices."

"Compliments. How gallant. This is going swimmingly."

"May I assume that you are here to allow your associates time to escape?"

"Mr. Mercier is still with me."

She had circled again and now pressed the rigid corset against the back of my head, her hands on my ears, caressing them.

"I am getting married in a few days, but then I realize you know that, Miss Fletcher will have told you."

She rested her chin on top of my head. I felt rather than heard her breathing.

"*Tant pis,*" she replied. Too bad.

I struggled, dislodging her head. My futile attempt to escape made her laugh. She stepped back and watched as though I were an entertainment for her alone. Finally, I stopped struggling. The ropes were closely tied and too binding to have been done by this near-emaciated girl.

"Why did you—"

She stopped my question by placing a finger on my lips. "Thomas, I am not here to answer your questions."

I ignored the warning. "Were you related to or merely acquainted with Jacques Perrine and the Mercier brothers?"

"You are boring me. I came here for fun!"

She pouted her rouged lips. The sound of her boot stamping the floor was muffled by the heavy dress. Her painted face, loose hair, distorted figure, and thin arms reminded me of a marionette. An evil, mad marionette.

"How came you to England, Camille?" I asked.

She narrowed her eyes, trying to decide whether to answer or not. "I came to be a governess. I answered an advertisement in Paris. England seemed like a good place. Quiet. I was here no more than a month before the father of the house raped me."

"What did you do?" I asked, trying to keep her talking.

"I did the only logical thing. I cut off his head. He was a doctor. His bag contained a scalpel and a bone saw."

"And the Metropolitan Police caught up with you."

"I waived my rights. After all, one prison is like another."

"Were you an inmate of Burberry Asylum?"

"My barrister claimed I was mentally unfit for prison and that I could never be returned to society without medical treatment. I was sent to Burberry Asylum for therapy."

"Where you met Dr. Pritchard."

"I did."

"Where, in fact, you became involved in a relationship with Dr. Pritchard. Did you wish to avenge his imprisonment by killing my employer?"

"The charges against him were not fully proven in court. They merely thought it expedient to lock him away in a place which is in every way worse than a prison."

"Obviously, the rigors of asylum life, coupled with questionable and experimental treatments, have damaged a fine man's reason. A great pity."

"Yes. For you. Did you think I had forgotten the two men who brought my lovely Edward to trial in the first place? Do you think me so weak-minded as to believe you sympathetic to my cause?"

"Oh, come now!" I argued. "You've blown our offices out from under us. You've put my employer in hospital. Isn't that enough?"

"No, it is not, *monsieur*," she hissed, her hands on her hips.

She moved to a small reticule lying on a windowsill, rummaging about in it for something the way women do. Finally, she found it and lifted it in triumph. It took a moment to work out what I was seeing, but when I did, my heart stopped in my chest. It was a scalpel, the point impaling a small cork, which she removed with a small sweeping gesture. It didn't matter whether or not it was sharp. I imagined that it was, which was enough to give me apoplexy.

Camille raised a boot to the front edge of the chair, forcing me to press against the back with my limbs splayed. Casually, she leaned forward and sliced my tie in half. Then she put a tear in the arm of my jacket. She made another on my trouser leg, so close as to leave a tingling sensation on my bare flesh.

She seized the tip of my collar and cut through it, though the stay made it more difficult. Cut after cut after cut. She was flaying my nice suit and she would flay me next.

At one point, she sliced open my waistcoat and shirt to such an advanced degree that she reached in and put her palm against my chest, wanting to feel my feverish heart. Whatever it did, she pulled the hand away again, satisfied.

There was something intimate about the experience which turned my stomach. The woman was dangerously mad. She whispered taunts in my ear that she could have spoken three feet away, but she wanted to personalize this for her own amusement.

"Oops," she said, as the knife ran along one shoulder. I felt a sharp, stabbing pain and I saw a bloom of scarlet appear on the lacerated white shirt.

"You know where the arteries run, don't you?" I asked.

"To the square inch," she replied. "Edward gave me a map of the nervous and circulatory systems. I don't know how he procured it. A Christmas present, he said."

"What is your intent?" I asked, trying to sound calm and to keep the panic in my voice from being too obvious.

"To be honest, I was going to flay you. I've always wanted to do that! But you've been such a dear. I think I'll just nick you here and there and let you bleed until you run out of blood. I wish I could stay, but I have plans today. I mustn't be late."

She cut across my arm then, not deeply, but enough to raise blood. I groaned as the scalpel sliced across my breast. She lowered the blade to a spot on the inside of my trouser seam.

"No," she said. "There's an artery here. You'd bleed out too fast. I think I'll give you a sporting chance. If your Mr. Barker is as clever as I think he is, he'll find you in time, or send that American. If not . . ."

She shrugged her shoulders as if to say it would be my fault, not hers. She had done all she could. She dug the blade a little deeper across my rib cage and I gasped in pain. She kissed my cheek like a disturbing parody of a mother kissing her child. I tried to shrug her off, but my body was stinging.

"Don't be petulant, Thomas. I may change my mind yet. One proper cut and you'll spray blood across the floor." She sighed. "I feel sorry for Mrs. Cowan. She will be a widow twice over. She won't get to have you, which I suppose makes you mine. Do you like being mine, my pet?"

I didn't respond. My body was growing weak. I heard the blood dripping on the wooden floor beneath my chair. As she had promised, none of the cuts would require more than a few stitches, but if I was not found until the morning, I'd be dead. It was as simple as that. She crossed in front of me in that frightful, twisted dress to her reticule again and consulted the time on a small watch.

"Oh, dear," she said. "I must away. I've got a train to board. *Au revoir,* dear boy. I'll see you in another life."

Then she was gone and I was alone. I listened to the steady drip of my life force onto the floor, like the ticking of a bomb.

I would have liked to be married. I had come so close. At least Rebecca and I had reconciled our differences. We had professed our love for each other one final time. Perhaps that was enough.

Suddenly, the door kicked open in front of me and a man entered. It was Caleb, I thought. And then I realized it wasn't.

"Oh, hell!" J. M. Hewitt cried. "She cut you good and proper!"

"What are you doing here?" I asked, raising my head.

"Following you, of course. You appear to be in front of this case since everything is happening to you."

He took off his jacket, pulled a jackknife from his pocket, and began cutting off the sleeves from his shirt. He seemed to know what he was about as he untied me and began to apply a tourniquet to my arm and another near my knee.

"You'll live another day, Thomas," he said.

My body was throbbing from the pressure administered to my limbs. His voice seemed to grow fainter and my mind was drifting.

Hewitt went out into the street and hailed a cab. Then he carefully loaded me into it. I was bleeding in several places, but the wounds were not deep and there was little blood.

"She was mad!" I said after he'd climbed in the other side. "Mad! She was going to kill me. She was going to flay me alive."

"Calm down, Thomas," Hewitt said. "You're scaring the horses."

"Look at my suit. It's cut to ribbons. What is wrong with that woman?"

"You said it right. Mad as a hatter."

"I've been shot at, stabbed, hung, even tortured. But nothing prepared me for that."

"I wish I'd got a single shot at her," he said.

"So do I," I muttered. "I'm cold."

"It's shock," he replied. "Have you a change of clothes at your offices? And some bandages?"

"Yes."

"Good."

I began to shake. My teeth chattered, despite the warmness of a September day.

"How did you find me?"

"I've been following you for days," he replied.

"I saw no one."

"I'm a professional, Thomas. What sort of agent would I be if I was easily spotted?"

"That witch was following me, too. Her lackey was after me. Not to mention Scotland Yard and the American legation."

"You're a popular fellow these days."

"How does Barker stand this kind of thing?"

"I don't think even he would be stoic under what you've just been through. Try not to talk."

We reached Craig's Court and Hewitt rushed me inside. I unlocked the door to number 7 and crossed to the rooms in the back. Jenkins came down and both men painted my wounds in iodine and then I changed into my spare suit.

So far, I had been injured twice in this case. That was more than enough for me.

# CHAPTER THIRTY-ONE

Back home in Newington, thanks to Hewitt, I was treated by Dr. Applegate, whom the Guv keeps on retainer. I had assumed I would need a good number of stitches, but the doctor said he was amazed with the way the epidermal layer had been cut with such precision that I required nothing more than sticking plaster over most of my wounds. Camille Archer had hoped that I would suffer for hours as the blood slowly pumped from my body. Instead, what could have been life-threatening was merely painful. Very painful, indeed.

"How are you feeling?" the Guv asked, propped up in the bed Mac had arranged.

"Some pain, but I'm managing," I said. "Although I am still grappling with what Camille Archer did to me."

"She has proven herself to be deadly dangerous, lad. You're fortunate Hewitt was following you."

"Sir," I said. "I'm assuming she is on her way to France with Mercier, since Pritchard is dead. We should cable Dover."

"Oh? Is she going to Dover?" Barker asked.

"I assume so, since Pritchard is dead. She will flee the country."

"How do you know Pritchard is dead?"

"I received a telegram from Burberry Asylum."

Barker nodded. He pulled his pipe from the table and began filling it. Orders be damned. "Did you test the knots?"

"I—"

No, in fact, I hadn't tested the knots. I had accepted the telegram as genuine merely because it looked official. The Guv would have sent off a telegram of his own, questioning the veracity of the first.

"Pritchard is alive," I said. "Strathmore was a diversion to split my efforts between two objectives. He had me thinking about the one under my nose while he plotted against us."

"Indeed," Barker rumbled.

My employer was being wily. He wouldn't tell me anything, just prod me along with questions.

"She's not going to Dover, then! She's going to Hampshire to see Pritchard with Mercier, who is a known bomb maker. They're going to break Pritchard from the asylum! We must warn them. I should send a telegram. With luck, it will arrive in time to stop them."

"If you think it the right decision."

"I do. But what about Mrs. Archer? Why did he have her tarry merely to torture me?"

The Guv lit his pipe with some degree of pleasure, then blew smoke into the air.

"Did he?"

"No. I suppose she must have decided to do it when she met me. She was flirting with me from the first moment."

"The Llewelyn charm," he said acidly.

"Sir, I cannot merely send a telegram. I have to go to New Forest. But is it really possible that Pritchard was feigning dementia? Would he be capable of plotting such a thing? I met him and found his faculties failing."

"Pritchard is mad, but he is single-minded and extraordinarily clever. He could act as if he were falling into dementia well enough to convince even the staff there that his mind was going." The Guv began to dig in the bowl of his pipe with a vesta. "And you do need to go, but not tonight. Burberry is remote and you must rest. I don't believe Mrs. Archer will meet with Pritchard until tomorrow morning. If you take the first express, you should be there in time."

I nodded, then winced. The slightest movement was painful.

"He must have enjoyed his little charade," I said. "Sticking pins in me and passing out mid-sentence."

"That aligns with his morbid sense of humor," Barker remarked, his pipe clenched between his teeth.

"What is his plan, then, sir? The Continent?"

"America, more likely, Thomas. They don't have many bogs, but plenty of heiresses. I think he could do very well there."

"If he can bring about the demise of all his associates merely to cloak his operations among a half dozen viable suspects, then appearing to slide into mental illness is facile by comparison. And what of your brother, sir?"

"For two days I have thought of him and little else. Of course we have quarreled, like all brothers before us, but I never gave him cause to come to London to kill me. Our unspoken arrangement to divide the world between us was satisfactory. On the other hand, if we found ourselves in the same city, it would be ill-mannered not to meet."

"You called him a loose cannon," I reminded him.

"I said so because he is one. He does not solve a problem, he augments it to the point of absurdity. Let us take the Wealden case. Caleb was sent on a routine matter to act as bodyguard for another agent, whom I assume was to speak as a witness at a trial. What was the result? Three men dead, no witness, and he being chased by officers of the American government."

"What is he really doing here, then? How do we know that he is not Mrs. Archer's lover, for example?"

"We don't. My brother is a conundrum. That being said, I do not connect his movements to the case."

I rested my elbow on the knob of his bedstead. "What of the theft at Cox and Co.? Perhaps he is out of money. He was very interested to see that you are well off. You have been a success, while he goes from catastrophe to catastrophe."

Barker relit his pipe and leaned against his pillow. He sighed with contentment. He was home, Philippa could not stop him from smoking, and he could ruminate on the case and cross-examine me to his heart's content.

"I think stealing from my bank account was another part of my life that Pritchard hoped to destroy, or to at least prove that he could interfere with it. At the same time, I believe the stolen funds paid for Mrs. Archer's hotels and meals, while some have been tucked away for their escape. Five thousand pounds will not last forever, but it will take you far away from here and pay to start a new life somewhere else."

"So, for now, we must assume our suspects are Mercier and Camille Archer. But we're left with the troubling question of why they visited several of the suspects."

"Why, indeed?" Barker muttered. "Let us say that they all colluded in a scheme to bedevil me. Their first concern would be how to escape; the second would be how to leave a thousand pounds richer. But all of them died, in one way or another. That means Mrs. Archer and Pritchard will make off with the rest of the five thousand pounds."

I had resumed pacing. The thought occurred to me that pipe smoking might be helpful to the mental faculties. The Guv certainly thought better with a meerschaum between his teeth. However, Rebecca had decided opinions about smoking and would never allow it.

"But what about Mercier?" I asked. "What will become of him?"

"This is your case, not mine, Thomas. What would you do in Pritchard's position?"

I thought, or tried to. "He's a loose end. Better to get rid of him."

"Agreed," the Guv answered. "Very good."

"Is it possible that there is someone else who wanted to kill you and who could have planned the entire operation? Someone who tricked all of them, and for whom Mrs. Archer works? Obviously, it would be someone not on the list of suspects."

"No, I trust your judgment. I'm certain you went through the files thoroughly."

"Yes, sir. Jenkins and I have put them all back in order. But suppose it was a relative of someone, a person we've never even suspected?"

"If that's true, you have to remember that not every case can be solved, lad. There is such a thing as a person clever enough to confound this agency. However, that is unlikely, in my opinion."

"I fear I have not the imagination for this."

"Nonsense. You have more imagination than five people. You must merely harness it to one cart and make it pull you."

I wanted help and he was giving me platitudes. "Yes, sir. Thank you."

"I have faith in you, Thomas."

I stifled a sigh of frustration. "I don't see why. If I can't solve a case after six years, what good am I?"

"Oh, that old chestnut," he grumbled. "You doubt yourself."

"It seemed that I was exactly the sort who would weigh you down, if you think about it," I said. "I was a failed scholar, and not suited in any way for the position. I was a bloody poet, of all things."

"Perhaps," he admitted. "But you were very keen that first day we met. You were the only one to apply for the position that seemed truly alive. Also, you were logical. It was a cold and blustery day, yet you were the only one to use the wall as a shield from the frigid wind. The rest stood in a row, each with a hand on their hat, following the man ahead of him by rote. You were thinking. I wanted that brain working for me. And now look at you. I am injured.

My office was bombed. My house has been set afire. Yet I am not concerned and have not shut down the agency. You are there, still keen as you ever were."

"Thank you for the confidence, sir."

"I must send Mrs. Cowan flowers," he said after a minute. "No doubt Philippa has already done so, but I shall choose these myself. I was brusque and rude to the good woman, proving that her fears were justified. Thomas, I owe not only her but you an apology. Husbands must love their wives as Christ loves the Church. There was no wish on my part to separate the two of you. Marriage is a wholesome and natural state for a man. I shall abjectly apologize to Mrs. Cowan and we shall form a strong bond. We will both have need of you, and it will not do to grasp from both sides. That would not be beneficial to anyone."

"I agree."

I took my leave and went out into the garden, where Harm was resting on a rock. The stream was gurgling. There was a light breeze and it was a trifle cool as I went to sit in the gazebo to think.

Pritchard had manipulated five suspects in addition to Camille Archer and Mercier. There had been a bombing and Perrine was a dynamiter. There had been a theft from our bank and Strathmore was a financier. I was attacked, and the Mercier brothers were devils with their canes. Rebecca's house was assaulted by Jack Hobson and his tribe of ruffians and thugs. That left Keller. How did he fit into this?

I thought for a good half an hour before it came to me. Joseph Keller didn't fit into this at all. He had been imprisoned because of Barker and had been visited by Camille Archer, but that was all. His purpose was to throw us off.

"I won't let you beat me, Dr. Pritchard," I said aloud, staring into the empty garden. "I'm not going to leave this case unfinished before my wedding. And I'm not going to bloody wait until tomorrow morning to track the lot of them!"

I jumped from my seat.

"I'm going to New Forest now, sir!" I said as I passed through the hall.

"Fine, then," he answered. "Go find him!"

Turning again, I ignored Harm, who chased me across the lawn to the back gate. I slipped through and bolted as fast as I could to the stable. Caleb's horse was gone. I had no time to think about him. I saddled Juno and was leading him out the door just as Caleb arrived.

"Where are you going in such a hurry?" he asked.

"Burberry Asylum," I replied. "It was Pritchard all along."

"No, Pritchard's dead."

"He wants us to think he is," I said. "Are you coming?"

"Wouldn't miss it!"

# CHAPTER THIRTY-TWO

We spent the next half hour cursing at slow vehicles, skirting dray vans, and occasionally stepping onto paving stones. It would not be the first time I would let Juno have her lead on the staid streets of London, and Pepper was doing his best to keep up.

We caused many a startled look and a blast from a constable's whistle, but he was afoot and we were not. By the time we arrived at Waterloo, both horses were blowing like bellows.

There threatened to be a delay. One does not arrive at a station with a horse and immediately have him stabled. There were procedures one had to follow.

"Procedures be damned, boy!" Caleb shouted. "How much money does it take to stable a couple of horses and give them a feed bag?"

So saying, he slapped two ten-pound notes on the counter. The porter's eyes went wide. Then they looked from side to side.

"That's more like it. Give us two tickets, first class. Bill Pinkerton's buying today."

"Yes, Mr. Pinkerton," the clerk said. "Anything you say."

We found our seats and I sat by the window, my nerve endings so rattled I could barely stay seated. My companion, on the other hand, took off his long coat, pulled the brim of his hat over his eyes, and promptly went to sleep. I could not believe a man could sleep under such conditions.

An hour later, he awoke. The compartment window was open, despite the order of a dyspeptic-looking porter, and Caleb lit another cigarette.

"So, I assume Dr. Pritchard planned this whole thing," he said. "He set the others onto you. How did you come to that conclusion?"

"He used the other suspects, while claiming to form a partnership. Strathmore provided the money, Perrine brought along the Mercier brothers and their bombs, and Hobson provided muscle and a good diversion."

"What about Keller? He was visited by Little Miss Muffet herself."

"I believe Pritchard used him as a ruse. Keller wanted nothing to do with them. I'd even say he had made peace with his maker and was ready for whatever came, good or bad."

"It's true that Keller didn't appear to have the same motives or abilities as the other suspects," Caleb said, settling back in his seat. "But how would Pritchard have known how to find out who had a grudge against my brother?"

"I've been giving this some thought. There are a few ways. He could have read about the cases in *The Times,* or he could have known some oily solicitor who harbored a resentment toward the Guv. Pritchard's case was before my time. I suspect he has been planning this for years."

"Could Pritchard have planned something this devious if he had truly been having electric therapy? Doesn't that addle the brain?"

"We only have Pritchard's word that he received such treatments. I believe he said it in order to convince us of his inability to make and carry out complex plans."

"Sounds reasonable. How is Mrs. Archer involved with this scheme?"

"From the first time I saw her, there was something about her that disturbed me. Looking back, I suspect she was an inmate at Burberry Asylum. Do you recall when we were there before, if there was a fence with all of the female prisoners on the other side? If we arrive and Pritchard's still alive and in their custody, we will see if Camille Archer, or whatever her name is, was an inmate."

"Do you suppose she's as barmy as Pritchard?"

"I've been in a room with her," I answered, remembering the feel of her scalpel on my flesh. "She might be worse than he is."

"Why did he hook up with her, then, if indeed that is what happened?"

"She was a means to an end. I think that he was looking for someone malleable and willing to do anything for him. Unless, of course, she was merely a mercenary who was after the money. Miss Fletcher said Camille has been spending money freely all over London. That would seem consistent with a person who had been incarcerated and unable to enjoy some of the finer things in life."

"Are you sure Miss Muffet's on her way to New Forest? I don't feel the need to take the air for my health."

"Have you ever gambled with a handful of seemingly random cards and found yourself with a low straight?"

He clapped me on the back. "Boy, you do know poker!"

"I prefer whist, but I have tried a hand or two."

After a couple of hours we arrived in New Forest and hailed a cab at the station. We were perhaps a few miles away when we first heard the din. I turned my head and looked over my shoulder.

"Bells!" I cried. "Someone has escaped!"

"Faster, man, faster!" Caleb called to the cabman.

The man whistled and snapped his whip and the horses doubled their speed. A mile flew by, then another half mile, and soon we came upon men dressed in gray guards' uniforms milling about. A few of them raised rifles at our approach. We pulled up and stood in front of them.

"We're hunting Henry Thayer Pritchard," I said.

"So are we," a guard replied.

"Is your warden here?" I asked. "Or someone in charge?"

"Dr. Lewis is standing by the front gate, waiting for the authorities. A man was found murdered."

"Was his throat cut, perhaps?" Caleb drawled.

"Yes, sir. As a matter of fact, it was."

"I thought as much."

"Gentlemen," the guard said. "I must take you to him, not knowing how the two of you are related to this incident."

"We want to see Dr. Lewis ourselves," I said. "Please lead the way."

When we reached the front gate, we were taken to see Dr. Lewis himself, who was directing the efforts to find Pritchard. Lewis was sturdy in a double-breasted suit and heavy brogues. He was a no-nonsense fellow, clean shaven, with short gray hair. I showed him my identification and explained our connection to the case.

"Who was found dead?" I asked the director.

"A stranger was found near the front gate," he replied. "A tall man with no papers of identification on him."

"Did he have a mustache?"

"Yes, he did. It was small and waxed."

I looked at Caleb. "The other Mercier brother."

"Dr. Pritchard has a knack for losing friends," Caleb remarked.

"Why are the bells ringing if the body is right here?" I asked.

"Pritchard escaped not more than an hour ago," Dr. Lewis replied. "He fled into the old Matley Wood with a former inmate."

"Is her name Camille?"

"You seem to know a great deal for a man who just arrived here."

"What is her surname, may I ask? Is it Perrine?" I remembered the note I had been given by Inspector Dacre at the Sûreté, stating that Perrine's daughter, Camille, had visited him in prison.

"In fact, her name is Ainsworth."

I suspected the girl lived in a world of aliases.

"My employer, Mr. Cyrus Barker, was the enquiry agent responsible for Pritchard's arrest. We believe Pritchard has been planning his escape for a long time. How did he escape?"

"There is a tunnel which comes out against the wall there, near those bushes. No one thought to look there because it is the farthest from Pritchard's cell. The tunnel must have taken years to dig."

"What do you know about Miss Ainsworth's relationship with Dr. Pritchard?"

"She was a patient here, in the women's ward," he answered. "She was committed after she murdered a man. I don't know how she communicated with Dr. Pritchard. The men and women are kept strictly segregated."

"It seems to me," Caleb said, "that this fellow has a knack for doing the impossible."

"He has not been a model prisoner, but he earned enough responsibility to be able to walk around the grounds on his own. He showed remorse for what he had done to his wives, and with his medical skills he has been able to treat other patients with minor injuries. We are understaffed and it seemed a good use of his abilities."

I thought Lewis a fool for allowing Pritchard to walk around the grounds and to interact freely with the other inmates, particularly with a medical bag. Not only did Pritchard have no remorse, he was probably incapable of it. Such a clever killer should never have left his cell unless under restraint. I had no respect for the latest scientific methods of treating prisoners.

"Is the forest being searched?" I asked.

"Of course," Lewis replied. "With dogs. However, it's bog land, and it's dangerous to walk among the moss and hillocks. One can easily be sucked down and drowned."

"Thank you for the information, sir. We volunteer for whatever service we can give."

"Thank you. We are working our way carefully around the edges of the forest and making sorties inside."

I nodded and followed after Lewis. We reached the edge of the forest and I peered in. Every tree trunk, every inch of ground, every rock, was covered in a thick, bilious layer of green moss. Frogs jumped into stagnant pools, and sphagnum hung over us like flailing arms.

"Oy!" a voice echoed through the forest.

We backed out, retracing our steps, and ran around the edge of the forest, trying to follow the sound. Gingerly, we made our way over slick, twisted knots of tree roots whence the voices came. We saw men circled inside and soon reached them. On the edge of a swampy pool, there were two small objects on the forest floor: a pair of green snakeskin boots. Women's boots.

"Those belonged to Camille Ainsworth," I said. "They match the dress she was wearing this morning."

The men looked at one another, and then a constable stepped forward to dare enter the bog. His comrades tied a stout rope around his waist and, taking a deep breath, he stepped into the pool.

He sunk to his knees immediately. There was no solid ground to cling to, nor water to swim through. It was a spongy mass trying to suck him down to his doom.

"Pull him out!" Dr. Lewis ordered, but the constable, whose name I learned later was Burroughs, held up a hand.

"A minute, sir! A minute! I know these pools since a lad."

He leaned forward, staining his crisp black suit, and thrust his arm into the vile water. We all took hold of the rope, preparing to pull him out. He flailed his arms about in the pea-green water.

"Now!" he cried, and we pulled with all our might. It had been a long while since I'd played tug-of-war, but the mechanics were the same. We pulled him from the bog inch by inch, and as he came he dragged a horrid, shapeless mass with him. When both were on solid land I took my handkerchief and wiped the muddy face, in order to see the features.

"It is Camille Ainsworth."

Her hair was slick with mud, her sightless eyes staring from a pale, soiled face. That nose would bewitch no man ever again.

"Dr. Pritchard has buried another wife," I murmured.

She had been insane. She had threatened my fiancée. The girl would have flayed me alive if given the chance. And yet I felt for that poor mad creature, used as a pawn, having fallen victim to the worst woman-killer in England.

I turned to say something to Caleb and found him gone. I wondered if he was connected to the case. For all I knew, he was escaping with Pritchard.

"Has anyone seen Caleb Barker?" I asked.

We all turned to look, but he was nowhere to be found. The mood of the party of men had begun to turn dark. One does not kill a woman and sink her in a bog. Not in England.

Dr. Lewis frowned. "Mr. Llewelyn, where is your companion?"

"I don't know, but I suspect he has gone after Pritchard himself."

We began to search for Pritchard, but it had been an hour since he had escaped, and if he knew his way through the bogs, there would be no way to know how far ahead he was, and no way to find him now.

I turned to one of the guards and asked to borrow his spyglass. I scanned the bog, looking for some sort of movement. It occurred to me that Caleb would look for the tallest tree in order to spot his quarry. My instinct was correct. I found him perched in a tall oak a couple of hundred yards distant. He seemed to be reaching for something inside his coat.

I ran to the foot of the tree and called up to him, but Caleb showed no sign of hearing me. He climbed ever upward. When he had reached the point beyond which he dared not climb, he wrapped a leg around a limb and leaned forward, pulling out a small metal shaft. As we watched, he began to assemble a rifle from parts inside the pockets of his duster coat, still dangling from his precarious position. There was silence in the clearing. We all looked up expectantly.

"There he is," Caleb said in a low voice. "He looks like he's just taking a walk in the woods. What say ye, gents? Shall I spoil his outing?"

There was a murmured agreement from all the men, especially Constable Burroughs, who had taken the fate of the dead woman seriously.

"Caleb, come down," I cried. "What do you intend to do?"

In answer, Barker's brother began screwing a wooden stock into the cylinder, and then affixed a sight atop it. My attempts to stop him were to no avail. The men began to encourage him now. Two of the guards took me by the shoulders, and I almost feared being thrown into the bog myself.

Caleb sighted for a full minute before pulling the trigger. The sound echoed through the forest. We all waited expectantly down below. Pritchard was at least half a mile away.

"Got 'im," he murmured after he took the shot. "That's for you, little brother."

All the men around us cheered.

# CHAPTER THIRTY-THREE

The strain of pulling Camille Ainsworth from the grip of the bog had proven too much for my injuries. I had bled through my shirt and could not travel. We found a hotel and a local doctor who gave me a few stitches. I ate a little food and went to bed. Caleb Barker met with some of the guards from the asylum, who paid for his drinks. I awoke the next morning stiff and sore, aware that in twenty-four hours I was to walk the aisle with Rebecca Cowan. We had a big breakfast and arrived shortly after lunch.

We were gathered in the sitting room that afternoon, Caleb and I in chairs at the side of Barker's bed. Caleb was his usual laconic self, indifferent to our opinions. In his mind he had done the right thing, and he was pleased with the result. His brother was not so sure, although under the circumstances he could not admit he would have handled it any differently. And I? I was relieved it was over, and trying to justify in my mind what had happened.

Pritchard had already killed three women, his brides, for their insurance money. He had tried to kill us. He had murdered Anatole Mercier and Camille Ainsworth. It might be difficult to prove, but I was certain he was also responsible for the death of Henry Strathmore.

Barker pushed his blankets down, his pale feet protruding from his nightshirt. He was running over things in his mind. We all were.

"They won't be long."

We knew he was speaking of Captain Yeager and the United States Marines, who were certain to arrest Caleb for murdering Pritchard and several others.

"I know that," Caleb rasped. He finished rolling a cigarette and struck a vesta underneath his chair.

"So, will you tell me now?" the Guv asked.

"Tell you what?"

"What you are not telling me, of course. I know you, Caleb. Something is happening. You completed your mission down south. You should have been in Chicago by now, getting your new assignment. Neither of us is sentimental, so there is nothing to keep you here."

"Well, that's a fine how-do-you-do," Caleb answered. "I don't know why I bother helping you at all!"

"You're obfuscating. You know I'll find out eventually."

Caleb said nothing, puffing on his cigarette and looking at a corner of the ceiling. Ten seconds went by. Twenty. Finally, he sighed.

"Oh, very well. My first assignment here was to protect Mc-Closkey, which didn't quite work out. My second was to scout property for Mr. Pinkerton."

"For a European branch of the Pinkerton Agency?" my employer asked.

"Yes, the first branch outside of the U.S. The boss wanted to buy some of the Earl of Harrington's holdings. He was going to offer top dollar, too."

"By the telephone exchange?" Barker asked.

"Wait, you mean in Craig's Court?" I nearly yelled.

"Yep," Caleb said. "This is the street of detectives in London. What better place for us to hang our shingle?"

I couldn't believe it. An American agency, a large organization, would drive us out of business, or at least steal away our clientele. People like Hewitt and Fletcher would lose their livelihoods. What kind of work would I find if we shut our doors permanently?

"Hmmm," the Guv said. "The one at the end of the court?"

"Yes," Caleb drawled.

"He'll never get it. I suspect it's owned by the government."

"That's what I found out. No one actually refused me, but there was always a new document to sign, and information to obtain, and then a form went missing. What in the hell is that building, anyway?"

Barker shrugged. "As far as I know, it is vacant."

I think I can tell when the Guv is not telling the whole truth. The thought that Barker might not know about a mysterious building in his own yard, so to speak, was suspicious.

"Hmm," Caleb said.

"Did you telegram Pinkerton?"

"I did," he said, leaning forward and putting out his cigarette in the ashtray.

Now that Mac was back, he had taken measures to prevent having Caleb's ashes all over the house.

"And what did you say?"

"I told him Scotland Yard was not pleased to have such an organization within arm's reach. It seemed as good an excuse as any."

"I can get them to corroborate your statement," Barker said, absently scratching under his chin.

"I suggested Paris; for now, anyway. We'll come eventually. The boss always gets what he wants."

"You wanted that to happen?" I asked, feeling the anger begin to rise in me.

"'Course not. I was in a strange city on an assignment. I

assumed Cyrus was dead years ago. How was I to know he would be here and in the same street where I was ordered to look? We may be estranged, but we're kin, and blood is blood. I'd better pack."

"Lad, you'd better go get Caleb's horse."

"I . . . yes, sir."

I patted Harm, the nonspeaking member of the party, who was watching us sagely, on the head. Then I left through the back gate. As I walked along the Old Kent Road on sore and bandaged limbs, I considered the situation. Caleb had done a number of things of which Her Majesty's government might not approve, not to mention the American government. He was close to starting an international incident all by himself.

Once back in Lion Street with Pepper, I brought him to the front door and tied him to a post. Then I went inside, just in time to see the brothers shaking hands.

"Take care of yourself, little brother," Caleb said.

"A letter every year or so would not come amiss," Barker rumbled. He turned his head and looked out the window. "Ah! Here they come, just as expected."

*"Adios."*

"Go with God, indeed."

"A Bible thumper to the last, eh?" he chuckled as he gathered his saddlebags and stepped outside.

"Go with him to the embassy, Thomas," the Guv instructed. "You are representing the agency. Mac! Top hat!"

Mac came out of his room and jammed the hat onto my head. I followed after Caleb.

There was a brougham in the street in front of the house. Three men were trying to work out how to tie the gelding to the back of such a fine vehicle. There was some kind of gold insignia on the cab door, but I didn't have time to inspect it.

"I'm coming with you," I called.

"And who are you, sir?" one of the men demanded. He was sturdy and bearded and very serious. I recognized him as a Scotland Yard inspector, having seen him once or twice in "A" Division.

"Thomas Llewelyn," I said. "I work for Mr. Barker. Cyrus Barker. His brother, Caleb, here worked for us."

The inspector turned and regarded Captain Yeager, who was standing behind him. He was holding Pepper's reins, still trying to work out where to tie them.

"There's no room," he snapped. "You can ride the horse, Mr. Llewelyn."

They put darbies on Caleb's wrists and pushed him into the brougham, and climbed in after him. I mounted Pepper and they rolled slowly out of Lion Street, with me following behind them.

I jogged over Westminster Bridge and passed the Abbey, where we all turned into Victoria Street, approaching number 123. It was one of the easier addresses in London to memorize. I followed the carriage up to the large granite mansion with the American flag flying in front of it, alternating stripes of red and white, with white stars on a field of blue. The carriage rolled to a stop and I came up behind it. Pepper nickered his opinion of the place and shook his head.

The inspector, having acquitted himself of his duty, left for Scotland Yard. If he were like all the other inspectors of the Met, he had far too many cases to dawdle over the delivery of an errant American. One of the men remained with the carriage, while Captain Yeager led us inside. I must admit he cut a fine figure. There was white piping all over his blue uniform, and I could have hung my hat on that curled mustache. I had been in enough embassies to not be particularly impressed by the decor, but for such a young country, they were doing well for themselves.

The officer led us through a tall door. Inside was a large, spacious room dominated by an enormous telescope. A sturdy-looking man was bent over the eyepiece. He stood when we entered.

"Have a seat, gentlemen," he said, as he returned to his observations. "Take off those handcuffs, Captain Yeager."

"Yes, sir," the officer answered.

We sat in front of the desk. Caleb suddenly sucked in air. I looked at him. He was glaring at a brass plaque before us with the owner's name on it: Robert Todd Lincoln. The late president's son.

Lincoln pulled himself away from the telescope with a sigh, and went to his desk, reviewing several papers on the blotter.

"This is not Abilene or Dodge City, Mr. Barker," Lincoln said. "You cannot shoot people with impunity. There are laws here. It reflects badly on our nation."

"No, sir. I mean, yes, sir."

For the first time since I had met him, Caleb was flustered. I suspected that to many of his countrymen, Lincoln was the closest thing to a king as they would ever know. However, the man looked nothing like his father. He was stout where his father had been lean. He had a gray, spade-like beard, and wore a pair of pince-nez spectacles. Only something about the eyes reminded me of the illustrations I had seen of the famous president.

"The report here says you shot at least two American citizens in Sussex."

"No, sir," Caleb said. "I was not in the building at the time."

"Mr. Barker," Lincoln said, removing the spectacles from where they were perched on his nose, and wiping them on a piece of silk from his desk. "Do you take me for a fool?"

"No, sir!" he replied. "Not at all!"

"You shot another man in Hampshire."

"A multiple murderer sir," I interjected. "He'd have escaped to kill again if it weren't for Mr. Barker here."

"And you are, sir?"

I set my card in front of him. "Thomas Llewelyn of the Barker Agency. We've been working with the Pinkerton Agency on a couple of enquiries."

"Barker?" Lincoln said, looking slightly confused.

"Cyrus Barker, sir. Caleb Barker's brother."

"English?"

"Yes, sir. Well, Scottish, but working in London."

"And they're both detectives."

"In a manner of speaking."

"I see. Now tell me, Mr. Barker, have you killed any other person in England that we don't know about?"

I tried to stop him, but did not succeed.

"Yes, sir. A fellow in an alleyway was beating Mr. Llewelyn here, and I jabbed him with my pigsticker!"

"Was the man English?"

"No, sir. French."

Lincoln closed his eyes and sighed. Then opened them again.

"Do you have any opinions about the Italians? Need I have any concerns for the Germans or the Dutch?"

"No, sir."

"Mr. Barker, it is obvious that you work in the far West, where law is subject to interpretation. However, I know for a fact that the Pinkerton Agency does not condone the use of extreme violence in the performance of your duties."

The corners of Caleb's lips went up, as if to say, "You, sir, have been misinformed."

Lincoln picked up a paperweight and thumped it on his blotter, like a judge with his gavel. "You are to be deported tonight. There is a ship leaving port within the hour. Do you possess anything you have not brought along with you?"

"No, sir, but my horse is outside. Can he be deported, too?"

Now it was Lincoln's turn to smile. "I've never deported a horse before, but there is a first time for everything."

"Will I stand trial in the States?"

The American minister shuffled the papers and looked at them closely. "Scotland Yard claims the shooting occurred between two groups. One of your side was killed, and both on the other side. The walls were studded with bullets. It sounds like a standoff to me."

"Yes, sir, it was."

"This so-called murderer you shot. He was killed from a far distance, is that correct?"

"That's correct," I confirmed.

"You," he said, pointing at me. "Explain what happened."

"The man who was killed, Dr. Henry Thayer Pritchard, had just escaped from a lunatic asylum, having killed both of his accomplices. He was a dangerous madman and was considered extremely dangerous. Mr. Barker saw him from far off, escaping across the moor, and he fired his rifle. He did not miss."

"Mr. Barker, where did you procure a rifle?"

"I brought it from America, sir."

Lincoln crossed his arms and regarded him as if he were a species with which he was not acquainted. "How were you able to do such a thing? You had to have gone through customs."

"Sir, the day a Pinkerton cannot get by a customs inspector is the day he hangs up his spurs."

"And your pistols. Did you smuggle those through as well?"

"No, sir. I acquired those here."

"From where?"

"From the Colt dealer in Glass House Street, Your Honor."

"He would not sell pistols to an American only briefly in the United Kingdom. They are heavily regulated."

"They are, sir, but I did not buy them. I have done a favor for Mr. Colt himself. After a telegram was exchanged, they were given to me gratis."

"Now this French business. You stabbed one of them. What happened to the other?"

"The girl, who was Pritchard's accomplice, cut his throat, presumably at Pritchard's request."

"I see."

Lincoln cleared his throat. "I have no control over the French government; they are liable to make suit against you. They are an excitable people. But I doubt the Court of King James is going to make a fuss over the death of a multiple murderer. As to the Wealden murders, I believe the Pinkerton Agency will have to answer for that. Say your good-byes to Mr. Llewelyn. You've got a boat to catch."

We rose and quit the room. Lincoln was already returning to his telescope. We had interrupted his contemplation of the celestial orbs. In the corridor, Yeager clapped Caleb in irons again. It didn't stop him from shaking my hand.

"That was Lincoln!" he said. "Robert Todd Lincoln. Can you believe it?"

"I know," I replied.

"If you're ever in the United States, come look me up."

"General delivery, The Open Plains?" I asked.

"Something like that."

"I wish you could have stayed for the wedding tomorrow."

He settled his wide-brimmed hat on his head. "I'm not much for ceremonies, Thomas, and even less for weddings. It's too much like a steer going to the slaughterhouse."

"Good-bye, Caleb," I said.

"Good-bye. Tell Etienne he can't cook a tin of beans without directions."

"Thank you. He'll probably quit for another week."

He turned and followed after Yeager, singing as he went. I'd set down the lyrics, but my ears burnt just hearing them.

# CHAPTER THIRTY-FOUR

And so the fated day arrived. I spent the morning feeling stunned, not very different from the moment after the explosion had taken place. I stood there holding one shoe, lost in thought, until Mac coerced me to put it on. It isn't every day a man gets married. Well, that *I* get married, anyway.

After bathing, shaving, dressing, eating, and sucking down a pot of coffee, I was ready to go. Mac inspected me for a full minute, removing bits of fluff too small to be seen by the naked eye until he was satisfied.

"That's the best I can do with what I've been given," he said. "Off with you. I've still got the Guv to dress. Not to mention my humble self."

"Thank you, Mac. But, before I go, there is something I'd like to discuss with you."

"Yes?" he asked, looking a bit testy. I was interfering with his times table.

"The thing is, Jacob, things are liable to change when I get back.

When *we* get back, I mean. It's all quite up in the air. We'll be deciding where to live, and if we stay here, I wouldn't want it to strain your relationship with Rebecca."

"Surely that couldn't happen."

"I hope not, because I have no wish to make sweeping changes in the way things are run here. That being said, I'm about to suggest a vast change in the way things are run."

"Mr. Llewelyn, I fear the day has unhinged your reason."

"Oh, come, that's no way to treat a man about to offer you a situation."

Mac had been looking at invisible dust falling on my shoulder, but his eyes suddenly linked with mine. "I beg your pardon?"

"I don't want you and Rebecca to be constantly trodding on each other's toes. You've been invaluable during some of our investigations. I thought I might suggest to the Guv that we call you in on a consulting basis."

"As an agent?" he asked.

"From time to time, if you are interested."

"Have you approached the Guv about this?" he asked.

"Not yet, but I believe I can convince him. This will be the perfect time, I think, when everything is in flux."

"Why would you do this?" he asked.

"Gift horses, Mac! Were I to convince the Guv to agree, would you be willing to join the agency on, shall we say, elastic terms?"

He crossed his thin, elegant arms, trying to decide if I was having him on. I knew he had wanted my position before I had been hired. Yet another applicant who had applied for my position.

"If anything," I went on, "this has shown me that when one of us is injured, the investigation slows, and we cannot afford that. We'll need another agent soon. Perhaps not full time, but you have your duties here and—"

"I accept."

We blinked at each other as if the word had shocked us both.

"Good. I'll bring up the matter with Mr. Barker when we return from the honeymoon, then. I'm not promising, of course."

"You'll be late," he said. "We all will."

"Thanks. I'll be off, then."

I opened the door and stepped out.

"Thomas!"

Mac stepped out onto the step. It was showing signs of being a beautiful day.

"Good luck today," he said, putting out a gloved white hand.

I tipped him a wink. "Don't go easy on me, now, Mac."

Cabs were easy to be found for once, and I chose one in which I would not mind arriving at the ceremony. When I reached my destination, Rabbi Mordecai of the First Messianic Church came out into the street and shook my hand. Then he crushed me in a hug and slapped me on the back.

"You grooms always make me nervous," he told me.

We had hoped to marry in Bevis Marks Synagogue, but they would not allow it until I became a convert, a decision I was not yet ready to make. Likewise, churches such as the Metropolitan Tabernacle would not accept a Jewess without a conversion of her own. We were stymied until I recalled a small congregation of "Christian-Jews" in Poplar who felt no need to compel people to change in order to get married. Mordecai, a Father Christmas of a fellow with a twinkling eye and a long white beard, was just the sort of man to lead the ceremony.

I entered and was immediately assaulted by Israel Zangwill, my closest friend. He was a columnist at *The Jewish Chronicle*. I'd known him since he was a teacher at the Jews' Free School. He was a spare fellow with a dry sense of humor.

"It's not too late to change your mind," Israel assured me. "Do you want to have a dragon for a mother-in-law?"

"She's worth the price," I told him.

"Yes, she is," Ira said. "Although Rebecca is bound to come to her senses before the vows and call the whole thing off!"

I turned and scanned the room. Philippa stood by the entrance to the chapel, regal and elegant in a light gray frock, speaking with one of the guests, with her eyes fixed on the doors.

The doors opened wide, then, and a bath chair holding my employer was wheeled in by an usher. Cyrus Barker was resplendent in his morning coat and striped trousers. His boots were polished to a high gloss and there was a diamond stud in his red tie. The wooden-slatted contraption was cinched around his trouser leg. He had a face like thunder. I murmured my apologies and moved through the crowd to his side.

"Sir, is something wrong?" I asked. "Are you sure you should be here?"

"Thomas, did you think that I would allow an assistant to wed without my participation and support? Would I stay at home while everyone I know is celebrating his nuptials?"

"We're glad you're here, sir. We wouldn't have it any other way. In a manner of speaking, you introduced us to each other. It wouldn't be the same without you. The question is, are you well enough to be here? That is what I want to know."

"I believe I am, and I have this cast and two stout sticks to help me."

It took a minute to work out what he had just said. "Sir, you didn't mention trying to stand. You know your doctors would not allow it. Mrs. Ashleigh would not allow it. Even Rebecca wouldn't!"

"I can manage."

"There is no need for you to stand. No one expects that."

Barker frowned and I saw a rare glimmer of light from the depths of his quartz spectacles. "I did not come here today to be an object of pity for our friends and acquaintances. I came to stand at your side on this momentous occasion."

"But, sir—"

"Save your breath to cool your porridge, lad."

A hand touched my wrist, gloved, scented, and fully in control.

"Thomas, mingle," Philippa said. "Leave Cyrus to me."

I nodded and watched as she moved around behind him and took control of the chair, wheeling him through the crowd while murmuring in his ear. I believe I heard the word "incorrigible" used.

"Thomas," a voice spoke in my ear.

It was Rebecca's aunt Lydia. I was deeply grateful that she had forgiven me after the shooting that had taken place in front of her and Rebecca.

"Yes, Aunt Lydia?"

"Rebecca wishes to speak with you."

She led me down a hall to a door at the far end and opened it for me. I stepped inside, my heart thumping in my chest. My bride-to-be was standing there looking like an angel, a vision in pale cream and lace. Her veil was cut and folded back in the Spanish style to represent her Sephardic heritage. I had never seen anyone more beautiful. And what do you suppose was tucked among the lace and fabric in her hair? Baby's breath.

"Thomas," she said in a low voice. "Are you ready for this? I'm frightened."

"I suppose it is normal to be afraid," I said, taking her hand. "What in particular frightens you?"

"What if I'm a bad wife?"

"Rebecca, you could never be a bad wife."

"But what if I am?" she asked. "What if I asked you to quit? What if I couldn't accept the work you do?"

I thought that a very good question. I considered it a moment and then posited one of my own.

"Would you ask that of me?"

"I don't think so, but neither do I want to receive a note or call someday saying you've been injured, as Mrs. Ashleigh has. I wish your situation was not so dangerous."

"I don't go out searching for it, but neither do I shrink from it. There was a time when you might have convinced me, five or six years ago, perhaps, but now I'm an enquiry agent. It's not just what I do, it's who I am."

"I know that. Don't mind me. I worry too much. Do you love me?"

"Of course I do," I said. It wasn't possible to tell her how much. "I don't go about marrying just anyone."

"Kiss me, then, and go."

I did as she asked. Then I straightened my coat and went into the lobby, where I was stopped every few feet by someone, a friend of Rebecca's or someone connected with our work. Jenkins was there, in a nicer suit that I had assumed he owned. Bok Fu Ying was present and so was Hewitt with Miss Fletcher. Sergeant Kirkwood shook my hand vigorously, reminding me of a dog off his lead. I found it all amazing that so many people had come for our benefit.

Rabbi Mordecai came up beside me and took my elbow, wheeling me about like a railway handcart and leading me toward the sanctuary.

I saw the chuppah there and the gallery above, which, though it now held guests of both sexes, was first built to keep them separate. For the first time, I felt butterflies in my stomach. Then I heard the squeal of a wheel behind me and the protest of leather and wicker.

Barker came up beside me, a stick in each hand, concentrating. One foot came forward, then the other dragged behind. I could almost hear his teeth grinding. Stubborn as a mule, I thought; hard on everyone but mostly on himself. I waited as he stood beside me.

"Thomas," he said.

"Sir. Thank you for being here."

"Wouldn't miss it for the world."

Then it came to me, a final revelation. "This was your doing, wasn't it?"

"Be more specific," he said.

I looked down the aisle, wondering if Rebecca was about to enter, whether or not I could say what needed to be said.

"You could have solved this case yourself. You gave it to me, perhaps as some sort of test, or to show me that I could do it on my own. You let me work it out, giving me little or no advice, save to not trust your brother."

He leaned his head to the side as if considering the matter, then grimaced at a reciprocal jolt of pain in his limb.

"Then, when I shot those two men in Rebecca's home, I suspect you dispatched Mac and Philippa to calm her and her aunt."

"Not strictly true," he said. "I dispatched Philippa alone. Mac was already there."

"I talked with Mac this morning. I think we need to discuss his duties now that Rebecca is here."

"It's something to consider," he replied, nodding. "We'll talk when the two of you return from your tour."

The crowd behind us hushed as Rebecca and her father appeared at the door. Everyone stood and I could feel the beating of my heart as I watched her walk down the aisle. She was soon at my side and the service commenced.

Rabbi Mordecai began by explaining that the ceremony would by and large be Jewish, but that he would relate each part of the ceremony to a verse in the New Testament. I thought that he had his work cut out for him. There were a few murmurs among the guests, but he was used to such things, having stood in the gap between these two faiths who worshiped one God for years.

First, we drank a ceremonial glass of wine together as Rabbi Mordecai explained it symbolized the joy of our union and the sanctification of a man and a woman to each other. The wine was terrible and I choked a little.

Next came the walk around the chuppah. As Mordecai chanted in Hebrew, we slowly circled the delicate structure together, symbolizing the journey we were about to begin together. I was about to do so without incident, but I think Rebecca must have trod on the front of her dress. She stumbled and bumped the chuppah. I caught her, but everyone gasped as the flimsy structure began to sway. I looked up to see her cheeks burn scarlet.

Afterward came the lighting of one candle with one of our own.

It was a simple matter, two lit candles lighting one, symbolizing the union as two became one. By then, both of our hands were shaking so violently that lighting the standing candle with the flame of a taper in our hands was difficult, but we managed to succeed.

The rabbi brought us in front of the assembled crowd and we went through the Christian part of the ceremony, the vows. My tongue cleaved to the back of my throat and I was certain that I would stumble over or even forget the two words I was going to say. Looking at Rebecca, I wondered if she felt the same.

"I will," I croaked.

At last, Rabbi Mordecai spoke a final prayer over us in Hebrew. The ceremony was almost over. He folded a cloth over a glass goblet and set it in front of us. He explained that the breaking of the glass suggests the fragility of human relationships.

"As this glass shatters, may your marriage never break," he intoned.

I stepped forward onto the bundle, but it didn't shatter. I saw a flash of surprise on her face. This was it, I was certain. She was going to bolt. The ceremony had been a shambles. I stepped forward again and the goblet slid out from under my foot and skittered a foot or two away.

There was a wail, then, and I realized as my stomach clenched that it was Rebecca. Then I heard laughter from the side of the marriage altar; loud, rumbling laughter. It belonged to Cyrus Barker. Then others began to laugh, too. I had never felt so mortified in my life. I looked up at Rebecca and I realized my own wife was laughing, too. In fact, she nearly collapsed, she was laughing so hard. Worse yet, I heard Rabbi Mordecai beginning to chuckle, as well.

In desperation, I jumped into the air and came down upon the goblet and the cloth, and at last, the glass gave a satisfying pop. Everyone jumped to their feet and spontaneously began to applaud. People were yelling and even whistling.

Then I understood, if a bit belatedly. They were laughing with us, not at us. We were loved in that room. The laughter bubbled up in my chest and burst forth. I had never laughed so loud in my life. I walked to my bride's side, put her arm in mine, and we left the chuppah as Mr. and Mrs. Thomas Llewelyn.

It was an interesting wedding. It would be an interesting marriage, as well, and we would not change even a minute of it for the world.

# CHAPTER THIRTY-FIVE

That day Rebecca Llewelyn gave up wearing black. The gown she changed into for the reception was a silvery blue. I looked at her with pride. She was mine now. All her worldly goods, but I didn't care about that. She was entitled to keep all she owned. Now that I had her, I needed precious little else.

Still, I owned a house, in the abstract at least. I had spent much of my life in hovels, garrets, cottages with too many people, usually no more than a bed to myself. I had skipped ahead of the rent. I had worked for my board. To think that I might own a place, any place in this world, was alien to me. No more so, however, than having someone for my very own, someone who loved me. Someone who, in fact, had just tethered herself to me for life.

Mac had delivered a change of clothing to the house in Camomile Street, and it felt strange changing into my gray cutaway in so feminine a guest room. When I had finished knotting my tie,

I stared at my reflection in the mirror. Thomas Llewelyn, married man. Thomas Llewelyn, husband.

I came down the stair and was stopped by Aunt Lydia. She took my arm and kissed me on the cheek.

"Welcome to the family, Thomas," she said.

"Am I a Mocatta now, or is she a Llewelyn?"

"Only time will tell, darling."

Rebecca came out with a spring in her step. Her dark eyes were livelier than I had ever seen them. There was a dimple in her cheek. She was exuberant when she came up and took me by the hand.

"You look beautiful," I said.

"You look glad the ceremony is over."

"I've had easier cases," I admitted.

The reception was at the Mocattas' house. Rebecca's father extolled the joys of converting to Judaism. Mrs. Mocatta actually touched my hand and I wondered for the first time if I might be able to build a relationship with her, too. I would try, for Rebecca's sake.

I heard a squealing wheel behind me and turned to meet the Guv.

"How are you, sir?" I asked.

"I'm fine, lad. The question is, how are you?"

"Never better. What will you do while I am away?"

"Philippa has convinced me to go with her to Sussex to convalesce. The offices will be closed until we both return."

"Excellent."

The Guv frowned as he inspected me. "Married now, eh?"

"So it would seem."

"It looks good on him, don't you think?" Philippa said, bending over his shoulder.

Barker mumbled in response. She was pressing him. Cyrus Barker does not like being cornered, but then Philippa Ashleigh is fearless. One would have to be in order to have a relationship with my employer.

"I expect you back from your tour on time, lad," the Guv said. "When we reopen the agency in a few weeks, there will be a surfeit of matters that will need our attention. You need to be rested and refreshed and ready to get back to work."

"Yes, Mr. Barker, sir."

The reception was under way. It became a blur of cutting of cake and speeches. Israel Zangwill spoke in lieu of Barker and gave a very jovial oration, completely at my expense. It was my own fault for revealing myself over the years to a now-treacherous friend.

The Scotland Yard contingent finished their punch and shook my hand, preparing to leave. Some people worked for a living.

"Now that you are a married man," Sergeant Kirkwood said, "you might want to set something aside permanently for bail."

"Droll, Sergeant," I replied. "Very droll."

The party went on too long. We had to reach Dover in a few hours if we were going to meet the ferry. My sense of time was lost. Some moments took forever, while others sprinted beyond me, calling for me to hurry or be left behind. I looked up and saw that Rebecca was smiling at someone, but I saw the strain in her eyes. I frowned at Israel.

"Everyone!" he said, rising. "A final toast to the young couple or they will miss their train, which would not be an auspicious start to the marriage."

They drank to us. We were unused to such good wishes, or at least I was. Rebecca was whisked off by friends and soon returned in a traveling dress of lavender-and-white stripes. It was a bit modern, but then we were going to Paris first. She kissed everyone in the room save my employer and then we were finally off.

"Drive along Whitehall Street!" she called to the cabman after I had helped her into the hansom.

"Dear, there is no time!" I argued.

"There is plenty of time, darling. I had Israel set your watch forward an hour."

"You clever little minx."

"One of us has to be clever," she replied. "I decided it would be me."

"What, pray tell, is in Whitehall Street?"

"Oh, government buildings, public houses, offices . . ."

"You're not going to tell me, are you?"

She smiled and we bowled down the Strand, with her hand in the crook of my arm. She looked at me with a smile. Our lives were about to begin. I wanted her to feel that way for her entire life. I was a lucky man, I who had blasted luck my entire life.

"Here, driver!" she sang out.

We came to the curb in front of the Clarence, right beside the gate at Scotland Yard.

"You intend to have me arrested," I said.

"Not yet, but I reserve the right."

She took my arm and propelled me in the direction of Nelson's Column.

"What's this all about?" I demanded.

We reached Craig's Court and Rebecca promptly stopped. She held out an arm to our offices. There was a new hoarding over the door:

### BARKER AND LLEWELYN
*Private Enquiry Agents*

It smote me. My eyes began to water. It was difficult to breathe.

"I don't deserve this," I stammered. "I nearly lost the case."

She wiped my eye with a morsel of a handkerchief. "That's not for you to decide, darling. It was Mr. Barker's wish."

I thought I was going to break down. Six years. Six years I had worked here. I had been shot, stabbed, very nearly hung. Barker had saved me countless times and I'd even saved him once or twice. I had doubted this day would ever come.

"Don't dawdle, Thomas," my wife murmured in my ear. "Remember, we have a train to catch."